Rege ...

From shopke ...

On a quiet stre ... unassuming biscuit ... you have the chance to ... a small slice of perfection. Belle biscuits are like nothing you could imagine! Though the shop would be nothing without the women who run it...

But it's not just confectionery delights that customers fall in love with—it's the shopkeepers, too! From a captain about to become an earl, to an officer who has just stepped back onto shore, there's an unexpected love story around every corner...

Escape to the Regency streets of Bath with:

An Unconventional Countess

Unexpectedly Wed to the Officer

and

The Duke's Runaway Bride

All available now

Look for Nancy and James's story

Coming soon!

Author Note

The Duke's Runaway Bride is the third and penultimate (probably) in my Regency Belles of Bath series. I find writing series quite hard because I usually either forget all the details I assume I'll remember or lose my notes, but I do have a soft spot for my biscuit shop. It's based partly on the places I used to visit in Bath with my grandmother and partly on a scene in the 1995 film version of *Persuasion* when Anne and Captain Wentworth meet in a coffee shop. That's become my ideal of how a coffee shop should look: wood paneled, cozy and with torrential rain pouring outside!

There's just one more book in the series to go. It's not hard to guess who the hero and heroine will be, but in the meantime, I hope you enjoy Quinton and Beatrix's story. A reader suggested the name Quin, so special thanks to them!

JENNI FLETCHER

The Duke's Runaway Bride

Recycling programs
for this product may
not exist in your area.

ISBN-13: 978-1-335-50607-8

The Duke's Runaway Bride

Copyright © 2021 by Jenni Fletcher

All rights reserved. No part of this book may be used or reproduced in
any manner whatsoever without written permission except in the case of
brief quotations embodied in critical articles and reviews.

This is a work of fiction. Names, characters, places and incidents
are either the product of the author's imagination or are used fictitiously.
Any resemblance to actual persons, living or dead, businesses,
companies, events or locales is entirely coincidental.

This edition published by arrangement with Harlequin Books S.A.

For questions and comments about the quality of this book,
please contact us at CustomerService@Harlequin.com.

Harlequin Enterprises ULC
22 Adelaide St. West, 40th Floor
Toronto, Ontario M5H 4E3, Canada
www.Harlequin.com

Printed in U.S.A.

Jenni Fletcher was born in the north of Scotland and now lives in Yorkshire with her husband and two children. She wanted to be a writer as a child but became distracted by reading instead, finally getting past her first paragraph thirty years later. She's had more jobs than she can remember but has finally found one she loves. She can be contacted on Twitter, @jenniauthor, or via her Facebook author page.

Books by Jenni Fletcher

Harlequin Historical

The Warrior's Bride Prize
Reclaimed by Her Rebel Knight
Tudor Christmas Tidings
"Secrets of the Queen's Lady"

Regency Belles of Bath

An Unconventional Countess
Unexpectedly Wed to the Officer
The Duke's Runaway Bride

Sons of Sigurd

Redeeming Her Viking Warrior

Secrets of a Victorian Household

Miss Amelia's Mistletoe Marquess

Whitby Weddings

The Convenient Felstone Marriage
Captain Amberton's Inherited Bride
The Viscount's Veiled Lady

Visit the Author Profile page
at Harlequin.com for more titles.

For Beatrice Gimson and John Bond,
always my favorite schoolteachers.

Prologue

Oxfordshire, March 1807

Quinton Everett Maximilian Roxbury, Twelfth Duke of Howden, squeezed on his reins, slowing his mount from a canter to a trot to a sedate, almost snail-paced walk. Unfortunately, no amount of squeezing, or leaning back in his saddle, or even willing his horse to sprout wings and fly off in the other direction, could prevent him from arriving eventually, and so it was only a matter of minutes before he found himself dismounting in front of the grey stone exterior of Howden Hall, low in spirits and heavy of heart. It made a sorry contrast. Just five minutes before, his heart had felt comparatively light. Not weightless, that condition being little more than a boyhood memory, but light*er*. Now, looking up at the vast facade of his ancestral home, he felt as though one of the stones had just settled in his stomach. And he detested those stones, every last one.

At least he was doing something about them these days, he consoled himself, as the sound of distant hammering attested. Thanks to his newly acquired fortune, he'd finally been able to order some essential repairs, *just* in time in the case of the roof, though even that wasn't enough to make him like the place. He never had. He never expected to. And yet there he was, trapped for ever. He was Howden and Howden was he; their identities entwined for life.

'Will that be all, sir?'

A groom came running from the direction of the stables and he nodded, forcing himself to relinquish the reins. A few moments of self-pity and resentment were all very well, but he had duties to attend to, a towering heap of them, in fact, and ten o'clock in the morning was quite late enough to start.

He made his way up the front steps, wondering if he looked as beleaguered and weary as he felt. Since inheriting the estate, he'd developed at least two new frown lines across his forehead, not to mention a seemingly ingrained furrow between his brows. Thankfully, his hair was still as thick and black as ever, but he expected it to start falling out and turning grey any day now.

It was almost comical in a bleak kind of way. Thirteen months ago, he'd been considered a prize catch in the Marriage Mart: young, handsome and the heir to a supposedly thriving dukedom to boot. Twelve months ago, on the other hand…well, it was fair to say that his reputation had suffered a blow, in the most mortifying and public way possible. After *that* not even the most ambitious Society mamas had sought him out, unwilling to lose their daughters to a life of public scandal and probable ruin. Which had been both a compliment to them and a lesson in self-worth for him.

He inclined his head to the footman who opened the front door and then stopped in the middle of the hallway, allowing himself to be divested of his outdoor garments while he waited.

One, two, three... He glanced longingly in the direction of his study door. Could he reach it in time? No, experience had taught him that any attempt would be futile. Better to stay and get it over with... *Four, five...* He planted his feet more firmly apart... *Six, seven...* That was unexpected. He didn't often get this far. Usually they were lying in wait... *Eight, nine...* Ah, there they were, footsteps approaching; three sets, if he wasn't mistaken. He rolled his shoulders and flexed his neck from one side to the other, bracing himself... *Ten.*

'You won't believe what he's done!' Seventeen-year-old Antigone was the first to exclaim, pointing accusingly in the direction of the library.

'Justin?' Quinton arched an eyebrow as their fourteen-year-old brother loped after her.

'It's a disgrace!' These words from his mother, descending the staircase. 'I've never been so insulted!'

He rubbed a hand over his chin, doubting the truth of *that* particular statement, though he supposed there was no way to avoid asking. 'How so?'

'Mrs Padgett is holding a soirée next week and I'm not invited!'

'I thought you didn't like Mrs Padgett?'

'I don't, but that's hardly the point. *I'm* still the Duchess.' A small crease appeared between her brows. 'Of sorts anyway. I ought to be invited everywhere, whether I choose to attend or not. Instead I have to read about it in a letter from Lady Fortescue.'

'How thoughtful of her to tell you.'

'She's a spiteful old cat. The next time I see her, I'll—'

'He read my diary!' Antigone refused to be ignored any longer.

'What?' Their mother's head snapped around. 'Justin, is this true?'

'Yes, it's true! I was writing in the library, but I had to get up to…you know, and when I came back he had his nose buried between the covers, the little sneak.'

'I don't know why you're so bothered.' The accused finally spoke up for himself. 'There was nothing interesting. She saw some daffodils yesterday, did you know? Fascinating.'

'You're an insensitive pig!'

'Justin, one does not invade another person's privacy.' His mother lifted her chin expressly for the purpose of looking down her nose. 'Although, I believe we've discussed your use of the library before, Antigone.'

'You *always* take his side!'

'I am not taking anyone's side. Strictly speaking, however, the library belongs to the gentlemen of the house. A lady ought to write in the comfort of the drawing room or her own bedchamber, where you have a perfectly charming escritoire, I might add.'

'I prefer the library!'

'And a lady does not use the words "sneak" or "pig".'

'This one does.' Antigone's green eyes flashed dangerously. 'I could call him other names, too. Corin taught me.'

'Go on.' Justin perked up immediately. 'I want to learn them, as well.'

'Enough!' Quinton held up a hand before his sister

could open her mouth again. 'Justin, you were in the wrong. Mother, rise above Mrs Padgett and Lady Fortescue. Antigone, whatever those names were, I order you to forget them immediately. In exchange, I'll take you out riding tomorrow. The woods are filled with daffodils.'

'Oh, yes, please!'

'What about me?' Justin sounded as if he'd just regressed to toddlerhood. 'I want to come, too!'

'Absolutely not. You can write an essay about why you were wrong and then translate it into Latin. It'll be good practice for school. And now, if you'll all excuse me, I have some paperwork to attend to. I trust that we can save any additional drama until luncheon?' He gave them each a stern look, making sure there were no additional protests before escaping swiftly towards his office.

'Masterfully done,' another voice drawled just as his hand touched the door handle.

Quinton closed his eyes, counting to ten—*again*—before turning around and lifting his gaze to the minstrels' gallery that ran along the top of the great hall. At twenty-five, Corin was only three years his junior, but sometimes the difference felt more like fifty.

'You're up early.' He couldn't resist the dig.

'I know. So much shouting…'

'I need to get on with some work.'

'I don't keep a diary myself,' Corin persisted, tapping his nose confidentially. 'It would be far too bleak.'

'Quite. I'll see you at luncheon, then.' He took a second look at his brother's unkempt hair and what appeared to be yesterday's clothes. 'I'd appreciate it

if you could make yourself look a bit more present-
able by then.'

'I'll do my best, but I can't make any promises.'
Corin lifted his shoulders. 'You'd know better than to
believe them anyway.'

Quinton gave a tight smile, opening his study door
and then shutting it firmly behind him. His family
were…well, they were his family. He loved them, he
was prepared to lay down his life for any one of them
if necessary, but the constant complaining and shouting and bickering and insinuating was exhausting. Even
on good days he was tempted to throw the whole lot of
them out onto the street, Helen excepted. And where
was Helen anyway? Hiding under a table somewhere,
probably. Life would be so much easier if he could
join her.

He leaned his shoulder against the door jamb for a
few moments, relishing the sudden descent of peace.
His study was his haven, his escape, the one place in
the house his family knew not to intrude upon without some life-threatening situation that required his urgent attention. Which was exactly the reason he spent
around eighty per cent of his time there.

Slowly, he crossed the faded red carpet to his leather-
embossed, walnut desk and sat down. At least Justin
would be going to Eton soon. That ought to reduce the
amount of shouting, though no doubt Antigone would
then begin wailing about how much she missed him.
She needed a companion, another woman to talk to,
or else she'd be left essentially alone with their mother
and *that* hardly bore thinking about. He ought to start
making arrangements, but it was difficult to decide
anything until…well, until a certain other matter was

settled. It was taking somewhat longer than he'd expected, but, as it turned out, people were even harder to manage than stones.

'Good morning, Your Grace.' His secretary, Harker, appeared in the doorway that connected their two studies. 'I trust that you had a pleasant ride? Not too cold?'

'*Very* cold, but still enjoyable.' He placed his hands flat on the table, determined to get straight down to business. 'However, it occurred to me that we ought to take a second look at those plans for the new labourers' cottages. I'm not sure the designs are quite large enough.'

'Of course, Your Grace, I'll go and find them now, only…'

'Yes?' Quinton quirked an eyebrow, surprised by his secretary's reticence. Usually he was straight to the point. 'Is something the matter?'

'Not exactly. Only the thing is…that is to say, a messenger arrived this morning. He brought a letter.'

'That's not so unusual, surely?'

'No, except that he came from Bath.'

'Ah.' It was a good thing, Quinton thought, that he was already sitting down. At that precise moment he couldn't have vouched for the stability of his own legs. 'I see.'

'Naturally, I haven't looked at the contents.' Harker pulled a folded piece of parchment from his inner pocket and passed it across the desk. 'Although I took the liberty of keeping it about my person.'

'To avoid prying eyes, you mean? Good idea.'

Harker took a tactful step backwards. 'I'll leave you to read it in peace. If Your Grace would excuse me?'

'Yes, thank you, that will be all for now.'

Quinton waited until his secretary's door had closed behind him before looking at the letter, then at a point in mid-air, then at the letter again. There it was, the very thing he'd been waiting for, and yet now that he held it between his fingers he was aware of a strange sense of foreboding. The very parchment itself felt hot, as if the words inside might actually brand him if he wasn't careful. Not that speculation was going to do him any good either… He took a deep breath, unfolded the parchment and read. The handwriting inside was small and neat, without any loops or flourishes, and the message itself concise, only two paragraphs long, containing no excuses or explanations, no pleas for help or declarations of feeling, just an expression of regret and an offer.

He leaned back in his chair, letting the parchment drop from his fingers onto the desk. Well, he had to hand it to her. Just when he thought that his wife was out of surprises, she gave him the biggest one of all.

Daffodils would have to wait. It was time for him to go to Bath and avert another scandal.

Chapter One

'Almost done,' Beatrix Roxbury, née Beatrix Thatcher, also known to the residents of Bath as Belinda Carr, slid one last pin into the mass of flaming-red curls before her and stepped back with a satisfied nod. 'There you go. Perfect!'

'Really?' The object of her ministrations sounded dubious.

'Take a look for yourself.' She held up a small hand mirror. 'Personally, I think you look lovely.'

'Oh!' Nancy MacQueen, her friend, fellow baker and resident of the adjacent bedroom, looked uncharacteristically stunned. 'It's so different. I don't know what to say.'

'That you like it?'

'Yes! I've just never seen it so neat. Usually it looks like there's a cluster of snakes on my head.'

'You're not Medusa.' Beatrix smiled fondly. 'Although I admit you're quite good at frightening people.'

'I take that as a compliment.'

'I know. I meant it as one, too, especially since I know you have a heart of gold underneath.'

'Harumph…' Nancy blinked at her reflection a few more times and then beamed. 'I love it. I look like the rest of you, for once.'

'What do you mean, "the rest of us"?'

'You and Henrietta and Anna. You're all so pretty and put-together.'

'I don't know about that. I mean, I still haven't met Anna, but I always feel so drab next to you and Henrietta.' Beatrix turned the hand mirror around and sighed. 'What colour is my hair anyway? Blonde or brown?'

'It's b…' Nancy paused. 'Light brown.'

'Exactly. Or dark blonde. Neither one nor the other. Drab.'

'Well, whatever it is, it's the exact same shade as your eyes.'

'So I'm doubly drab?'

'Co-ordinated.' Nancy laughed and stood up. 'All right, you've made your point. Maybe we should both just agree to feel pretty this evening. It's a special occasion, after all, the grand opening of Henrietta's Tea Shop!'

'I know!' Beatrix forgot all about her drabness, bouncing up onto her tiptoes with excitement. 'I can't wait to see what they've done, and so quickly, too. It's hardly been two months since they got back, though of course they've had a lot of help from Mr Redbourne. *He* was the one who found them premises so quickly.'

'Mmm.'

'*And* with rooms above for them to live in. Which,

you have to admit, saved us from having to move out. We couldn't all have fitted in here.'

'Yes. It was kind of him.'

Beatrix felt her jaw drop. *'What?'*

'Nothing. I said it was kind.'

'You just complimented Mr Redbourne!'

'I did not!'

'You did!'

'I gave credit where it was due, that's all. Anything else I might think about him hasn't changed.'

'But why—?'

'And I'm *not* going to discuss it!' Nancy thrust her chin into the air. 'Now, you'd better change so we can get going.'

'You go ahead.' Beatrix stretched her arms above her head, knowing better than to pursue the subject any further. When it came to James Redbourne, Nancy was even more intractable than usual. 'I want to sit down for five minutes first.'

'Oh, dear.' Nancy looked immediately contrite. 'I've made you late.'

'Don't be silly. I offered to do your hair and mine won't take more than a few minutes. Now hurry along and I'll catch up.'

'Are you sure?'

'Perfectly.' She dropped down onto the bed behind her. 'It's been a long day and my feet need a rest.'

'The shop *was* busy,' Nancy agreed from the doorway. 'Just don't fall asleep or I'll come back and fetch you.'

Beatrix yawned and wriggled back against the pillows, closing her eyes for a few seconds as the sound of footsteps receded. Nancy was right, if she stayed there then she was liable to fall asleep and miss the celebrations completely, but her bed was *so* comfortable. Or if it wasn't in reality then it was to her. *Her* bed in *her* room beside *her* rickety old chair by *her* scratched maple wood table in the corner; they were all perfection.

Belles was the first place she'd thought of as home in twelve years, ever since the death of her parents had left her one of the wealthiest heiresses in England—one of the wealthiest middle-class heiresses anyway—and she treasured everything about it. The shop had given her a place to live, a profession to learn, friends she could trust and a sense of contentment she hadn't felt since she was ten years old.

There was only one grey smudge on her conscience, but now that she was settled, she was doing her best to set that to rights, too. After two months of humming and hawing, the letter she'd been dreading to write was finally sealed and sent—unbeknownst to Nancy, who would have tried to stop her—so now all she had to do was wait. In the meantime, she could get up and enjoy the party.

She heaved herself upright, removing her shop dress and giving herself a quick wash from the basin before twisting her long, *drab* hair into a knot on top of her head and sliding into her new, apple-green muslin gown. It wasn't very elaborate or even particularly good quality, with only a thin strip of white lace around the neckline, but she'd purchased it with her own earnings especially for the occasion, and that fact alone made her feel like a princess. As a final touch, she added a small pair of topaz earrings and then headed downstairs barely five minutes behind Nancy.

Stifling a yawn, she made her way out through the shop, wrapping a shawl around her shoulders as she locked the front door behind her. In the early evening, the sky was a brilliant shade of cerulean blue and a family of finches were busy chirruping their farewells to the day from the opposite rooftop, filling the air with a cheerful, harmonious melody. She looked up and smiled, wishing she weren't already late so that she could stay and enjoy their song for longer. Maybe if she walked slowly…

'Beatrix?'

She froze with one foot in mid-air, feeling as if her heart had just slammed hard into her ribcage and then plummeted all the way down to her stomach, not with fear so much as surprise. No, that was too mild a description. Utter, total, stupefying amazement was better. There was no mistaking that voice, which was odd considering on how few occasions she'd actually heard it, but then she supposed some voices were memorable, her husband's particularly so.

Quinton.

A thin layer of perspiration broke out on her palms and forehead, though she didn't move so much as a muscle, her thoughts whirling as she wondered how to react, whether to faint, run or do the sensible thing and face him. Fainting, apparently, wasn't something a person could will upon themselves, and what would happen if she ran? Would he pursue her? Yes, of course he'd pursue her, she thought in mortification. He was *there*, wasn't he? After coming in person—*and what on earth was he doing there in person?*—it wasn't likely that he'd simply give up at the sight of her retreating back. Brief as their acquaintance had been, he hadn't struck her as lazy or unfit. Quite the contrary, in fact. He'd struck her as quite robustly healthy. And even if he didn't chase after her himself, he was a duke. No doubt he had attendants with him. He'd probably send one of them to catch her, which would be doubly mortifying. No, running away—*again*—was a foolish impulse, but she still wasn't ready to see him, not here and not now. She was supposed to be going to a party! And he must be thinking she'd turned into a statue...

Slowly, she turned around, willing her imagination to be playing tricks on her, but there he was, looking every inch the haughty peer of the realm that she remembered, swathed in a black cape and wearing a top hat that made him appear a full two heads taller than she was. She ran her tongue along her lips and swallowed, hoping she didn't look as intimidated as she suddenly felt.

'Good evening.' He inclined his head as if they were mere acquaintances, which to be fair seemed a more fitting description than husband and wife.

'Your Grace.' She dipped into what hopefully passed for a curtsy, amazed by how calm her voice sounded when her mouth felt like a desert and her insides like a quivering mass of jelly. 'This is a surprise?' Somehow the statement came out sounding more like a question.

'You wrote to me.'

'Yes, but surely the messenger only arrived yesterday?'

'Nonetheless, here I am.'

'Oh.' She dug her teeth into her bottom lip, unable to think of a single other thing to say. She wasn't sure what she'd expected to happen when he'd received her letter, but it certainly hadn't been for him to turn up on her doorstep the next day. A lawyer perhaps in a week or two, but not *him*! From what she could see, he was alone, too, without a single attendant to manhandle her. Which was a relief, although it still didn't explain what he was doing there…

After running away on their wedding day, she'd assumed that he'd never want to see her again. She'd assumed that he'd be furious. Surely he *was* furious! Only he didn't look furious. He looked…nothing. Whatever he was feeling inside, his expression was just as austerely handsome and inscrutable and…*ducal* as it had been on their wedding day. As if no time had passed and nothing else had happened…

'You look well.' He removed his top hat, reducing the difference between them to a single head, not that it made her feel much better. The initial shock was subsiding, but her pulse was still thudding painfully hard and she was getting a crick in her neck from looking upwards.

'Do I?'

'Yes. Bath obviously agrees with you.'

'I suppose so,' she agreed warily, trying not to blink under the intensity of his blue gaze. 'I like it here.'

'Indeed.' He turned his head to look at Belles. 'So this is it?'

She blinked. 'This is what?'

'Your biscuit shop. I've been wondering what was so special about it.'

'You've been wondering…' It took her a few moments to fully comprehend his meaning. 'You mean you *knew* I was here?'

'Since December, yes…' there was a momentary pause while he examined the window shutters '… *Belinda*.'

She gave a start at the sound of her 'other' name, the one she'd been living under for the past three and a half months. 'But how? Why didn't you—?'

'I'd prefer not to discuss my private business on the street.' He turned his head back sharply towards her. 'Perhaps we might talk inside?'

'That depends on what you want to say.' She stiffened her spine, determined not to let him take control of the situation. She'd spent too much of her life allowing other people to do that. 'If you've come because of my letter then you know my offer. Do you accept?'

'No.'

'What?' She pressed a hand to her mouth with a gasp. So much for not letting him take control. She felt—no doubt she *looked*—stunned. 'But I offered to free you. I offered either an annulment or a divorce!'

'Yes.'

'I said that you could keep all the money and that I wouldn't contest it or make any fuss.'

'I know.'

'Then *why not*?'

'Call me eccentric, but I have a strange revulsion against stealing another person's fortune.'

'But it's not mine any more! Legally everything I inherited became yours on our wedding day.' She strove to keep the bitterness out of her voice. 'You wouldn't be stealing.'

'As good as.' His eyes seemed to spark with some emotion, though it came and went so quickly she couldn't be sure whether or not she'd imagined it. 'However, despite what you may have thought, I was never happy about the idea of marrying for money. I did what I needed to do, but I'll be damned if I don't fulfil my side of the bargain, as well.'

'But I'm saying that you don't have to!'

'And I'm saying that I do. Ironic as those two words sound under the circumstances.'

'I don't... *You* don't understand.' She clenched her teeth and fists at the same time, panic making her indiscreet. She'd been so sure of him accepting her offer, she hadn't even considered the alternative. 'I don't *want* you to fulfil your side of the bargain!'

'Yes, I believe you made that point abundantly clear. However, as your husband I vowed to protect and take care of you.'

'*I* can protect and take care of me. I admit, I wasn't particularly good at either to begin with, but I am now. I've made myself a home and I'm happy here. How dare you think you can just come and claim me?'

'I dare because it's the truth, as I think we both know.'

Beatrix sucked in a breath, her emotions swinging wildly between fear, resentment and anger. He was right, she *did* know. By law, he could demand whatever he wanted and there was nothing anyone could do about it, least of all her. A wife had no independent identity, no personal freedom, no way to even petition for a divorce; as good as a prisoner at the whim of her husband. And now here she was in the exact situation that Nancy had warned her about! A shudder racked her body at the thought. If only she'd listened instead of trying to set things right by sending that letter...

'As it happens, however, I haven't come to claim anything.' He sounded maddeningly calm. 'I've simply come to talk.'

'*Just talk?*'

'Given the circumstances, I thought a conversation wasn't too much to ask. After all, how many bride-grooms can say they've been abandoned on their wedding day? And *after* the wedding, too? From what I understand, most brides make a run for it beforehand.'

'Ye-es. About that...'

'Not here,' he repeated firmly. 'Inside.'

Beatrix narrowed her eyes suspiciously. He'd struck her as cold and forbidding the first time they'd met, an ice-capped mountain in human form, but now there was something different about him. He looked tired. Care-worn. Oppressed even. If she were going to labour the mountain metaphor even further then she might have said there were cracks in his cliff-face, as if he were trying to hold back an avalanche. None of which told her whether or not she could trust him.

'If I wanted to *claim* you then I could have done so at any point since December.' He sounded impatient, seeming to guess her thoughts. 'You've nothing to fear from me, Beatrix, I give you my word.'

'Oh, all right.' She lifted her key to the door and then hesitated. If she didn't make an appearance at the party soon then Nancy would assume that she'd fallen asleep and come back to fetch her, and the *last* thing she needed was for her housemate and husband to meet. She'd never seen fireworks, but she'd heard about them and, Duke or no Duke, she imagined the effect would be similar. 'But not here.'

He was the one to look suspicious this time. 'Any particular reason?'

Yes, an extremely belligerent one with red hair, as it happened... 'I'm just not sure that we'd have privacy.'

'Very well. In that case, I'm staying at the George Hotel. Would that be more amenable?'

She stiffened in shock. 'You mean go to a hotel together?'

'Yes, since we apparently can't use a biscuit shop. It's not particularly scandalous when you consider that we're already married.' He paused and looked thoughtful. 'It's not scandalous at all, in fact.'

'But what if somebody sees me? What if they think that I'm…you know…?'

'I do know, although I'm not sure what you want me to say.' His gaze swept down to her feet and then back up again. 'You're hardly dressed like one.'

'I still don't look much like a duchess!'

'True. However, it's either here or there. You decide.' He pinched the bridge of his nose between two fingers. 'Only preferably before it gets dark. I've had a long journey and I'm tired.'

Beatrix drew her brows together. *He* might not care about other people's opinions, but *he* didn't live in Bath. What if they were seen together by someone who knew her? It could start all kinds of rumours. On the other hand, it was still safer than being caught by Nancy.

'Fine. Just give me a moment to write a note for my friend. I'll tell her that something's come up and I can't be…where I'm supposed to be.'

'As you wish.'

'It's not a trick. I won't run out the back door, I promise.'

A black eyebrow rose upwards. 'The thought never crossed my mind.'

She gave him a withering look, then hurried inside and up to the parlour, scribbling a message about having a headache and going for a walk. It wasn't particularly believable, but it was better than nothing. Nancy wouldn't be able to read it herself, but she could show it to Henrietta.

Satisfied, she ran back down the stairs, propped the note up on the shop counter and closed the door behind her.

'You're not sending the note?' Either her husband hadn't bothered to lower his eyebrow the first time or he'd just raised it again.

'No.' She shook her head, knowing that Nancy would ruthlessly interrogate any messenger. 'She'll find it. Trust me.'

'Very well, then.' He lifted a hand, gesturing ahead of them down the street. 'Shall we?'

Beatrix tightened her shawl around her shoulders and started walking, relieved when he didn't offer an arm. Frankly, the thought of any physical contact with him was unnerving. They hadn't touched very often, only twice, now that she thought about it—once when he'd kissed her hand after his proposal and again when he'd slid the wedding ring over her finger—and both times had left her feeling hot, trembly and decidedly uncomfortable in a way that she hadn't understood *or* appreciated. Even walking beside him now, she was aware of her pulse beating twice as fast as usual.

'This way.' She swung away from him abruptly, crossing to the far side of Great Pulteney street to avoid walking right outside Redbourne's General Store and its new neighbour, Henrietta's. A quick peek through the windows showed that the tea room was already full of guests, almost bursting at the seams, in fact, though the new sign above the door was still draped in cloth, waiting to be unveiled. She only hoped that her conversation with her husband wouldn't take too long and she'd be back in time to see it happen.

'Acquaintances of yours?' Quinton turned his head in the same direction.

'Friends, actually. Good ones,' she answered pointedly. At least that would tell him she *had* friends—ones who would help her, or try to anyway, if she needed their support—even if she was currently trying to get past them as quickly and stealthily as possible.

Fortunately, it was only a few minutes until they were safely over the bridge and making their way up Milsom Street towards the George Hotel, an elegant, honey-coloured building with large Doric columns on either side of the main doorway.

'You'd better wait out here and I'll send a page to escort you up.' Her husband stopped on the threshold. 'That way we won't leave your reputation completely in tatters.'

'Oh…yes…' She felt her cheeks flush at the reminder. 'Thank you.'

'I'll see you upstairs in a few minutes?' He gave her one last penetrating look before turning away, vanishing inside without waiting for an answer.

Beatrix stared after him, wondering whether it wouldn't be wiser to turn and run back to the safety of Henrietta's and her friends after all, but somehow her feet refused to budge. For one thing, because he was giving her a choice, not compelling her. For another, because he was right, a conversation wasn't too much to ask; it was the least that she owed him. And for a third…well, for a third because if she was going to get a divorce then it seemed they needed to talk. And she needed to be a lot more persuasive.

'Miss?' A page came out and bowed discreetly. 'Are you…?'

'Yes.' She pulled her shoulders back and herself together. 'Yes, I am.'

'Very good, miss. This way.'

Chapter Two

'You came, then?' Her husband opened the door himself, tossing a coin to the page before stepping aside to let her in.

'I said that I would.' Beatrix lifted her chin as she crossed the threshold.

'If memory serves, you also said "I do".' He closed the door behind her and made a face. 'Forgive me, that was a low blow.'

'Yes, it was.' Annoyingly, it was also true. Given their history, she could hardly expect him to put a great deal of store in her word. 'Here. You can take these as an apology.'

She thrust her shawl and gloves at him, not waiting to see his reaction before walking ahead into the suite. From the look of it, there were three rooms beyond the entrance hall: the drawing room she'd just entered, a dining area to the left and—she turned her face away quickly from the sight of a large four-poster bed through the open doorway—a bedroom to the right.

'You look different.' Her husband's voice came from behind her shoulder.

'Do I?' She didn't bother to turn around, though she could feel his gaze like a touch on the nape of her neck. It sent an unusual, not entirely unpleasant, but definitely unnerving shiver down her spine.

'Yes. You look older.'

Older. She pursed her lips as he came to stand beside her. It wasn't much of a compliment, not that she ought to have expected one. He'd never given her so much as an approving glance before so it was hardly likely he'd start now. Still, at least it gave her licence to be honest, as well…

'So do you.'

'I know. My mirror reminds me of the fact every morning. However, I wasn't talking about your appearance exactly. I meant more your demeanour and…' He gestured at her dress. 'This. I like it better than your wedding dress.'

'So do I, but then I chose this one myself.'

'You mean you didn't choose your wedding gown?'

'No.' She was faintly offended by the suggestion. 'My aunt chose all of my clothes before.'

'Ah. That explains the frills, but this style suits you. The colour, too.'

She jerked her head back. That was *almost* a compliment. 'Green is my favourite.'

'Good to know.' He nodded slowly as if he were filing the information away for future reference. 'I suppose that's the sort of thing a married couple ought to know about each other, although for myself I've never really considered the matter. Blue, probably.' He shrugged and then gestured towards a small round table set in a bay window. There was a chair on either side and a bottle of what appeared to be red wine in the centre. 'Take a seat. I took the liberty of preparing.'

'I don't drink.'

'That's for me, although I could ring for some tea if you like?'

'No, thank you. This shouldn't take long.'

'Indeed? Shall we sit and get it over with, then?'

She clenched her teeth at the sarcasm, not that she disagreed with the sentiment, taking the chair facing the hall while he took the one opposite.

'So.' He placed one hand on the table between them, tapping his fingers lightly against the surface. 'Perhaps we ought to get straight to the point. What happened? *Something* happened, I presume?'

She glanced at his hand, tempted to pretend that she didn't know what he meant. She didn't want to talk about their wedding day, but if she were going to persuade him to apply for a divorce then apparently she needed to tell him the truth, more—*and maybe a little extra*—of it than she'd intended. Surely he'd be glad to be rid of her then.

'Not exactly, although it wasn't planned either.' She lifted her gaze back to his as she spoke. A new feeling of tension seemed to have settled over the room, like a low-hanging cloud with tiny lightning bolts flashing across the ceiling. It made her far too aware of her own breathing—of his too—as their eyes locked and held across the table. Strangely enough, now that she looked at him properly, he was a lot more handsome than her memory had given him credit for, the almost razor-sharp lines of his face lending him a strong and commanding aspect. 'I had no intention of running away when we said our vows. I swear it never crossed my mind until afterwards.'

'A burst of inspiration, then?'

'Impulse.' She corrected him. 'The opportunity was there so I took it. There was no one watching me. For the first time in months, I was all alone, free to make my own decisions…' She shook her head, squirming beneath the intensity of his gaze. 'My only defence is that it seemed like the right thing to do at the time. Although I appreciate it must not have looked that way to you.'

'You're right, it didn't. One moment your uncle was raising a glass of champagne, the next your aunt came running into the room in a panic. She was extremely concerned about you.'

'No, she wasn't.' Beatrix bit back a laugh. 'If she was worried about anyone then it was herself. She was probably frightened about how you were going to react.'

'I see.' He didn't contradict her, his expression turning thoughtful instead. 'I admit that was my impression afterwards, too.'

'Out of interest…' she leaned forward, unable to resist asking '…how *did* you react?'

'You mean did I shout and throw things?' His lips curved sardonically. 'I'm afraid not. We discussed where you might have gone and then I went to my lawyer's, engaged the services of a detective and returned to my own house. It was all rather anticlimactic.'

'Oh.'

'You sound disappointed.'

'No.' She tossed her head. 'I could hardly have expected you to care. We hardly knew each other.'

'Quite.' His blue eyes glittered, seeming to turn silver for a moment. 'However, if it's any consolation, I remember drinking an ill-advised amount of brandy that night, enough to cause me a significant amount of regret in the morning.'

'Sorry.'

'Not at all. That part was my own doing. In retrospect, I suppose I ought to be grateful you didn't run away *after* the wedding night. There's only so much a man's pride can take.' There was another silver flash before he laid a hand down flat on the table. 'So what do you mean about it being "the right thing to do"?'

'Well…' She cleared her throat, wishing the interview over and done with. 'There were—*are*—certain things you didn't—*don't*—know about me. Things you ought to have known before the wedding, only I didn't have any opportunity to tell you.'

'I'm listening now.'

'Ye-es.' She took a deep breath, her pulse accelerating again as she summoned the courage to go on. 'The truth is, I'm not the kind of woman you think I am.'

'Really? Then what kind of woman are you, exactly?'

'I'm…' She squeezed her eyes shut and waved her hand in the air.

'A windmill?'

'Promiscuous!'

'Ah.'

She waited a few seconds and then opened her eyes again, surprised to find that his expression hadn't altered at all. He looked just as inscrutable as before.

'I just said that I'm promiscuous!' she repeated, irritated by his utter lack of reaction. 'Aren't you shocked? Don't you have anything to say?'

'I'm reserving judgement. Perhaps you might start by providing me with some evidence. Details perhaps? How many men exactly are we talking about?'

'One!' She wrenched her shoulders back, offended by the question.

'Forgive me, but you made it sound…' He untied his cravat, leaving it hanging on either side of his neck. 'On how many occasions?'

'One!'

'Ah. Again, you made it sound—'

'So you see,' she interrupted him, aware that her cheeks were flaming now, 'I'm not suitable to be a duchess!'

'Is that what you think?' He rested one elbow on the table and rubbed his knuckle against his forehead. 'Might I ask when this *indiscretion* occurred?'

'Eight months ago.'

'Before our engagement, then?'

'Of course *before*!'

'And the man's identity?'

She sat back in her chair, pressing her lips together tightly as if the name might escape by accident.

'Beatrix?' His tone sharpened.

'I'd prefer not to say.'

'Believe me, I'd prefer not to ask.' He frowned. 'All right. Were you—*are* you—in love with him?'

'Would it make any difference?'

'Yes!' His gaze fixed upon hers so intently that she almost flinched. 'I'm not entirely heartless, no matter what you might think. Now as to my question, are you in love with him?'

She drew in a deep breath, startled by his sudden burst of vehemence. *Not entirely heartless...* No, she had to agree, he wasn't that. He was asking for her side of the story as if he really were reserving judgement.

She licked her lips and then shook her head. 'No. I thought I was in love with him when we…or I would never…only it turned out that he wasn't the man I thought. I only loved the man I thought I knew.'

'And was it him you went to after you ran away?'

'You know about that?' She jerked her head up in horror.

'Not until this moment. My man tracked you down in Bath, but I presumed you must have had some kind of plan beforehand.'

'Oh…yes, I went to him. I hadn't heard from him in months, but I knew where he lived and I thought that he'd help me. I was wrong.' She sucked in her cheeks, fighting back tears at the memory. 'It's not something I wish to discuss.'

'Then just one more question.' To her surprise, he sounded almost sympathetic. 'Are you still in communication with him?'

'No. I hope I never see him again in my life.'

'I see.' He nodded slowly, his eyes never leaving her face. 'Then did it never occur to you to come back to me afterwards? The streets of London can be dangerous, especially for a woman.'

'Honestly, I didn't think that you'd want me. And as for going back to my uncle and aunt's…' She shuddered. 'Fortunately, I remembered the address of my old governess in Bath so I came here. I didn't find her, but I found Belles instead.'

'I'm relieved you made it here safely.' He leaned back in his chair. 'You know, I've thought about what happened a great deal over the past three months and what I don't understand is why you didn't just say if you didn't want to marry me. Why didn't you refuse my proposal? I would never have agreed to the match if I'd known you were unwilling.'

She shifted uncomfortably in her seat. Her uncle and aunt would have made her life a misery if she'd refused, but they hadn't actually compelled her down the aisle. 'It's hard to explain. I wasn't unwilling, not exactly. Maybe I wasn't thinking straight after my... indiscretion, but I thought that my choices were either marry you or spend another three years under my uncle's roof and you seemed like the lesser of two—' She bit her tongue.

'Evils?' he finished for her. 'Not the greatest compliment I've ever received, but possibly a fair one. However, if you wanted to run away then why didn't you do it *before* the wedding? You could have saved us both a great deal of trouble.'

'Because it was never a possibility before. I was never allowed out of the house except with my aunt and then only rarely. Do you know, I lived in London for twenty-two years and yet I've never even seen the Tower? I spent most of my time indoors and my maid locked us both into my bedchamber at night. She even slept with the key beneath her pillow.'

'You make it sound like a prison.' His brow knotted. 'I confess that when I met your uncle, he seemed somewhat...'

'Avaricious and insincere?'

'Something like that.' He tipped his head in acknowledgement.

'It all happened so quickly, too. My uncle told me that he'd arranged a match, but he never explained to me how it had all come about or why. I could hardly believe it when he said you were a duke.'

'Yes, he did seem particularly impressed by that point.' His frown deepened as he reached across the table and poured himself a small glass of wine. Surprisingly small considering the circumstances. 'It was thanks to my lawyer. He made some enquiries on my behalf and came up with your uncle.'

'You mean you asked your lawyer to find you a rich wife?'

'That's about the long and short of it, yes.' He tossed the wine back in one mouthful. 'It was necessary. Once I inherited the Dukedom it didn't take me long to realise that my family estate was close to ruin. And by close I mean teetering on the brink of a precipice.' He paused and then seemed to think more explanation was necessary. 'My father and I had been estranged for a number of years.'

'You mean you didn't know things were so bad?'

'No. I was in France.'

'France?' She gasped. 'But there was a war!'

'That probably explains why they gave me a sword and pistol.' His eyes glinted with a hint of amusement. 'I was a Major in Wellesley's army.'

'Oh!' She opened her mouth and then closed it again. 'Nobody told me about that.'

'There appears to be quite a lot of things we don't know about each other. More things than we *do* know, truth be told, favourite colours excepted.'

'But that doesn't make sense!' She shook her head, confused. 'You're a duke so you must be a first-born son, mustn't you?'

'Yes.'

'Well, I thought that *second* sons joined the army?'

'Usually.'

'So…'

'Like I said, my father and I were estranged. He wouldn't have cared if I'd gone on a one-way expedition to the North Pole.'

'Oh…' Judging by the tone of his voice, it wasn't a subject he wished to pursue any further. 'So you left the army after he died?'

'A little before that. I resigned my commission and returned to England at my mother's request when his health began to decline. I only inherited eleven months ago.'

'And then your lawyer found my uncle?'

'Eventually, yes. They agreed on a marriage contract.'

'Exchanging my fortune for your influence?'

'Exactly.'

She dug her teeth into her bottom lip. It made sense. At the age of twenty-two, she was only three years away from gaining her fortune and her independence. Her uncle would have had nothing to lose by arranging a marriage for her except the yearly stipend he received for letting her live under his roof, but obviously he'd thought a connection with a duke would benefit his mercantile business enough to compensate.

'I'm sorry.' He was looking at her strangely, she noticed, as if he were seeing her properly for the first time. 'I ought to have told you all of this before our wedding. I had a lot on my mind, but that's not much of an excuse. How many times did we actually meet before we got married?'

'Once. The day you proposed.'

'*Once?*' He swore softly. 'I wasn't much of a suitor, was I?' He put up a hand. 'Wait. On second thoughts, don't answer that.'

'To be fair, I wasn't much of a bride either. I should have told you about my…indiscretion, but there was no opportunity. Our engagement was so short and since it was all about the money anyway…' She lifted her shoulders. 'I truly thought that I only had the two choices, marrying you or staying with my uncle and aunt, but then after the wedding, when there was no one guarding me, I suddenly realised that there *was* another choice. I could run away and be free. So that's what I did. I changed out of my wedding dress, grabbed a few belongings and ran down the servants' staircase to the back entrance. I thought that if I left before the wedding night, then our marriage could still be annulled.' She leaned across the table. 'And it still *could*, couldn't it? We haven't had a chance to consummate the marriage.'

'Actually, I'm afraid it's a little late for an annulment.'

'It is? Why?'

'Because nobody knows you ran away except for my family and yours and they're all sworn to secrecy. Fortunately we chose not to have a big wedding.'

'You mean…'

'That as far as the rest of the world is concerned, we were married three and a half months ago and have been happily *consummating* at Howden Hall ever since.' He refilled his glass, raising it as if he were making a toast and then lowering it again without drinking. 'There might be rumours, but for the moment that's all they are, just rumours.'

'But…why? Why didn't you denounce me?'

'Because my family's been involved in enough scandal over the past year. For myself, I'd prefer not to be the butt of every *ton* joke, but I have a thick skin. For my family...' The line of his jaw tightened, a muscle flexing beneath the skin. 'I don't want them humiliated any more than they have been already.'

'Oh.' She tilted her head to one side curiously. 'How have they been—?'

'The point is,' he interrupted before she could finish the question, the muscle flexing again, 'a divorce would be difficult, messy and a national headline. Is that really what you want?'

'Of course not, but if we can't get an annulment then we'll *have* to get a divorce and—'

'No.' His tone was unequivocal.

She opened her eyes wide. 'But surely you don't want to remain married? Not after what I just told you?'

'I do. To be honest, I was as enthusiastic about the idea as you were, but it was my duty to marry and so I did. Now that I *am* married, moreover, I intend to stand by my word. You're my Duchess. For better or worse. Windmill or...otherwise.'

She was vaguely aware of her mouth dropping open, though it seemed beyond her power to close it again.

'Beatrix?' He lifted an eyebrow.

'So you're saying that you want to stay married *despite* my running away?' Somehow she got her jaw working again.

'Yes.'

'*Despite* my being damaged goods?'

'There's no need to be quite so dramatic.' His voice was laced with irony. 'Unless the act itself caused you damage in some way, which I doubt, that seems a rather ugly way of putting it.'

'It's what a lot of men would call it.'

'A lot of men are hypocrites. I would hardly describe myself as a rake, but I haven't led a celibate life either.'

'Then what about my working in a biscuit shop? Doesn't that bother you?'

'As to that, it appears no one else has any inkling. You must be a very convincing baker.'

'I am. What I'm *not* is a duchess.'

'Like it or not, you already are.'

'Only in name.' She stood up, stalking halfway across the room before realising that she was heading for the bedroom and swinging quickly around again. 'I don't understand. After what I did, I thought you'd be furious with me. *I* would have been furious with me! Why *aren't* you?'

Chapter Three

*W*hy wasn't he furious? It was a reasonable question, Quinton supposed. He had to admit he'd been somewhat disturbed and irritated at the time. Even today he'd been aware of a few brief sparks of temper before he'd managed to wrestle his emotions back under control again. Now that he had, however, he was simply concerned with finding a resolution to their current predicament, one that *didn't* involve a divorce.

'I can't say that I'm particularly pleased with our situation.' He made a point of speaking as calmly as possible. 'However, I choose not to waste my time with unhelpful or extreme emotions, nor do I let them control me. Therefore, I believe it would be best to put the past behind us and move on.'

'Just like that?' She looked and sounded bewildered.

'Just like that. Since I was, to an extent, culpable, too. At the very least, I ought to have visited you more than once before our wedding ceremony. I presumed that we'd get to know each other afterwards, but it was misguided of me. If we'd had a conversation beforehand then this whole situation might have been averted.

I can hardly blame you for acting on impulse when I behaved so coldly. For which, I apologise.'

'You apologise...?'

Her voice trailed away as if she were struggling to believe the evidence of her own ears. It was, however, the truth. He *was* sorry. He ought to have treated her like a person and not a banker's draft. He'd agreed to the marriage in exchange for her fortune, but he'd arrogantly assumed that his title would be enough to tempt her. He'd misjudged her; no, worse than that, he'd dismissed her. They'd barely discussed the weather before he'd proposed and, having got that formality out of the way, he'd seen no point in further conversation. He hadn't bothered to enquire too far into her relationship with her uncle and aunt either, taking her uncle's assurances at face value, or allowing himself to. It was somewhat galling to discover that she'd been so reluctant to marry him, but it was no good simply blaming her uncle. He'd been equally at fault, seeing what he'd wanted to see. And what he'd seen was her fortune.

Quinton gritted his teeth against a wave of self-disgust. He'd needed the money—correction, *the estate* had needed the money—but that was no excuse. He might as well have gone to market and bartered for a bride. That would have been more honest. Now it seemed that her uncle had barely bothered to involve her in the decision, which no doubt meant that he hadn't told her anything about the history of the Roxbury family either. And she *ought* to have been told about the scandal before she married him. *He* ought to have told her. He ought to tell her now, especially after what she'd just confided about her own past. Only he wasn't accustomed to discussing his private affairs with strangers, which was what she effectively was.

The feeling was exacerbated by the fact that she was nothing at all like he remembered. His initial impression had been of a mouse: timid, unobtrusive and apparently devoid of spirit, with brown eyes, brown hair and the kind of average prettiness that blended into a room rather than stood out from it. As it turned out, he'd been wrong on almost every count. The woman standing in front of him now had the same heart-shaped face, round cheekbones and small, slightly pointed chin, but somehow the combination struck him as far more attractive today than it had before. She even smelled different, like sugar and soap mixed together; not a combination he would have expected to like, but that struck him now as oddly appealing. She was also markedly less pale and gaunt than she'd been on their wedding day and, as for spirit, if anything she'd developed too much of it. There was a new confidence and vitality about her that made him think he would have noticed her in *any* room.

As for her confession about having a lover, he had to admit that he'd been taken aback. He couldn't say he was entirely unperturbed by the discovery either since a large part of the reason he'd married her was because she'd seemed so eminently respectable, precisely the kind of woman who *wouldn't* be involved in any scandal, but since it had happened before their engagement and there obviously hadn't been any consequences, he was prepared to let the matter rest. Which, he congratulated himself, was a lot more than most husbands would do.

'Well, then.' He nodded, pleased to be getting matters settled. 'I suggest that we return to your bakery and collect your belongings.'

'What?' Her head swung back towards him. 'Why?'

'So that you can return with me to Howden Hall and take your place as the Duchess. We'll leave first thing in the morning and put all this unpleasantness behind us. We'll never speak of it again, if you wish.'

'But I haven't agreed to anything.'

'Nonetheless—'

'No!'

'No?'

'No,' she repeated, more firmly. 'As much as I appreciate the offer, I just told you I don't want to be a duchess. That was all my uncle and aunt's idea. I want the life I have now.'

He stared at her in dawning horror. 'Are you saying that you'd prefer to remain here as a baker than be my Duchess?'

'Yes. It's not personal. I know I should never have gone through with the marriage and I'm truly sorry I did, but that's why I wrote to you, so that we can put things right. Properly.'

'And I told you, I don't want a damned divorce!'

She started as he slammed his hand down hard on the table, her expression turning guarded. 'You said you hadn't come to claim me. You gave your word that we'd only talk.'

'Because I assumed that you'd see reason! I'm offering you a position in Society and a life of comfort and security!'

'I don't want it. I'm happy here.'

He stood up and turned towards the window. The street outside was swathed in darkness now, illuminated only by an occasional street lamp. He'd thought that she'd be thrilled to be forgiven so easily. Surely any reasonable woman would be? Unfortunately, it seemed that his wife wasn't a reasonable woman. She preferred a life of drudgery in a biscuit shop to life as a duchess! What was he supposed to say to that? And damn it all, why should he *have* to say anything? She was his wife! Legally he could order her—hell, he could drag her—away from Bath and nobody would bat an eyelid. Only he didn't want to order or drag her. Even if he could have justified that kind of tyrannical behaviour to his conscience, there were enough miserable people at Howden Hall without him adding another.

He took a deep breath and then expelled it again slowly. 'I want to put things right, too. That's why I came. However, if you're truly happy here then I suggest that you stay and continue to live under your assumed name. We'll remain as man and wife and each live our separate lives; be married and not married, as it were. Then we can divide your fortune equally.'

'Divide it?' Her gaze was arrested. 'You mean you'll give me half of it back?'

'Yes. I don't like the idea of depriving you of even that much, but I'm afraid a significant amount has already been spent on repairs to the hall and estate, ones that couldn't wait any longer. The best I can offer now is a repayment of the rest when the farms become profitable again, as I hope that they will.'

'But you don't have to pay any of it back. No court in the land would say otherwise.'

'*I* say otherwise. I don't believe in taking something for nothing and you'd be living outside my protection.'

He paused. 'Although, if you were in trouble, you could always call on me.'

'That's very generous.' She sank back down into her chair. 'I don't know what to say.'

'Start with a yes.'

'I don't know…' Her brows knotted. 'It's not that I'm not grateful, but…'

His heart sank. 'But?'

'It's just not very practical, is it, being married and not married? I mean, won't people wonder where I am? A duchess is supposed to *do* things, isn't she?'

'Yes, but I have a mother and two sisters. They can perform those duties for now.' Although the thought of *that* made his spirits sink even lower. 'As for people wondering where you are, believe me, they've wondered enough already. However, I can let it be known that we've separated. They'll simply assume that you've moved to one of my other estates.'

'But what if you fall in love with someone else?'

'Are you asking for me or for yourself?' He narrowed his eyes suspiciously.

'You.'

'That's absurd.'

'You think that falling in love is absurd?'

'For my own part, yes. Like I said, I don't care for extremes of emotion and, after this, I certainly wouldn't consider marriage again.'

'What about an heir? You're a duke.'

'A duke with two younger brothers. I have enough heirs in waiting.'

'But surely you must want your own son?'

'Must I?' He came back to the table and sat down

again. 'You know, for a runaway bride you seem to have remarkably prosaic ideas.'

She pushed her hands into her hair, dislodging a few pins in the process. 'I'm not trying to be difficult. It just doesn't seem *right* to stay married.'

'In what way?'

'I mean that we made vows and this just seems so *cold*. I know that sounds hypocritical when I was the one who ran away, but I couldn't see things clearly back then. Now I know who I am and what I want and I value my independence. I want the freedom to make my own decisions and choices.'

'You can still have that freedom.'

'A married woman is never truly independent.'

'Whereas a divorced woman is the object of scandal.'

'I don't care about scandal.'

'Really?' He could feel his temper rising again. 'Maybe because you've never had to face the consequences before.'

'That may be so, but I just don't think I can do it. I can't be married and not married.'

'It's what you *have* been doing. For three months!'

'Yes, but I was never comfortable with it. I've felt guilty for the whole time. I'm sorry. I know I've caused you enough distress already.'

'*Distress?* What a very polite word.'

He muttered an oath and twisted his face away. If he were the kind of man who lost his temper, he had a feeling that 'distress' might have been the last straw. He wanted his Duchess. Saving that, he wanted to remain married at a distance. What he *didn't* want was a divorce and more scandal and yet his wife—his formerly placid, obedient mouse of a bride—was proving surprisingly adamant. He was starting to wish that she'd never written to him so they might have left well enough alone…

'I know I can't insist.' Her brown eyes—no, not brown…for he could see a hint of green, too—opened very wide. 'I know that a wife can't petition for divorce, but…please?'

He groaned. She was right, a wife couldn't petition for divorce. He had the law on his side, but how could he refuse to listen when she appealed to him so plaintively? He didn't want to be a tyrant. And was it so much to ask that one person, just one person in his life didn't cause him any more problems than he already had? A wife was supposed to be a helpmeet, wasn't she? Someone to stand by his side and support him, not tear his life apart all over again.

On the other hand, she was only his wife and Duchess in name. She had no idea of the kind of life he could offer her. All she knew of the world was her uncle and aunt's house and now some blasted biscuit shop. Maybe she was simply alarmed by the thought of more upheaval. In which case, if he could persuade her to return with him to Howden, to see the house and the estate, not to mention the life of luxury he could provide and all the potential good she could do there, maybe she'd change her mind?

'All right. I'll apply to Parliament for a divorce, but *only* on one condition.'

'What?' She straightened up at once.

'That we give this farce of a marriage a chance first. Obviously we shouldn't have done it, obviously it was a huge mistake, but it's where we are now. So let's give it a chance and if by the end of three months, say, you still want a divorce then I'll find some grounds.'

'You would? What?'

'I have no idea, although insanity looks like a strong possibility right now.'

She ignored the comment. 'So what do you suggest? That you stay here in Bath?'

'No. That would look far too suspicious. It would ruin your assumed identity, too. You'd have to come to Howden Hall and live as my Duchess. That way we could be seen together and you'd learn what you'd be letting yourself in for if you changed your mind. You never know, we might even come to like each other.'

She looked sceptical. 'You think that liking is enough for a marriage?'

'I think it's a great deal more than some marriages have.' He frowned. 'Or is your heart set on love?'

'No.' Her expression seemed to clamp shut. 'That idea is absurd for me, too. But I *do* want freedom and I *won't* change my mind.'

'Then coming to Howden will prove it.'

She hesitated, a faint blush spreading over her cheeks. 'Surely you aren't suggesting that we live as man and wife?'

'In separate bedrooms, obviously. That's my final offer.'

He waited, tapping his foot as she stared across the table at him. Their conversation-turned-negotiation had taken longer than he'd anticipated. It hadn't exactly gone the way he'd expected it to either, but it was his best chance. He needed to get her out of Bath and into Oxfordshire and then do his damnedest to persuade her to stay.

'Why did you wait?' she asked quietly at last.

'What do you mean? Wait for what?'

'For me to write. If you knew where I was this whole time, why didn't you come and find me sooner?'

'I almost did. When you were close to starving, that was. Then you ended up in that biscuit shop and, by all accounts, you were...' he spread his hands out as if he were searching for the right word '...content. So I decided to wait for you to be ready to contact me. I thought it would make this conversation easier. I didn't want you running away again.'

'That was thoughtful.'

'Was it?' He made a face. 'I'm starting to think it was a mistake. I didn't expect you to be *this* content. I thought you'd be glad to be rescued.'

'I thought you'd be glad of a divorce. What you're offering...it's unbelievable. Incredible.'

'Acceptable?'

She folded her hands on the table. 'Three months is too long. Make it one.'

'Not enough. Two.'

'One and a half. Six weeks. That's forty-two days, starting tomorrow. And, I won't ask you to repay me when—*if*—we divorce. After everything that's happened, we'll divide the money equally and leave it at that.'

'Absolutely not...'

'Take it or leave it. That's *my* final offer.'

He clenched his jaw, grinding his teeth for a few seconds before inclining his head. 'As you wish. In that case, do we have an agreement?'

'We do.' She plucked the glass from the table in front

of him, swallowing the contents and then spluttering violently into her hand. 'Argh! What *is* this?'

'Port.' He took the glass back and refilled it, allowing himself a small twitch of the lips before drinking. 'To marriage!'

Chapter Four

'You can leave me here.' Beatrix stopped in front of Redbourne's General Store, far enough away for them not to be visible through the windows of Henrietta's. Her husband had insisted on escorting her back, but the risk of him meeting Nancy increased with every footstep and she had no intention of letting him go any further. 'I'll be quite safe.'

'You don't wish to introduce me to your friends?' He lifted an eyebrow sardonically.

'Not tonight, thank you.' She gave him an equally expressive look back. 'I need to explain a few things to them first.'

'Such as your real name and identity? You haven't shared those small details, then?'

'I've told Nancy, my best friend, just not the others.'

'Then I'd better leave you to it.' He glanced over her head towards the sounds of revelry within. 'It sounds like quite a celebration.'

'It's the grand opening.'

'Of a tea shop?'

'Yes.' She pulled her shoulders back indignantly.

'It's not such an outrageous idea. Or don't you think tea shops are worth celebrating?'

'I don't recall ever thinking about tea shops before at all. I've never been inside one.' His gaze wandered back to her face. 'And since I won't be remedying that state of affairs tonight, I'm afraid I shall have to reserve judgement.'

'Yes, well, you'd like it. I helped to choose the tablecloths.'

'Then I'm sure they're charming.' He tipped his hat. 'Until tomorrow morning? Nine o'clock sharp?'

'I'll be ready.'

'As will I.' He reached for her hand before she realised what he intended, lifting it to his mouth and pressing his lips against the back of her glove. 'Goodnight, Beatrix. Enjoy the rest of your evening.'

'Goodnight.' She blinked, faintly alarmed by the wobbly-kneed feeling his kiss left in its wake as he marched off down the street, swinging his cane, with long, ground-eating strides. She stared after him for several strangely breathless seconds, telling herself that she was just making sure he was leaving before shaking her head, opening the door of Henrietta's and mentally bracing herself for what she expected to be the second difficult interview of the evening.

'Where have you been?'

Nancy came barrelling across the room at once, practically barging her way through a group of revellers.

'It's a long story.' Beatrix fixed a polite smile onto her face. 'But I'm here now.'

'Eventually! I've been back to Belles twice looking for you.'

'Didn't you find my note?'

'Yes, not that it made any sense. Why would you go walking in the dark with a headache?' Nancy's hands slid to her hips, making it clear that she wasn't about to let the subject drop. 'What's really going on?'

'Not so loud! I don't want to spoil the evening.'

'There you are!' Henrietta came over, somewhat more gracefully, to join them. Since her marriage to Sebastian, the owner of Belles, she seemed to have grown even more beautiful, her already impossibly perfect features glowing with happiness. 'Nancy showed me your note. Are you feeling better?'

'Yes. It wasn't really a headache, just something I needed to do, but I'll explain later.' Beatrix gestured at the scrubbed oak floors, blue-and-white-striped flock paper and collection of round linen-and-lace-covered tables. 'You've done a wonderful job with the place.'

'I know. I can hardly believe we're opening tomorrow.' Henrietta's smile grew even wider. 'I'm so happy I could cry.'

'Well, don't, or everyone will assume that I'm the cause.' Nancy gave her a nudge in the ribs before turning back towards Beatrix. 'Now stop trying to distract us. What's happened?'

'I can't talk about it here.'

'Then we'll go back to Belles.'

'I've only just arrived!'

'There's a parlour upstairs.' Henrietta gestured towards a staircase at the back of the room. 'Although I suppose that might draw more attention.'

'You can use my office next door, if you like?' a deep male voice offered. 'Then everyone will assume you've just stepped outside for some air. Forgive me, but I couldn't help but overhear.'

'Because you were listening.' Nancy's face snapped into a frown. 'Wh—?'

'That's very kind of you,' Beatrix interrupted quickly, wondering for probably the hundredth time why a man as kind, intelligent and attractive as James Redbourne was still unmarried. Not to mention why Nancy, despite his obvious interest in her, was always so rude to him. 'We won't be long.'

'Take all the time you need.' He smiled, though his eyes, as usual, were on Nancy. 'I'll wait outside.'

'Wait, I want to come, too.' Henrietta put a hand on her arm. 'Just give me a moment to tell Seb.'

Beatrix groaned inwardly. At this rate it wouldn't be long before everyone was heading next door to hear her story.

Fortunately, Sebastian was busy regaling a group of guests with some naval anecdote so it was just the four of them who made their way to the neighbouring shop, led by James.

'Make yourselves comfortable.' He went through to his office and lit a pair of candles on the desk. 'I'll leave you in peace. Just let me know when you're done.'

'Right.' Nancy didn't waste any time, looking at Beatrix expectantly as soon as the door closed behind him. 'This is something to do with what we discussed in December, isn't it? You sent that damned letter.'

'What letter?' Henrietta settled herself into a green leather armchair. 'Ooh, this is comfortable.'

Beatrix chose a more businesslike mahogany chair behind the desk, putting some distance between herself and Nancy's interrogatory expression. 'I wrote to my husband, yes.'

'Your *what*?' Henrietta stopped rubbing her hands over the leather to gape.

'My husband.' Beatrix threw her an apologetic look. 'Do you remember the day I first came to Belles? I told you that I hadn't done anything wrong, just something very foolish? Well, here it is…'

'I don't believe it,' Henrietta concluded when Beatrix finally finished talking. 'I mean, I *do* believe it. I'm not accusing you of lying, but I still don't believe it. No wonder you didn't tell us at first. I wouldn't have believed it then either.'

'You would probably have thought I was mad.'

'It's possible.' Henrietta rubbed her palms over her face. 'No offence.'

'None taken.'

'You're really a *duchess*?'

'Who bakes for a living.' Nancy perched herself on the edge of the desk. 'It's like some strange fairy tale, only the Duke isn't much like Prince Charming.'

'No-o…' Henrietta sounded thoughtful. 'Although, I must say, he seems quite reasonable. He's not demanding that she goes with him. He's only asking her to give their marriage a chance.'

'So what does he expect? That she'll take one look at his big house and fall into his arms?'

'I don't think he cares much about that,' Beatrix interjected. 'He claims he doesn't care for extremes of emotion. I suppose he's hoping I'll like the place enough to stay, but, most of all, he doesn't want a divorce. He mentioned something about avoiding another scandal.' She dug her teeth into her bottom lip and started chewing. She'd tried to ask what he'd meant by that, but there had been so much else to talk about that she'd forgotten.

'But if you don't want to go then why not just agree to his idea of a separation?'

'Because I want a clean break. Complete independence, no matter what the scandal. And if the only way to get it is six weeks in the country pretending to be a duchess—'

'*Being* a duchess,' Henrietta corrected her.

'Either way, it's a price I'm prepared to pay. It's not like I'm going to fall in love with— Oh, no!' She stopped and swung towards Nancy. 'I didn't think about Belles. You can't do all the baking on your own for the next six weeks!'

'I'll help,' Henrietta offered.

'But you have the tea shop now.'

'I can still come and do the baking in the morning. Seb, too. We'll manage somehow.'

'Are you sure?'

'I'm not.' Nancy perched on the edge of the desk. 'Not about any of it. How do you know he's not just saying what you want to hear so that you'll go with him?'

'Because he doesn't *have* to say any of it. He's known where I've been since December. He could have come and claimed me at any time, but he waited until I wrote to him. That says something.'

'But what if he changes his mind once he's got you? How can you be certain he'll go through with a divorce in the end?'

'Because I trust him.' Beatrix nodded firmly. 'He might be stiff-necked and severe and about as warm as an ice sculpture, but I believe that he's honourable.

He's not pretending to care about me. He admits that he only married me for my money. Now all he wants is six weeks to persuade me to stay married. He won't succeed, but it's my only hope of a divorce.'

'Ahem.' James gave a small cough from the doorway. 'Seb's asking for you, Henrietta.'

'What did you just hear?' Nancy sprang off the desk immediately.

'Probably a little more than I should have.' He held his hands up. 'I'm sorry. I did knock.'

'It's all right. I trust you.' Beatrix smiled and stood up, too, somewhat relieved by the interruption. 'It's time to get back to the party anyway.'

'How are we supposed to celebrate now? I'm going to stay here for a few minutes.' Nancy wrapped her arms around her midriff and shot a truculent look towards James. 'If you don't mind?'

'Of course not.' He looked surprised to be asked. 'Whatever you need.'

'I'll be back before you know it.' Beatrix squeezed Nancy's arm before making her way discreetly after Henrietta, leaving the pair of them alone. 'I'll see you in a few minutes?'

To her surprise, it was over an hour before either of them returned to the party.

Chapter Five

He wasn't sorry, Quinton reflected, surveying the world from the top step of the George Hotel, to be leaving Bath. It was a pretty enough city, he'd give it that, but after an hour spent wandering the streets, appreciating Palladian architecture and generally brooding in the early morning sunlight, he was more than ready to depart.

He wasn't sorry to be leaving the George either, since he appeared to have traumatised the hotel's proprietor by arriving, arranging a room and finally settling his account all by himself, without so much as a valet to tie his cravat. In the rush to leave Howden, he hadn't seen the point in bringing anyone else, but thank goodness he'd only registered under his surname and not his full title or the man might have expired from shock.

He adjusted his hat and then reached into his waistcoat for a pocket watch. The dial read half past eight in the morning. Thomas, his groom, the one servant he *had* brought with him, was scheduled to meet him at Belles with a hired carriage and driver at precisely nine o'clock, ready to collect Beatrix for the journey into Oxfordshire. He supposed he could only hope that she hadn't run away again during the night, although, considering how much she wanted a divorce, he doubted it. More likely, she'd be standing on the front step with a calendar ready to mark off the days, if not hours, of their agreement.

In the cold light of day, he wondered if he might have made something of a tactical error in proposing a trial period. At the time, it had seemed like the only way of getting her to Howden and giving himself a chance to talk some sense into her, although how he was actually going to achieve that was another matter. Given the circumstances, not to mention his family, six weeks hardly seemed long enough. On top of which, he was now honour bound to give her a divorce if he failed. Which would mean sticking his head back into the lion's jaw of Society's opinion and getting savaged all over again.

He closed the watch with a snap, refusing to dwell on that particular scenario. He'd convinced his wife to accompany him home and that was enough for now. All things considered, he could regard his trip as a success. A qualified success anyway.

Briskly, he made his way through the busy thoroughfares of the city, past street vendors, smartly dressed businessmen and scruffy-looking urchins until at last he reached Belles, pushing the door open to find his path immediately blocked by a scarlet-haired woman with a decidedly unwelcoming expression.

'It's you, isn't it?' She looked him up and down,

blue eyes flashing as if she were trying to scorch him on the spot. 'You're *him*!'

Quinton inclined his head, acknowledging that he probably was *him*. It wasn't exactly the kind of subservient or formal greeting he was accustomed to, but he couldn't deny that it suited the situation.

'Good morning.' He gave a deliberately obtuse smile. 'Is Beatrix ready?'

The woman didn't answer, storming towards him as if she were daring him to flinch, before veering away at the last moment to turn a sign over and slam the bolt on the door.

'Closing early?'

'Just for a while. She's upstairs.'

'Ah. I'm obliged to you.'

'Don't be. I'd rather you weren't.'

'Duly noted.'

He stepped behind the wooden counter, inhaling the mouth-watering aroma of fresh baking as he made his way through a narrow hallway and up a staircase to a landing where a dark-haired man with pre-emptively folded arms stood waiting. Another member of the welcoming committee presumably.

'How do you do?' Quinton squared up to him. 'I've come to collect my wife.'

'So I heard.'

'Sebastian,' a female voice interrupted. 'That's not going to help. Come in, Your Grace.'

'Thank you.' Quinton turned towards the voice, surprised to find the most breathtakingly beautiful woman he'd ever beheld sitting in the window seat of a warm and cosy-looking parlour. Her expression, he was both relieved and faintly chagrined to find, was sad rather than unfriendly.

'Beatrix will be down in a moment.' She stood up as she spoke. 'She's just saying goodbye to her room.'

'I see. Then please allow me to introduce myself. I am Howden, at your service, Miss…?'

'Mrs.' The dark-haired man answered for her. *'Mrs* Henrietta Fortini, my *wife.'*

'The very same.' The woman looked simultaneously amused and exasperated. 'And this is my husband, Sebastian.'

'An honour to meet you both.' He bowed politely, trying to remember where he'd heard the woman's name recently. No, not heard—*seen.* Now that he thought of it, it had been on the sign above the tea shop where he'd left Beatrix the night before. At least now he knew who the 'good friends' were… 'I presume that Beatrix has told you about our agreement?'

The pair exchanged a look before the man nodded tersely. 'She has, although it sounds like a strange kind of arrangement to me.'

'I suppose it is. However, it's what we've agreed on.'

'So long as you keep to your side of the bargain.'

'You doubt my word, sir?' He stiffened at the implication.

'Of course not.' The woman came to stand beside her husband. 'This is Beatrix's choice and we support her.' A dainty elbow nudged outwards. 'Don't we, Sebastian?'

Fortunately the man himself was prevented from answering as Beatrix appeared at that moment, already dressed for travel in a forest-green cloak and plain, cream-coloured bonnet.

'I thought I heard your voice.' She gave Quinton a half-hearted smile, as if she'd been hoping their conversation of the night before had been nothing more than a bad dream. 'You're very punctual.'

'I always am.' He glanced towards the window. If he wasn't mistaken, he could hear the rumbling of carriage wheels outside. 'Are you ready? We have a long way to go.'

'Ready as I'll ever be.' She turned to clasp the woman's hands. 'Goodbye, Henrietta. Thank you for everything.'

'You're more than welcome.' The other woman gave a suspicious-sounding sniff. 'We'll be right here if you need us.'

'Just send word.' The man threw Quinton another black look, though whether that was for Beatrix or for making his own wife cry, he had no idea.

'A coach just pulled up outside.' The red-haired woman stomped up the staircase, glowering so fiercely it made the man look as if he were smiling. 'No insignia on it though.'

'It's hired,' Quinton answered, vaguely resenting the need to explain himself. 'Since Beatrix has managed to keep her true identity a secret for the past three months, I saw no point in drawing attention to it today. Now, shall we?'

'Just a moment.' Beatrix hugged both of the women at once, closing her eyes as if she, too, were on the verge of tears. It was like a scene from a painting, Quinton thought, with the three women all holding onto each other like a trio of tragic heroines. It might have been quite touching if he hadn't been cast as the villain.

'Where's your luggage?' His voice was somewhat

louder than necessary, but the sooner he got her out of that place, the better.

'Over there.' She gestured towards a single valise by the staircase.

'That's *all* of it?'

'I didn't have much chance to pack before I ran away.'

'Evidently. Well, then...' He picked the bag up himself and went down the staircase, feeling even more like a villain when the women all hugged for a second time on the pavement.

'I'm sorry I've delayed the opening of your tea shop.' Beatrix was speaking to the beautiful blonde again. 'On your first day, too.'

'Don't be silly. You're *much* more important.'

'I'm going to miss you both so much!'

'But we'll see you in six weeks.' The redhead shot him another dagger-like glare as she spoke. 'Not a day more.'

Quinton declined to comment, rolling his eyes instead at the sight of another man coming along the pavement to join them.

'I came to say goodbye, Miss...' The man, whose handsome visage only served to increase Quinton's exasperation, looked momentarily stumped. 'I mean—'

'Goodbye, Mr Redbourne.' To add insult to injury, his wife's smile was a little too warm for his liking. 'Please call me Beatrix from now on.'

'Shall we?' Quinton opened the carriage door with a jolt, causing it to creak and groan in protest.

'Oh, very well.' Beatrix threw him a reproachful look and climbed inside. 'Goodbye, Nancy, goodbye, Henrietta, goodbye, Sebastian, goodbye, Mr Redbourne.'

Quinton followed her inside once the tally of names was complete, slamming the door and banging his cane on the roof so violently that the carriage lurched forward almost at once, albeit not a moment too soon for his temper. Not that he ever allowed himself to lose his temper, of course, but he was starting to wish that he'd chosen to ride alongside the carriage on his own horse like Thomas. A gallop was just what he needed, but he'd thought it polite to keep his wife company for a while. Judging by her expression as she pulled her head back inside after waving out of the window, however, she would have preferred solitude.

Fortunately it was a good morning for a drive, bright and mild and yet not too busy on the roads, allowing them to make quick progress out of the city and into the countryside. In the absence of conversation, Quinton turned his mind to the mile-long list of tasks requiring his attention on their return to Howden: checking on the roof repairs, redecorating the bedrooms that had suffered worst from all the leaks, approving the revised plans for the cottages, finding an engineer for the new drainage project, making arrangements for Justin's departure... No doubt a dozen more urgent matters had piled up on his desk during his absence, and those were *aside* from the most important task of all: persuading his wife against a divorce.

He should probably say something, he thought, glancing sideways. He should probably try to be charming, too, although he hadn't the faintest idea how to start. Corin would know, though, on the other hand, charm smacked of duplicity and he had no intention of feigning any more affection than he felt. Which was little enough considering the trouble she'd already put him to. No, charm was out of the question. He would be honest. Maybe not as brutally honest as he'd been before their wedding, but still…forthright…scrupulous… *civil*. Their marriage was a business agreement of sorts and so their quandary also required a businesslike solution. He just needed to work out what that might be.

There was a small sniffing sound and he reached into his pocket, extracting a handkerchief and handing it to her. 'Here.'

Beatrix turned her head, regarding it and then him with something like surprise. 'It's all right. I'm sad, but I'm not crying.'

'Ah.' He tucked the handkerchief away again, confirming the truth with his own eyes. 'Forgive me. Force of habit.'

'Habit? You mean you're accustomed to women crying?'

He made a face, realising how incriminating it sounded to agree. 'Not usually *because* of me, but yes. My family can be quite…emotional.'

'Really?' She twisted in the seat to get a clearer view of him. 'You know, I assumed that you were an only child since none of your family came to the wedding, but yesterday you said that you had two brothers and two sisters.'

'Yes.'

'So…?' She prompted him. 'Tell me about them. It seems about time that we started getting to know each other.'

'Ah. Well, their names are Corin, Antigone, Justin and Helen.'

'So there are five of you altogether?'

'Correct.'

'And you're called Quinton?' She looked thoughtful. 'And yet you're the oldest?'

'It's a family name. One of my ancestors was a fifth son and somehow inherited the Dukedom so eldest sons have been called Quinton ever since. The number of my siblings is merely a coincidence.'

'How strange. Are you close?'

'In some ways.' He sidestepped the question. 'Although we're somewhat spread out in age. My youngest sister, for example, is eighteen years my junior.'

'So she still lives at the hall?'

'They all do.'

Her eyes widened. 'You mean they're *all* at Howden?'

'For the time being, although Corin goes up to London regularly and Justin will be starting at Eton soon.'

'So they'll *all* be there when we arrive?'

'I expect so, yes.'

'Oh.'

'Oh?'

'I just didn't realise that there would be quite so many people.'

'It's a big house. You can avoid them all if necessary.'

'I didn't mean that I wanted to avoid them. I just hope they don't resent me too much, given the situation.' Her voice wavered slightly. 'I presume *they* know about me running away?'

'Yes. I'm afraid there was no way to avoid it.'

'What about your mother?'

He cleared his throat, staring fixedly at the opposite seat of the carriage. 'What about her?'

'Is the dower house close by?'

'It is, but she still lives at the hall, too.'

'Oh...' *Oh, again...* 'Then what does she think of it all? I suppose she must have been angry at me for running away?'

'She was...' he sought an appropriate word '...*offended* on my behalf.'

'Does that mean yes?'

Yes. He winced. 'She can be difficult, but her heart's in the right place.'

'And your siblings? Are their hearts in the right place, too?'

He sighed. He'd hoped to avoid this subject until they'd put at least a hundred miles between them and Bath, but it seemed there was no way of avoiding it.

'I should imagine their hearts are in the same place as your friends' were. They certainly won't be any more unwelcoming.'

'I'm sorry about that.' She looked genuinely apologetic. 'I explained our agreement, but they're very protective.'

'Not a bad quality to have in friends.'

'They're more like a family now. Henrietta and Nancy are like sisters to me.'

'What about the man who arrived just as we were leaving?' Despite a determination not to, he couldn't resist asking. 'Is he a brother?'

'Mr Redbourne? Sort of. I think he's in love with Nancy.'

'Indeed?' He was surprised to feel a faint sense of relief. 'He hasn't declared himself to her, then?'

'He probably would if she'd give him half a chance, but she won't. She's very stubborn.'

'I noticed. She doesn't like me.'

She didn't contradict him. 'If it's any consolation, she doesn't like any men.'

He made a harrumphing sound. 'It hardly seems fair to generalise.'

'She has her reasons, but they're not mine to share. I just keep trying to convince her that there are *some* good ones, like Sebastian and Mr Redbourne.'

'Quite.'

He turned his face to glower out of the window. Mr Fortini, in particular, hadn't struck him as a particular paragon of virtue, not that he was going to lower himself by arguing or exhibiting any emotion that might be misinterpreted as jealousy.

'Care for a biscuit?'

He turned around at the sound of rustling to find Beatrix holding an open muslin bag out towards him.

'What are they?'

'Belles. We baked them fresh this morning.'

'You baked this morning?'

'It needed to be done. Nancy tried to stop me, of course, but I insisted. She's going to have enough to do for the next six weeks. Now, there are three flavours: plain, rose water, and cinnamon.'

He reached dubiously into the bag. He didn't have a particularly sweet tooth, but perhaps just this once...

'I'll try a plain one.' He examined it sceptically for a few seconds before taking the smallest of small bites and then nodding in approval. 'This is delicious.'

'You needn't sound so surprised.'

'Forgive me, I simply had no idea of your talents.'

'Hard work and practice more than talent. Nancy despaired of me to begin with.'

'Coffee.'

'I beg your pardon?'

'This would go very well with coffee. I'll order some when we stop to rest the horses and then we can have another. With your permission, that is.'

'Of course. I brought them to share.' She wrapped a ribbon around the top of the bag with a smile. 'So how long until we reach Howden?'

'If the weather stays fine, we should be there by to-morrow night.'

'*Tomorrow?*' A shadow crossed her face. 'But doesn't that mean we'll have to stay at an inn tonight?'

'I'm afraid so. I can hardly ask the driver to drive in the dark.'

'No-o.' Although she sounded as if she were considering the option. 'I *suppose* not.'

They lapsed into silence again afterwards. If someone had opened the carriage door and hurled a bucket of water inside, it could hardly have had a more damp-ening effect, Quinton thought, watching his wife out of the corner of his eye. He wasn't sure what else she'd expected them to do that night, given the distance be-tween Bath and Oxfordshire, and she didn't give him any opportunity to find out, responding in monosyl-lables to all his further attempts at conversation. She seemed to become more and more tense throughout the day as they made small, *very* small talk over cof-fee, then over luncheon and then lapsed into com-plete silence for the rest of the afternoon. By the time they drew up outside a coaching inn that evening, he couldn't even remember the last thing either of them had said.

He stepped down from the carriage with a sense of relief, stretching his limbs as he took stock of the neat and pleasant-looking establishment before them. The sky above, he noticed, was in the process of turning from rich royal blue into darkness, making it just over twenty-four hours since he'd first met Beatrix outside Belles. Funnily enough, that was *how* he now thought of it, as their first meeting, as if the brief time they'd spent together in London didn't count.

'I can manage, thank you.' His wife ignored his hand and climbed down from the carriage herself, walking stiffly into the inn and taking a seat in the dining parlour while he went to speak with the landlord.

'There are no suites available, I'm afraid,' he informed her a few minutes later, sitting down just as a waitress arrived carrying plates of beef doused in gravy and accompanied by a veritable mountain of potatoes and carrots. 'There's some kind of local horse race tomorrow so the place is busier than usual. There *are* a few rooms left, however, so we'll just have to share for tonight.'

'Share?' Her whole body seemed to tense. 'But you promised…'

'Separate rooms, yes. Which we'll have as soon as we reach Howden, but right now, you're travelling without a maid. It would hardly be advisable for you to sleep in a room on your own.'

'I don't see why. I could lock the door or barricade it.'

He picked up his fork. 'Beatrix, flattering though it is that you'd prefer a barricade over a night in my company, this isn't an attempt to change the terms of our agreement. It's simply common sense.'

'Mmm…' She stared down at her plate, taking a few

small mouthfuls and then moving her food around in a desultory manner until he couldn't stand it any longer.

'Don't you like your meal?' Her silence seemed even louder compared to the dozens of conversations going on around them.

'It's not that. I'm just not very hungry.'

'You need something. We haven't eaten for hours.'

'I've had enough.'

'Very well, then.' He took one last mouthful before putting his cutlery aside and pushing his chair back. 'Shall we go upstairs?'

'Now?' She gave him a startled look. 'Aren't you going to finish?'

'I'm not particularly hungry either.'

'As you can see, it's busy tonight, sir.' The innkeeper led them up a flight of stairs, opening a door at the top to reveal an old-fashioned, but comfortably furnished chamber dominated by a four-poster bed so tall there were actual steps leading up to the mattress. 'But this is one of our best rooms.'

'It will do nicely.' Quinton went to warm his hands in front of a roaring fireplace while Beatrix remained standing stiffly beside the door.

'Thank you, sir. Will there be anything else?'

'Not tonight, thank you.' He glanced over his shoulder as the innkeeper departed again. 'For pity's sake, it's just one night, Beatrix.'

Her eyes narrowed. 'And just one bed.'

'I noticed. However, it looks quite big enough for the both of us. Fortunately, I'm far too tired for any ravishing.'

'That's not funny.'

'No, I suppose not.' He sighed heavily. The words

were somewhat ungallant, but, after that morning, he was getting weary of slurs on his honour. 'Beatrix, I gave you my word. You're perfectly safe with me, I promise.'

'Oh, all right.' She moved away from the door finally. 'But can I at least undress in privacy?'

'I suppose you won't be satisfied with me just closing my eyes?' He fought the urge to sigh again. 'Very well, I'll wait in the corridor. Call out when you're ready.'

It was strange, he thought, leaning back against the timbered wall of the corridor a few moments later, for a woman who described herself as promiscuous to be quite so disturbed by the idea of sharing a bed, especially when he'd promised that he had absolutely no intention of doing anything other than sleeping. Then again, by her own admission, she'd only slept with her lover once, probably not enough to overcome a natural modesty. Or perhaps the experience hadn't been very pleasant... The thought of that made his brows snap together. Not that he was particularly thrilled by the idea of her enjoying herself in another man's bed either, but still, that would explain her trepidation.

There was a faint call from inside and he opened the door to find Beatrix already lying in the bed, her back turned towards him and with at least three layers of blankets pulled up to her chin. She was so far over to one side that she looked in imminent danger of rolling onto the floor, which, given the height, seemed likely to result in injury.

He rubbed a hand over his jaw. Modesty was all very well, but even if she didn't break an arm, she was going to roast under so many layers of wool. And since his word apparently wasn't convincing enough, the sooner he proved that she was safe with him, the better.

'I don't think I'll need all of these.' He folded the top two blankets back, forming a wedge in the middle of the bed before removing his jacket, waistcoat and boots, and sitting down on the side. When she didn't object, he swung his legs up and then lay carefully down beside her, folding his arms over his chest and rolling his shoulders to get comfortable. Which he suddenly couldn't.

He stiffened, almost sitting bolt upright again in surprise as a hot ache suffused his body, making his blood surge and his nerve endings all tingle and start vibrating with tension. It was utterly bizarre. As far as he knew, he had absolutely no physical interest in his wife. She wasn't *un*attractive, just not particularly to his taste. And yet the moment he'd lain down beside her he'd felt as though his whole body had just been struck by lightning, positively electrified and pulsing with sensation.

He turned his face into the pillow, stifling a groan. Now that he thought of it, he hadn't shared a bed with a woman for over a year. Hell, his own wife had been more active in that department than he had. But at least *that* would account for the force of his reaction...damn it, his whole body felt rigid...although he'd had long periods of celibacy in the past without ever experiencing anything like this afterwards. *This* was decidedly uncomfortable. *This* was maddening. This was—

'Goodnight.' She murmured the word softly, her shoulder still turned towards him. Which, at that moment, was something of a relief. If she'd been anxious before, she would be horrified if she saw him now.

'Goodnight.' Somehow he managed to inject his voice with an appropriate note of exhaustion while staring, entranced, at the braid of hazel hair trailing across the pillow behind her. For a rousing moment, he allowed himself the fantasy of reaching for it, of curving his hand around her neck, twisting her face back towards his, claiming her lips and delving beneath all those blankets.

But they had an agreement. He'd given his word and he needed some sleep, a *good* night's sleep if they were going to get up early enough to reach Howden and his family the next day… And if *that* thought wasn't enough to dampen his ardour, he didn't know what was.

He leaned over, blew out the candle and concentrated on thinking about roof repairs.

Chapter Six

Week One. Day Two

Beatrix stared out of the carriage window, anxiously twisting her hands together in her lap. It was a good thing that she was wearing gloves, she thought, making one final concerted attempt to keep them still by clasping her fingers together, or she would have torn her nails to shreds by now. The carriage had just rolled beneath the curved archway of a massive, three-storeyed gatehouse and was driving at what felt like a breakneck speed towards what, from a distance, resembled a great grey shadow. And a driveway could only last so long. At this rate they'd arrive at their destination within minutes, just in time to be interrogated by Quinton's family before dinner, in fact. Her empty stomach heaved. It had been one thing when she'd assumed that her 'visit' to Howden would involve just the two of them, but two brothers, two sisters *and* a mother-in-law, all of whom doubtless resented her for abandoning him, were a lot more than she'd bargained for. Unfortunately, it was much too late to turn back.

'They won't eat you.' Quinton, on the seat beside her, tipped his head closer. 'There's no need to be quite so nervous.'

'Easy for you to say. I feel like I'm going to be sick.'

'That would certainly make for a memorable arrival.' His lips quirked. 'However, perhaps you'd like me to stop the carriage so you can walk around for a few minutes instead? A little fresh air might help.'

She took a deep breath and then shook her head. No, she didn't want to stop, not unless it could be for a few hours, and even then... She suspected her queasiness wasn't going anywhere until she got this meeting over with. In which case, she *wanted* to get it over with, no matter what kind of welcome lay ahead.

'You can withdraw to your rooms as soon as you wish.' To her amazement, Quinton laid one of his hands on top of hers as she started to fidget again. 'Remember, Howden is your home now, for six weeks anyway. You can do whatever you like.'

She dropped her gaze, her body tensing at the contact. They were both wearing gloves, but she could still feel the warmth of his hand against her skin, raising the temperature in the carriage by several blistering degrees. Suddenly she felt very aware of his proximity, not to mention his thigh on the seat next to hers, making the whole side of her body tingle.

It was the same tingle she'd felt when she'd woken up beside him that morning. Sleeping in the same bed had been a nerve-racking, nail-biting and ultimately confusing experience. She'd been dreading it, worried that Nancy had been right and that she'd made a mistake by trusting him, memories of Alec spinning around her mind so fast that she'd felt as though her head was going to burst, and yet, oddly enough, the moment Quinton had lain down beside her, all of her worries had seemed to dissipate into thin air.

She'd felt safe. Unexpectedly, unfathomably and utterly safe. Maybe because he'd come to bed with half of his clothes still on—she'd paid attention to the sounds of rustling. Maybe because the closest he'd come to seduction was telling her she suited green. Or maybe simply because he was so completely *un*like Alec. Now that she thought about it, the two men were almost complete opposites, both in appearance and personality. Quinton was dark where Alec was fair, cold where Alec was warm, remote where Alec was—or had been—all too approachable. And yet despite his obvious faults, her husband's behaviour had been by far the more honourable. She'd *known* that she could trust him. And so she'd surrendered to sleep, waking up in the early hours feeling surprisingly well rested and headache-free; *vindicated* even as she'd rolled over on her pillow and found him still slumbering, as if she'd made the right decision by trusting him.

She'd lain completely still for a few minutes, watching the rhythmic rise and fall of his broad chest before moving her attention to the muscular outline of his arms, clearly delineated beneath his crumpled shirt. They were larger and thicker than she would have imagined, like the arms of a man who did manual labour occasionally. From there, she'd moved on to his shoulders, also broad, then the strong column of his neck, dotted with a fine layer of dark stubble, and finally to his face. Interestingly, his sharp features looked less severe in sleep, his brow clear and unknotted, tempting her to reach out and touch it, stroke it even, which had led to the strange tingly feeling in the pit of her stomach, like an instant, uncontrollable fluttering, which had itself led to another near-silent day in the carriage trying to understand what it meant.

Almost twelve hours later, she still had no idea.

'No one will insult you, I promise.' Her husband was talking again, she realised suddenly. 'Or, if they do, they'll answer to me.'

She lifted her eyes back to his with a jolt. On the one hand, the words made her feel even worse, implying that she was right to be nervous. On the other, the formidable tone of his voice was reassuring, making the fluttering intensify all over again. He was looking at her strangely, too, she noticed, with a querying glint in his eye as if he were wondering what she was thinking. As if he wasn't entirely sure what he was thinking either. Which made two of them.

She pulled her hand away, genuinely shaken by the exchange. Obviously, she was even more nervous than she'd thought. For an insane moment, she'd actually been tempted to turn her hand over and slide her fingers through his.

Fortunately, the carriage juddered to a halt at that second, the door opening to reveal a line of people standing outside the portico of an immense and quite spectacular-looking house. Howden Hall, she presumed, although hall didn't seem a big enough word to encompass so many Ionic columns and Venetian windows. Mansion would have been better. Or Baroque Castle.

A footman lowered the steps and Quinton descended first, turning around and reaching a hand out to help her, which, this time, she accepted.

'Welcome to Howden.' He led her towards an imposingly long flight of front steps. 'This is my family.'

'Oh...' She fought an impulse to shudder. Viewed from below, the row of people standing at the top resembled a line of granite statues, their grim expressions blending perfectly with the grey building and even greyer sky above. There were only four of them, however, meaning someone was missing.

'My mother, Lady Morgana, the Dowager Duchess of Howden...' Quinton continued, gesturing to a woman with auburn and silver-flecked hair '...my brothers, the lords Corin and Justin, and my sister, Lady Antigone. Everyone, this is Beatrix, my wife.'

'Pleased to meet you.' She dipped into a respectful and only slightly wobbly curtsy. The sister and younger brother, she noticed, took after their mother with reddish-hued hair, whereas the other brother had much paler colouring, with grey eyes and hair so blond it looked almost white. Not one of them acknowledged her curtsy by so much as a twitch of an eyelash. She was just starting to wonder if they were going to stand there all night when the Dowager's lip finally curled.

'So you're my runaway daughter-in-law?' A swift look up and down managed to convey both disappointment and distaste, as if Beatrix were a stray dog grovelling for scraps at their feet. 'You came to your senses, then?'

'Mother.' Quinton gave a low murmur.

'I can see why you might think that, Your Grace.' Beatrix lifted her chin, refusing to be cowed. 'However, the situation is a little more complicated.'

The Dowager pursed her lips. Judging by the intricate array of wrinkles around them, it was how they spent most of their time. 'I don't care what it is. You ought to be crawling on your knees, begging for forgiveness.'

'Beatrix and I have talked about what happened and come to an agreement.' Quinton's tone hardened. 'I see no need for any further discussion. And *definitely* no begging.'

'I disagree, especially if she thinks she can simply walk in here and take *my* place after the disgraceful way she's behaved!'

'I'm truly sorry for what happened.' Beatrix tightened her hand over Quinton's as he opened his mouth to speak again. 'And I would never presume to—'

'Do you have *any* idea of the trouble you've caused, the scandal you might have unleashed, the ruin you could have brought on this entire family, you ungrateful, hare-brained, self-centred—?'

'Mother!' Quinton ignored her hand this time. '*Inside!*'

Beatrix watched as the whole family turned their backs at the same moment, as if pulled together on an invisible string. The two women were wearing identical expressions of disdain, she noticed, though thankfully the men seemed slightly less severe, the elder one throwing Quinton an ironic look while the younger seemed to wish himself a hundred miles away.

More to the point, at that moment, so did she.

She tipped her head backwards, gazing up at the massive, triangular-shaped pediment above the front door. It looked forbidding and ominous, like the portal to a gilded prison. Maybe staying in Bath and accepting a separation wouldn't have been such a bad idea, after all.

* * *

'Dunstan. Mrs Hastings.' Quinton was relieved to find the housekeeper and butler hovering by the staircase as the family entered the hall, looking as if they weren't sure how to behave. The rest of the staff were conspicuously absent, no doubt by his mother's orders, but he'd rectify that situation later. Right now, he needed to get Beatrix out of the way so that he could deal with his family. 'This is my wife, Beatrix, the new Duchess of Howden. Mrs Hastings, perhaps you might show her upstairs for a rest before dinner?'

'Of course, Your Grace.' The housekeeper dipped into a curtsy, though not without a subtle, swift glance at his mother first.

'I'll meet you in the drawing room in an hour.' He turned towards Beatrix with what he hoped was an encouraging expression. Her own face was pale and drawn and no wonder. Gorgons would have been more welcoming. As first meetings went, their arrival could hardly have gone any worse. 'Unless you'd prefer to have dinner in your room?'

She opened her mouth and then hesitated, obviously contradicting her own inclination. 'No, I'll come down.'

'Good.' He gave a terse nod and watched as Mrs Hastings led her upstairs, waiting until their footsteps had receded before unleashing a thunderous glare on his family.

'Drawing room. All of you. Now.'

For once, none of them argued, trailing into the room one after the other.

'First things first.' He closed the door firmly behind them and then stood in front of it, blocking the route of escape. 'Where are the servants?'

'Busy.' His mother settled herself on a sofa.

'*All* of them? You were obviously aware of our carriage approaching since you managed to come outside yourselves. You *ought* to have arranged a proper reception.'

'I didn't think you'd want me drawing attention to her arrival.' His mother sniffed. 'Especially when she's supposed to have been here for the past three and a half months.'

'Officially, yes. Unofficially, I think it's fair to assume the servants have noticed the truth.'

'I've no idea what they've noticed. I simply thought it was enough that *we* were there to welcome her.'

'You call that a welcome?'

'It was all she deserved.'

'We discussed how I expected you to behave towards Beatrix *before* I left.'

'Did we? It must have slipped my mind.' His mother looked unrepentant. 'And what on earth do you mean about coming to an agreement? What is there to agree on? She ran away to who knows where with who knows whom. Who is *she* to think that she can just come and live here now as if nothing ever happened?'

'*I* know where she went and who she's been with.' Quinton clasped his hands behind his back. 'And the reason she thinks she can live here is because I told her she can. The details are nobody else's business. It's enough for you all to know that she's here.' For six weeks anyway, he added silently, not that he had any intention of telling his family that particular detail...

His mother harrumphed loudly. 'I *cannot* believe that you expect us to share a house with a woman like that. Why not send her to one of the other estates?

Somewhere in the north where she can't disgrace us any more.'

'I'm not sending her anywhere. This is her home now and we're all going to live together *peacefully*.' He gave a tight smile. '*You're* going to be polite and pleasant, Mother, and if you can't manage that then there's a perfectly good and conveniently vacant dower house close by.'

'You wouldn't!' His mother started coughing on the amount of air she dragged into her lungs suddenly.

'Wouldn't I? Whether you like it or not, *she's* the Duchess now, which means that you need to treat her with respect.'

'*Respect?*' His mother's face turned puce-coloured.

'Yes, respect. And that goes for the rest of you, too.' He looked at each of his siblings in turn. 'Or there'll be consequences. Do I make myself clear?'

'Perfectly,' Corin drawled from his recumbent position on a sofa by the window. 'Although I'm curious— where will you send me if I misbehave?'

Quinton narrowed his eyes. 'That depends on what it is you intend to do.'

'Oh, nothing.' Corin held his hands up innocently. 'You know me, I've no intentions at all.'

'Good. For once.'

'She's quite a pretty little thing, actually. Although more my type than yours, I would have thought. As I recall, you always preferred—'

'*Corin!*' Their mother's voice recovered just enough to sound horrified.

'Sorry, Mama.'

'What does he prefer?' Justin's head swivelled towards the window.

'*Justin!*'

'I'll tell you later.'

'*Cor—*'

'I need a bath,' Quinton interrupted, rubbing a hand over his eyes. 'It's been a long day. I'll see you all at dinner.'

'Well, *I* have a headache.' Antigone got to her feet with a speed that belied her statement.

'Meaning?'

'Meaning that I'm going to bed. I don't want any dinner.'

'I don't care. You'll be at the table.'

'But I have a headache!'

'And yet you appear to have no trouble with shouting. You'll come down to dinner as normal and be polite.'

'That doesn't sound normal.' Justin smirked.

'You, too. No provoking each other this evening.'

'Or you'll send them away somewhere, too?' Corin folded one leg lazily over the other. 'You'll need a different threat, I'm afraid. You're already sending Justin to Eton in a few weeks.'

'Don't remind me.' Justin sounded morose.

'Then I'll send him even sooner. Tomorrow if necessary. As for Antigone, I'm sure I can find a finishing school for young ladies somewhere.' Although how any school was going to finish what nobody had ever started was beyond him. 'Now, if you'll excuse me...' He reached for the door handle and then stopped. 'Where's Helen?'

Chapter Seven

Helen, as it turned out, was safe and sound up in the nursery, or so one of the maids informed Quinton on his way up the main staircase. He thought briefly about going to visit her before dinner and then decided to wait until morning. The opportunity of being alone with his own thoughts for an hour was too irresistible to miss.

He climbed into a copper bathtub with a groan of relief, allowing the deep, steaming-hot water to soak away some of his cares. It had been a trying few days, but at least he was making progress. Beatrix's arrival hadn't quite gone as he'd hoped, but she was there now at Howden, under his newly-repaired roof. He'd retrieved her, if that was the right word, which it undoubtedly wasn't, and now all he had to do was convince her that she liked it enough to stay *despite* his family, though fortunately, he had another five weeks and five days to compensate for their behaviour.

He looked at the wall separating his bedroom from the next, usually vacant, chamber. Would Mrs Hastings have placed her in there? He hadn't thought to ask, though since it had doubtless never occurred to his mother to vacate the Duchess's suite at the front of the house, it seemed likely. In all likelihood, she was taking a bath at that very minute, too, on the other side of the wall, in fact… He lay still, listening for any sound of telltale splashing. Just the idea of it stirred his blood to a surprising degree. She would be naked, of course, or wrapped in a sheet perhaps, her limbs soft and wet and pink from the heat…eminently touchable, strokeable, kissable…

Damn it. He'd hoped his reaction to her the previous night had simply been an aberration, but it appeared his body had other, increasingly visible, ideas. He closed his eyes and slid under the water, holding his breath for a few seconds until the feeling passed before scrubbing himself vigorously with a cloth. Then, when he was satisfied that everything was back to normal, he climbed out of the bath, shaved, dressed himself in evening clothes and made his way back down to the drawing room for six o'clock sharp, irritated but not surprised to discover that only one other member of his family had managed to arrive on time. Still, under the circumstances, one wasn't too bad, he supposed.

'Justin.' He gave his youngest brother an approving nod.

'I've finished that essay you asked for.' Justin leapt up from the armchair where he was lounging, his expression eager. He looked taller than he'd been two days ago, Quinton observed in surprise, although more likely he was only just noticing.

'Essay?'

'About why I shouldn't read Antigone's diary. You wanted it in English and Latin.'

'Oh…yes. In that case, I hope you've learnt your lesson.'

Justin looked dubious. 'I suppose so. Although, to be honest, I didn't want to read her diary again anyway. It might have been better to write about how boring other people's diaries are. Sisters especially.'

'Mmm.'

'You know she's going to be late for dinner?'

'Antigone's late for everything.'

'Later, then. She and Mother are plotting.'

'Really?' Quinton drew his brows together with annoyance. 'What else have they been saying?'

'I'm not sure, but Mother says the only way she'll move to the dower house is if you drag her there by her hair.'

'That sounds suitably dramatic. She shouldn't tempt me.'

Justin grinned. 'Corin told me, by the way.'

'Told you what?'

'That you like tall blondes.'

Quinton paused with his hand on a decanter of sherry, annoyed that, for once, Corin was right. He *did* prefer tall blondes, the taller and blonder, the better. Beatrix's friend Mrs Fortini had been a perfect example of that type, not that he'd paid her a great deal of attention. For a start, because he'd suspected her husband would have ripped his head off if he had and, for an end, because he was a married man now. He might not know much about the blissful state of wedlock, but he knew that married men didn't go around noticing their wives' friends, no matter how stunning they might be.

'Good evening.'

They both spun around at the sound of his average-sized brunette wife's voice.

'Good evening.' Quinton made a stiff bow, wondering how much of his conversation with Justin she'd just overheard. Judging by the heightened colour in her cheeks, more than he would have liked. 'How do you like your new room? I trust that everything is to your satisfaction?'

'It's very nice.' She darted a quick look at Justin, who was now studying the carpet with an unusual degree of interest. 'Mrs Hastings was very helpful.'

'Good. Excellent. Sherry?'

'No, thank you.' She sat down on one of the sofas, emulating Justin by examining a rug at her feet. She was wearing the same green dress from that first evening in Bath, he noticed, the one that brought out the green flecks in her brown eyes and turned them hazel. Judging by the size of the valise she'd brought with her, it was likely the only evening gown she owned.

'Well, then…' He poured out a glass for himself before going to stand beside the mantelpiece. 'The others should be down shortly.'

'I expect so, yes.'

He passed the time by looking at his younger brother, thinking up punishments while waiting for him to lift his gaze sufficiently to be glared at. It would have to be more than a Latin essay this time. Maybe a whole book on the subject of minding his own damned business, keeping his voice down and how *not* to offend people's wives…

'Well, here we all are.' Corin appeared in the doorway a few awkward minutes later, arms spread wide in a way that suggested he'd already imbibed a few private glasses of sherry. 'A few of us anyway. How charming.' He made a beeline for Beatrix, taking her hand and lifting it to his lips. 'May I say how lovely you look this evening, Duchess? Or may I call you Sister?'

'Um…' She looked somewhat taken aback by the attention. 'Thank you and yes, if you like.'

'Any sign of Mother?' Quinton hadn't realised he'd been grinding his teeth until he had to unclench them.

'Not yet.' Corin didn't bother turning his head, still gazing at Beatrix in a way that made his elder brother want to storm across the room and physically remove him. 'No doubt she's busy fulminating somewhere. Can't you sense the storm clouds gathering?'

'I can, but some metaphors aren't helpful.'

'Your Grace?' The butler cleared his throat from the doorway.

'Yes, Dunstan?'

'A message from the Dowager, Your Grace. She's been unavoidably detained.'

'Of course she has.' Quinton took a mouthful of sherry to rinse the bitter taste from his mouth. 'How so?'

'I'm afraid that her maid didn't share the details, Your Grace.'

'And my sister? I presume that she's been detained, also?'

'I…' Dunstan looked flustered. 'I don't know, Your Grace. I could send someone to find out, if you wish?'

'No need. Is dinner ready?'

'Yes, Your Grace, but…'

'But there are only four of us present. However, that's still more than half so I think we ought to consider it a quorum.' He slammed his empty glass down on the mantelpiece. 'I'm too hungry to wait.'

'Very good, Your Grace. I'll inform the waiting staff.'

Quinton came to stand beside Beatrix, resisting the urge to shoulder Corin out of the way. 'Shall we?'

She hesitated briefly before looking up at him, her gaze wary. And definitely hazel. 'Don't you think we ought to wait a little longer?'

'No. They know what time dinner is served.'

'But if there are already storm clouds…?'

'Trust me, some storms are unavoidable.'

'If you say so.' She stood up, shrugging her shoulders slightly. 'I confess that I'm hungry, too.'

'We're eating in *here*?' Beatrix stopped in the doorway of the dining room, certain there must have been some kind of mistake. The table before her was at least twenty feet in length and ten in breadth, so huge that conversation would surely be impossible without shouting. They might as well all sit in separate rooms. Unless that was the point?

'Yes.' Quinton sounded unperturbed, waving a footman aside and pulling a chair out for her at one end of the table.

'But it's immense! You could hold a ball in here!'

'Except that it's the dining room.'

She sat down, unable to refute that particular statement, waiting the dozen or so seconds it took for him to reach the opposite end before picking up the glass of wine a footman had just filled for her. If she were going to face his mother again at some point then she had a feeling she might need it.

'Soup, Your Grace.'

She gave a start as another footman slid a bowl of steaming, green-coloured liquid in front of her. It was going to take a while to get used to being called *that*, she thought, although she could get used to the food easily enough. The soup smelled delicious.

'It's a bit like a cave, isn't it?' Corin chuckled from his seat halfway down the table. 'You know, Quin and I used to play pirates in here when we were boys. We used to duel on the table with wooden swords. Remember, Quin?'

'I do, although, as I recall, *you* were the pirate.'

'And you were the noble sea captain.' Corin turned towards Beatrix. 'He refused to play a villain. He always had to fight for King and country, honour and duty and all that.'

'You make them sound like bad things.' Quinton lifted an eyebrow. Or at least she thought he did. At this distance it was impossible to be sure.

'Personally I've always thought them rather overrated.'

'Then that's where we differ.'

'*Quinton?*' His mother chose that moment to sweep into the room, Antigone at her heels. '*What* is the meaning of this?'

'Dinner, Mother.' He dabbed at his mouth with a napkin. 'Served at the usual time. You said you were detained. Unavoidably, as I recall.'

'You still might have waited.' The Dowager's gaze travelled the full length of the table, looking as scandalised as if they were all doing something obscene on top of it.

'And *you* might have mentioned how long you expected to be. Some of us have had long days.'

His mother's eyes narrowed. 'And where exactly would you like me to sit?'

'Anywhere you like.'

'I would *like* my chair of the past thirty years.'

'That's where the Duchess sits.'

'I can—' Beatrix started to rise and then subsided again as both her husband and mother-in-law turned implacable faces towards her.

'Very well, then.' The Dowager took a seat two thirds of the way down the table, as far away from Beatrix's end as possible, gesturing for Antigone to follow. 'Am I permitted to eat the soup or is it too late?'

'Eat as much soup as you like, Mother.'

The meal descended into desultory silence afterwards. It was strange, Beatrix thought, just how heavy and uncomfortable it felt, drawing attention to the sound of her own chewing and the scrape and clatter of cutlery. She was used to being excluded at meal times. Her uncle and aunt had mostly ignored her presence and never included her in the conversation, but at least there *had* been some conversation. Here, both the Dowager and her daughter seemed determined to keep their lips tightly sealed and their faces averted, casting a pall over the whole room.

'So, Beatrix...' Corin spoke up eventually, taking the opportunity of the dessert arriving to slide his chair further towards her. 'Tell us about Bath. Quin says that's where you've been living.'

'Did I?' Quinton's voice sounded sharp.

'Maybe it was your coachman.' Corin shrugged. 'I happened to pass by the stables earlier and he mentioned that you'd hired him in Bath. Or was he mistaken?'

'That hardly seems likely, does it?'

'Not really. So…' Corin twisted back in her direction, his face the picture of innocence. 'How did you like Bath?'

Beatrix glanced down the table, trying to judge from her husband's expression what he was thinking, but as usual his expression was inscrutable, or so it seemed from a mile away. She was still adjusting to hearing him referred to as Quin, too. The name sounded far too carefree to suit him, but she liked it. It made him seem less severe somehow. Perhaps she might ask if she could use it, although at that moment she had far more pressing questions, such as how he might want her to answer. Despite all their time together in the carriage, they hadn't discussed what to tell his family about her three-and-a-half-month absence. He'd told them about her running away so she'd simply assumed that he'd told them the rest, too, but obviously not. Then again, why *shouldn't* she talk about Belles? She wasn't ashamed of her time there. On the contrary, she was proud of the skills she'd learned. She loved it and missed the shop horribly already.

'I liked Bath very much. I found a job baking biscuits,' she answered finally.

There was an abrupt clatter as the Dowager's spoon fell to the table. *'A job?'*

'Yes. I only had a little money when I ran away so I had to do something.' She dipped her own spoon into her trifle. 'I'm actually quite good at baking these days.'

'A *lady* does not work.' Antigone expressed what was obviously uppermost in her mother's mind.

'That's probably why I was so bad at it to begin with, but thankfully even a lady can learn.'

'Perhaps it depends on her breeding?'

'Or her intelligence?'

'Touché.' Corin chuckled. 'So did Quin have to fight some strapping baker fellow to get you out of there?'

Beatrix darted another glimpse up the table, surprised to see a flicker of something other than inscrutability on her husband's face. Annoyance? She wasn't sure whether it was directed at her or Corin, but, either way, he wasn't stopping her from talking…

'Actually, I worked with a woman called Nancy. She and I would get up early and do all the baking together. Then we'd have a rest before opening the shop.'

'You *served* in a shop?' The Dowager's voice was pained, as if every word were a dagger in her heart.

'Oh, yes, Belles is very popular in Bath.'

'I don't doubt it.' Corin smiled lazily.

'Of course, that used to have a lot to do with my friend Henrietta.' She popped a spoonful of trifle casually into her mouth and then couldn't resist adding: 'She's very beautiful. Tall and blonde.' Another spoonful of trifle. 'A lot of men like that. Or so I hear, anyway.'

'Well!' The Dowager pushed her chair back. 'I seem to have lost my appetite for dessert. I'm going to bed and so is Antigone.'

'By all means, if that's what you want.' Quinton laid his napkin aside and stood up with what appeared to be deliberate slowness. 'Sleep well, Mother.'

'Antigone!' The Dowager shot a stern look at her

daughter, who was endeavouring to shovel the remainder of her trifle into her mouth in one go, before storming to the doorway.

'Just us again, eh?' Corin didn't bother to stand up for his mother and sister, lounging further back in his chair instead. 'Now do tell me more about biscuits.'

'Actually, if you don't mind, I think I'll have an early night, too.' She put her spoon down, losing her own appetite suddenly. 'It's been a long day.'

'Of course.' Quinton was still on his feet, his gaze hooded. 'Sleep well, Beatrix.'

Chapter Eight

Week One. Day Three

'Good morning,' Quinton announced to the empty-looking breakfast room, making his way to the sideboard and preparing two plates of scrambled egg, mushroom, sausages and bacon and then carrying them both back to the table. 'It looks like it's going to be a pleasant day.'

No answer.

'I'd rather hoped you'd be outside with the others yesterday.' He slid one of the plates under the table-cloth, waiting until it was plucked from his fingers before continuing. 'I know you're shy around new people, but there's no need to worry about meeting Beatrix. She's very nice, trust me.' He almost smiled at the words. They were true. She *was* very nice, if a little unconventional for a duchess. 'In any case, I'd be grateful if you could make an appearance at luncheon. You don't have to eat with us, just show your face. Will that be all right?'

A small bump on the table answered in the affirmative.

'Good. Now, do you want toast?'

Another bump.

'Butter and marmalade?'

Two bumps.

'Just butter, then?'

One bump.

'Quinton?'

He lifted his head at the sound of his wife's voice. She was standing just inside the doorway, regarding him with an expression of perplexity mixed with alarm as he pushed a piece of bread under the table.

'Beatrix?' Fortunately, the toast was pulled from his fingers at that moment, allowing him to stand up and make a small bow. 'You're awake early.'

'I got used to early hours at Belles.' She seemed somewhat reluctant to come any closer, looking from him to the table and back again. 'Who were you talking to? Is there a dog under there?'

'No-o, no dog.' He gave a small cough. 'Can I fetch you anything?'

'Um…no, thank you. I can manage.' She regarded him suspiciously for another moment before reaching for a plate, appetite obviously outweighing caution. 'Don't let your own breakfast get cold.'

'You slept well, I trust?' He sat down again, wondering how to explain.

'Very well, thank you. And you?'

'Not bad,' he lied. Truthfully, he'd had a wretched night, kept awake by a combination of anger at his intractable, ill-mannered family and a sleep-thwarting awareness of her on the other side of the wall. If she *was* on the other side of the wall, that was. He still hadn't asked Mrs Hastings. For all he knew, he'd been lusting after a completely empty bedchamber...

'Can I pour you some coffee?'

'Please.' She took a seat beside him. 'So...why were you just talking to the table?'

'Ah. Well, about that... I wasn't talking *to* the table exactly.' He passed her a small silver milk jug. 'Beatrix, meet my youngest sister, Helen.'

'Your sister?' Her eyes widened, flashing with something like panic.

'Again, *not* the table. The little girl sitting under it. She's a little reserved.'

'Oh...' Beatrix lifted a hand and pointed a finger downwards. 'So I shouldn't...?'

'It's usually best to wait until she comes out. I'm afraid it might take a few days before she actually says anything.'

'I see. Well, then, it's very nice to meet you, Helen. I'm Beatrix.'

There was a momentary pause, followed by a faint bump.

'I hope that we're going to be friends.' She leaned towards Quinton, lowering her voice slightly. 'How old is she?'

Ten bumps, one after the other, answered for him.

'Thank you.' She laughed delightedly, her face lighting up in a way that was completely different from all the tight, forced smiles she'd given him so far. She looked transformed. Radiant. Captivating. *Beautiful*. Enough to make him forget all about the piece of bacon he'd been about to pop into his mouth. People rarely smiled like that at Howden. Or anywhere, come to think of it. The sight seemed to warm his insides. And as for her laugh…

'What's the matter?' To his dismay, the smile faded as her eyebrows lifted instead.

'Nothing.' He gave his head a small shake, returning his attention to the bacon. 'It just occurred to me that I've never heard you laugh before.'

'I've never heard you laugh either, but then I suppose we haven't had a great deal to laugh about together so far, have we?'

'True. Although to be honest, I don't remember the last time I laughed at all.'

'Hmm.' She looked thoughtful rather than shocked by the observation. 'I suppose I never used to laugh much either. There was a time, when I lived with my uncle and aunt, when I wasn't even sure that I could. Of course, that was before I met Nancy.'

'She's amusing?'

'Very, although not always intentionally. She has the worst temper and biggest heart of anyone I've ever met.' She chuckled quietly to herself before bending down to speak under the table. 'Would you like anything else, Helen?'

Two bumps.

'That means no,' Quinton interpreted. 'I gave her a full plate earlier.'

'Ah. What a kind brother you have.'

A single thud, louder this time.

'So…' He gave a small cough of embarrassment. 'I was hoping to show you the park this morning, but I'm afraid there's a problem with the roof that requires my attention. Perhaps we might take a ride after luncheon instead?'

'I'd like that. Although I'm afraid I don't have a riding habit.'

'Antigone can loan you one. You must be about the same size.'

'I don't know...' She picked up her coffee cup with a grimace. 'I'd rather not make the situation any worse.'

'Nonsense. I'll send a message up to her maid in a moment.' He nodded, pleased to have plans in place. 'Now, if you'll excuse me, I ought to get started...'

'Wait!' She put a hand up as he pushed his chair back. 'Before you go, there's something I'd like to ask you.'

'Yes?'

'Well... I noticed that your brother calls you Quin and I wondered if you'd mind my calling you that, too?'

He paused, considering. When he'd left home and joined the army, he'd gone from a Quin to a Quinton overnight. Major Quinton Roxbury, in fact. Now only his brothers and sisters still used his old, boyhood name. Not that he had any objections. On the contrary, he found himself quite liking the idea... 'Very well, if you prefer.'

'I do.'

'Then Quin it is.' He was halfway out of his chair before stopping again. 'What about you? Is there a shorter form of Beatrix?'

'Ye-es.' She frowned slightly, sinking her teeth into her bottom lip as if she wasn't sure whether or not she wanted to answer.

'Of course, if you prefer Beatrix...?'

'No, it's just...when I was little, my parents called me Bea. No one's used it in twelve years, but it's less of a mouthful.'

'And you wouldn't object to my using it?'

'No.' Her lips twitched and then spread into that radiant smile again. 'It'll be easier to get used to than Your Grace.'

'Bea…' He let his gaze linger on her face for a few seconds before tearing it away. 'I'll see you at luncheon, then.'

Beatrix—*Bea*—watched Quinton—*Quin*—depart, blowing her cheeks out as she wondered what had just happened. The way that he'd just looked at her, as if he couldn't *not* look at her, had caused the strange tingling feeling that had lain dormant since their arrival at Howden to flare up all over again, only this time accompanied by a tightening sensation in her abdomen that made it downright impossible for her to continue eating.

She put down her knife and fork and looked around the breakfast room instead, relieved to find that not every meal was served in the cavernous dining room. Not that *this* was small exactly, but it was infinitely cosier. East-facing, too, allowing rays of soft morning sunshine to filter in through two floor-length windows and bathe the room in a lustrous, golden light. At any other time, she might have been quite happy to sit there, basking in warmth and nursing her coffee for hours, but the rest of the family would probably be down soon and the thought of *that* was enough to dispel any residual tingling and make her eat up the rest of her eggs in a hurry.

She was just standing up when a plate slid out from beneath the tablecloth.

'Oh!' She put a hand to her chest, startled by the sudden movement. 'Helen. You were so quiet I forgot you were there. Can I fetch you anything else before I go?'

To her surprise, a small face framed with an abundance of black curls followed the plate, staring up at her with the wide-eyed stare of an extremely solemn puppy.

'Maybe another piece of toast?' Beatrix offered, crouching down and then almost tumbling backwards when the girl spoke.

'No, thank you.' Her voice was as solemn as her expression. 'Are you *really* married to Quin?'

'I am.'

'I thought that you ran away?'

'Yes.' Beatrix felt her cheeks flush guiltily. 'But we talked and…well, I'm here now.'

The girl nodded. 'I'm not supposed to know about it, but I hear things.'

'From under tables?'

'And behind doors. And curtains. They're all angry at you.'

Beatrix couldn't help but smile at her bluntness. Children had a way of getting straight to the point. 'I've noticed.'

'Don't worry. They get angry a lot.' Helen made a face that on an older person might have been described as jaded. 'I can show you around if you like?'

'Would you?' Beatrix's smile widened. Mrs Hastings had also volunteered a tour, but the little girl's offer was too touching to resist. Besides, she had a feeling that Helen's might be more interesting.

'Yes, but we'll have to hurry. Mama has breakfast in her room, but the others will be down soon. Except for Corin because he's been playing billiards all night. Come on.' Helen crawled the rest of the way out and scurried towards the door, peering around it like some kind of Napoleonic spy. 'All clear.'

'Where are we going?' Beatrix whispered as they crossed the hall at a scamper.

'There's a way out through the music room.' Helen stopped abruptly at the sound of footsteps, then darted into the shadows beneath the staircase.

Beatrix followed, flattening herself against the wall obediently and wondering how it would look if they were discovered.

'You *have* to come with me!' It was Antigone's voice, an imperious echo of her mother's as the footsteps came closer, thankfully on the far side of the staircase. 'I'm not having breakfast with her on my own.'

'Where's Justin?' The second voice belonged to a weary-sounding Corin.

'He's still in bed.'

'Lucky him. That's where I'd like to be.'

'Why can't you sleep at night like normal people? Please, Corin, I need some moral support.'

'Why not just try and be pleasant? It's not *that* hard.'

'Because she's an ungrateful, ill-bred upstart and I refuse to pretend that she isn't.'

'Good grief, Antigone, you really *are* turning into Mother, and that's not a compliment, by the way.'

'Mother's right! After what that woman did to Quin, she ought to count herself lucky I haven't spat in her face.'

'Try it and Quin will lock you in your room for a month. Remember what he said last night.'

'I know, I know, be polite and pleasant. I can't understand why he's being so forgiving.'

'Because he's a better man than I am and he's determined to save this family from ourselves.' Corin sounded dead on his feet. 'Which is a losing battle in my opinion, but he always did tilt at windmills. Personally I think we're doomed.'

'Corin!'

'Oh, fine. I'll come to breakfast with you, but just this once.'

Beatrix pressed her lips together, fighting back tears as the footsteps faded into the distance. She'd known that her husband's family didn't have a particularly high opinion of her, but Antigone's words made her feel as if she were back at her uncle and aunt's house all over again, barely tolerated and overtly despised.

'Don't cry,' a voice whispered as a small hand slid into hers. '*I* like you.'

'Do you?' She looked down, feeling almost pathetically grateful for the words.

'Yes. I'll prove it.'

The little girl tugged on her hand, pulling her through three almost identical, and identically vast, reception suites into a room containing a piano and a large, wooden harp.

'There's a way out over here.' Helen unlocked a French door on the far wall and led her out onto a long, stone-flagged terrace.

Beatrix caught her breath, looking out past a low grey wall at the landscape beyond. Darkness had already been falling when they'd arrived the previous night, but now she could see the rolling parkland in its full splendour. At a guess, the estate had been remodelled at some point during the last century, the gentle slopes and occasional clumps of trees suggesting that either Capability Brown or one of his students had taken a hand in the design. If she wasn't mistaken, there was a bridge to the east, where a hill slid sharply downwards, indicating a river, and if she followed the curve of the land beside it…yes, she could just spy a thin, glittering ribbon of blue. It was all quite beautiful, she had to concede, albeit with a chill in the air that made her wish she'd brought a shawl. Not that wild horses would have dragged her back inside the house at that moment. She only had one friend there and she wasn't about to risk losing her.

'This is the herb garden,' Helen explained as they made their way down the terrace steps, then along a pathway between two mostly empty flowerbeds. 'The greenhouses are over there, but the maze is this way.'

'There's a maze?' Beatrix felt her heart give a little bounce of excitement.

'Yes. The others don't visit very often so it's mostly mine.' She looked back over her shoulder. 'And Quin's the only one who knows the way to my secret den.'

'In the centre?'

Helen gave her a faintly pitying look. 'That would be *much* too obvious. It's this way.'

She could only hope, Beatrix thought a few twists and turns later, that Helen wasn't secretly in league with Antigone and plotting to abandon her. The maze was so large and intricate that she'd be lucky to find her own way out again without help before nightfall. Fortunately, they stopped eventually, turning a corner into what looked like another dead end before Helen dropped onto all fours, crawling towards a small gap in the hedge and burrowing inside.

Beatrix followed suit, ardently renewing her wish that she wasn't about to be abandoned, pushing her way through a tunnel of branches and leaves and then sitting up in surprise as she found herself in a triangular-shaped gap between the hedges, big enough for three or four people to stand up in. Closer inspection revealed that someone, presumably Helen, had trimmed away one side of the hedge, making a small domed shelter, beneath which were stored several cushions and a blanket.

'How wonderful.' Beatrix looked around approvingly. It was a perfect child's den. 'Did you do it all by yourself?'

'Yes, I found the gap and—' Helen twisted her head at the sound of a purr. 'Oh, there you are. I haven't seen you for a few days.' She reached over to pick up a large tortoiseshell cat with white socks. 'This is Paws.'

'Hello, Paws.' Beatrix tickled the animal under the chin. 'Pleased to meet you.'

'I think she belongs to one of the gardeners, but she likes to come and visit me.' Helen reached into the pocket of her skirt and pulled out what appeared to be a piece of dried kipper. 'Nobody else knows about her, not even Quin. So now you *know* that I like you.'

'I like you, too.' Beatrix smiled. 'And for what it's worth, I never meant to hurt your brother.'

'That's what he told the others last night.' Helen crossed her legs, letting Paws curl up in her lap. 'They thought I was in the nursery, but I was behind one of the sofas.'

'And your brother told everyone to be nice to me?'

'Yes. Or he'd send Mama to the dower house and Antigone to a finishing school. They'd both hate that.'

'Oh, dear. What about your brothers?'

'He said something about Justin going to Eton

sooner, but he didn't threaten them exactly. They kept on talking about it after he left and Corin said that looking stern was giving him a headache and Justin said that he didn't want to write any more essays in Latin. Then Antigone called them both traitors and Justin called her a harpy.'

'Oh…' Beatrix drew her brows together, unsure what essays in Latin had to do with anything. 'What about you? I hope that Quin hasn't said anything severe to you.'

The look in Helen's blue eyes suggested she'd just taken leave of her senses. 'Quin would *never* be mean to me. He's the kindest brother in the whole, wide world!'

'Oh.' Beatrix sat back on her haunches, thoroughly chastened. There was really nothing she could say to that.

Chapter Nine

To Beatrix's relief, luncheon was also served in the breakfast room, though the atmosphere at noon was unfortunately similar to that of dinner. To be fair to her husband, he made a few valiant attempts at conversation, one brief remark about the weather and another longer comment about the progress of the roof, but the rest of his family, Corin and Helen excluded— the former being in bed and the latter eating in the nursery—seemed determined to respond with apathetic murmurs followed by silence. There were no more malicious comments or glares. They were all being perfectly 'polite and pleasant', as Antigone had put it, but that was *all* they were doing. There *had* been a moment when Justin had seemed about to contribute something, but a sharp look from his mother had put paid to that. Judging by the way the table shook briefly, it was also accompanied by a kick from his sister, one that was reciprocated a few seconds later, causing the salt cellar to topple onto its side with a thud. If Quinton had announced a royal visit, she doubted any of them would have given more than a half-hearted murmur of acknowledgement.

'Well, much as I hate to leave such a scintillating conversation…' Quinton arched an eyebrow sardonically once the dessert had been cleared '… I promised Beatrix a tour of the park this afternoon.'

'You're going for a ride?' Justin sat up eagerly.

'Beatrix and I are, yes.' Quinton pushed his chair back and stood up. 'Naturally, I'd invite you and Antigone to accompany us, but you both seem *so* tired. I can't remember the last time we had such a quiet luncheon.'

'Usually you complain that we argue too much.' Antigone's chin jerked upwards.

'True. However, one extreme to the other isn't necessarily an improvement. I recommend a nap before dinner or I might have to suggest that you start taking your meals back in the nursery.'

'The *nursery*?'

'Where childish behaviour belongs, yes.'

'And what about me?' His mother's eyes flashed across the table. 'Will you condemn *me* to the nursery, too?'

'Of course not.' His neutral expression didn't alter. 'Although if you wish to eat in complete silence then there's always that house we spoke of yesterday. I've asked Mrs Hastings to start preparing some furniture just in case.'

'You've done what?'

'The decor is in good condition, apparently. All the place needs is a bit of paint and a good airing.' He looked at Beatrix as if he were entirely oblivious to the effect of his words. 'Are you ready?'

She nodded and got up, covering her mouth with her napkin until she felt able to suppress a burble of laughter. Part of her was tempted to intervene and insist that his brother and sister join them, but another, more realistic part doubted that the gesture would be appreciated or do anything to improve their opinion of her. More likely, their company would simply spoil the afternoon.

'Thank you.' She threw Quinton a grateful look as they stepped out into the hallway. 'I probably shouldn't admit it, but I enjoyed that.'

'So did I.' One side of his mouth twitched upwards. 'But it was no more than they deserved.'

This time she couldn't prevent a small giggle from escaping her lips. 'They did, but perhaps Helen could join us?'

'Helen?' He looked surprised.

'Yes. She showed me her den in the maze this morning and I'd like to repay her. Only if she wants to come, of course.'

'You mean, she came out from under the table?' Surprise turned to approval. 'You're honoured.'

'I think she felt sorry for me at first, but now we're officially friends.'

'I'm delighted to hear it.' The other side of his mouth tilted upwards as well, easing into what appeared to be a real, bona fide smile before he strode across the hall and picked up a brass bell sitting on top of a large oak chest. Even though she watched him do it, Beatrix was still unprepared, almost jumping out of her skin at the near-deafening clanging sound it made as he swung his arm up and down.

'It's our signal!' Quinton shouted over the din. *'She knows to come here when I ring! It saves us all wandering about the house shouting!'*

'Good idea!'

'I've always been afraid she might hide herself away and forget to come out otherwise!'

'Why does she hide?'

He put the bell down again, pausing thoughtfully before answering. 'She was only two years old when I left to join the army, but, from what I gather, it's just something she's always done.' His brows compressed. 'Perhaps it was the atmosphere. Neither of our parents was easy to live with. I might have hidden away if I'd ever thought of it, growing up.'

'Does she have a governess?'

'No. One of the maids looks after the nursery, but most of the time she does what she likes. It's hardly ideal, I know.'

'Definitely not. What about Antigone and Justin? Do they have tutors?'

'My secretary, Harker, is helping to prepare Justin for Eton. As for Antigone...' He rubbed the bridge of his nose. 'She can read and write and play music, of course, but my mother doesn't approve of too much education for women.'

'And what do *you* think?'

'I think that she's a clever young woman and a governess would do her a world of good, but it's frankly hard to imagine anyone wanting the job.'

'Then we'll just have to find somebody who likes a challenge.' Beatrix nodded firmly. 'Either that or pay them a hundred pounds a month.'

'Do you think that would be enough?' He smiled again as Helen came scampering down the staircase. 'Ah, there you are. How would you like a ride out on your pony?'

After the chill of the morning, the afternoon was glorious for mid-March. Beatrix tipped her face upwards, basking in the sun's warmth as her chestnut palfrey trotted slowly across the park. No doubt her new mother and sister-in-law would call such behaviour unladylike, but freckles seemed a small price to pay for such a blissful feeling. Besides, this was England. It would doubtless be raining again soon enough.

'Is that Antigone's riding habit?' Helen asked, riding alongside on a pretty grey and white dappled pony.

'Yes. She's letting me borrow it.' Beatrix threw a worried glance towards Quinton. 'I think.'

'It looks good on you.' He ignored the implied question, turning his head to look her up and down approvingly. 'You suit bold colours.'

'Thank you.' She felt her cheeks warm under his scrutiny. Personally, she would never have chosen anything so bold as magenta, but, she had to admit, she liked it, too. Looking at her reflection in the bedroom mirror, she'd been surprised at how well the vibrant shade brought out the few golden threads in her brown hair. It even made her eyes look bigger and brighter.

'You're brave,' Helen commented.

'Am I?'

'*Very.* I tried on one of Antigone's bonnets a few weeks ago and she sat on me.'

'She *sat* on you?' Quinton sounded horrified.

'For ten minutes.' Helen nodded placidly. 'So that I'd learn not to go into her bedroom again.'

'Good grief.'

'It worked. I haven't been in there since.'

'Fortunately, I didn't go into her bedroom,' Beatrix reassured her. Although whether that would make any difference was another matter. She wouldn't be surprised if Antigone refused to wear the habit ever again, claiming she'd made it smell of the shop.

'The only way to escape is to tickle her,' Helen continued. 'I can't do it because she's so much stronger than I am, but you probably could. That's why she daren't sit on Justin any longer. He says the best place is—'

'There'll be no more sitting on anyone,' Quinton interrupted firmly.

'But just in case—'

'No more!'

'This is a lovely park.' Beatrix changed the subject tactfully, dropping back to give Helen a conspiratorial wink and to mouth the words 'you can tell me later' behind Quinton's back.

'Yes.' He threw her a suspicious look. 'My grandfather had it all landscaped fifty years ago.'

'Can we go to the copse?' Helen chirped up again. 'The bluebells will be coming soon.'

'They won't be flowering yet. Not for another few weeks.'

'But they'll still be growing.'

'In that case, you'd better ask Beatrix. This is her tour.'

'Can we, Beatrix? *Please?*'

'Mmm.' She tapped a finger against her chin, laughing at the little girl's imploring expression. With her blue eyes and black hair, she looked like a miniature female version of Quinton. Beatrix couldn't imagine him ever imploring her for anything, but if he did, she could imagine he might be similarly hard to resist. 'Well, how can I refuse a plea like that?'

'Oh, thank you!'

'This way, then.' Quinton flicked on his reins, directing them towards a small woodland in the distance.

'Here we are.' He brought them to a halt beside a pair of tall horse chestnut stumps that obviously marked the start of a pathway.

'Can I go and explore?' Helen jumped down from her pony, her small face bright with excitement.

'So long as you come back when I call you.'

'I promise!'

'She's very sweet.' Beatrix smiled as the little girl hurried away. 'Quite adorable, too.'

'She is.' He agreed, smiling back. Which was three times in almost an hour, Beatrix thought in amazement, though this particular smile seemed the most natural, reaching all the way to his eyes and softening his sharp features until he looked almost relaxed. She had to admit he looked surprisingly handsome this afternoon, too, his tall figure encased in brown breeches, a buff-coloured jacket and Hessians so bright they seemed to sparkle like mirrors in the sunshine.

'And she really does like you,' he added. 'She would never have agreed to come along if she didn't.'

'I'm glad.' She felt a wistful pang in her chest. 'I always wanted a sister. I would have given an arm or leg for one growing up.'

'But you had cousins, I thought?'

'Jaspar and Cordelia, yes, but they were both older than me and my uncle and aunt didn't like us spending time together.'

'Why not?' His brow knotted as he dismounted and came towards her.

'Oh…' She hesitated, fiddling with the reins. 'It's complicated. They resented me in a way, I think.'

'What on earth for?'

'Just for being an heiress, I suppose. My father's will left me in the care of my uncle, but I don't think he ever really understood how his brother felt towards him, let alone me. You see, my father had been successful where my uncle hadn't and it caused bitterness between them, on my uncle's side anyway. Then my uncle thought that he should have been left more in his will, but, instead, all he got was me and a yearly stipend for looking after me.'

'And he took it out on you?' Quinton's expression darkened.

'In a way. He and my aunt never wanted me. They made that obvious from the start.' She shuddered at the memory. 'At first, I thought it must have been something I'd done so I tried to make it up to them by being good and obedient, but everything I did only seemed to make things worse. They were so cold and unwelcoming… I was only a little older than Helen's age now and I felt so lonely and unlovable. Wretched.'

'I'm sorry. I had no idea.' He reached his hands up to help her down. 'Truly.'

'Fortunately, Miss Foster came along.' Despite the subject, her pulse quickened at the touch of his hands on her waist. 'I'm sure that my uncle only hired her for appearances' sake, but she was so kind, she made me feel like I had some value again.'

'Miss Foster was the lady you went to find in Bath, as I recall?'

'Yes.' She slid to the ground, catching her breath as her skirts brushed against his trousers. 'Then when I turned eighteen, my uncle said that I didn't need a governess any more and sent her away. I was heartbroken, but we kept up a correspondence. Or we *did*. Her letters stopped around the same time as our engagement. Looking back, my uncle probably intercepted them so that she wouldn't influence my decision. That's why I didn't know she'd married and left Bath.'

'But then you found your biscuit shop?'

'Yes.' She dropped her gaze as her heart began to thud far too heavily against the walls of her ribcage. His hands were still around her waist and the feeling of them, never mind his close proximity, seemed to be having a disturbing, somewhat chaotic effect on her body. It didn't make sense. How could her heartbeat accelerate for a man she'd run away from and had every intention of leaving in another five and a half weeks?

'Yes,' she repeated, her voice sounding strangely throaty. 'Henrietta and Nancy rescued me.'

'And you were truly happy there?'

'The happiest I'd felt in twelve years.' She looked up again and then wished that she hadn't. His pale gaze was searching her face so intently she felt her stomach start to tie itself in knots. 'I don't know what I would have done without them.'

He released her suddenly, turning his head to one side and uttering something she couldn't understand, but that sounded a lot like an oath.

'You're very good with Helen.' She decided to change the subject again.

'She's easy to get along with,' he murmured, looking back to his usual severe self as he moved away to tie their horses' reins around the branch of a birch tree. 'Unlike the rest of my family, I might add. I apologise for their behaviour today. And last night. And tomorrow probably. Unfortunately, my mother is the worst of all, but for what it's worth, you're dealing with her admirably.'

'Really? I don't feel like it.'

'Believe me, I've seen grown women reduced to tears with less.'

'You mean she behaves this way with other people?'

'Frequently. My mother has never exactly been easy to get along with.'

'Then no wonder you didn't tell me about her before.' She lifted an eyebrow ironically. 'Although, as much as I appreciate your defending me, you don't have to threaten her with eviction.'

'Yes, I do. You're the Duchess of Howden now, whether she wants to accept it or not. She needs to understand that things have changed.'

'*Temporarily,*' she corrected him. 'But it's all right. Truly. It might not be very pleasant, but I can understand why she hates me.'

'She doesn't hate you.'

'No?' She gave him a disbelieving look.

'No.' He leaned a shoulder against a tree trunk, looking in the direction Helen had gone. 'My mother's an angry person. She has been for as long as I can remember. You're an easy target, that's all.'

'How reassuring. Why is she angry?'

'Because of my father. Even now he's gone, she's still angry.'

'They weren't a love match, then?'

He snorted. 'I believe it was more like hate at first sight. They were both equally volatile.'

'But they married anyway?'

'It was a good match on paper.'

'Oh.' She pressed her lips together, finding the words a little too close for comfort.

'My father wasn't a good man,' Quinton continued, his jaw clenching as he spoke. 'His vices weren't particularly original, but he never made any effort to mend his ways either. He drained the estate of every last penny and humiliated my mother whenever he could. There must have been occasional breaks in the hostilities, I suppose, since they managed to have five children, but most of the time they loathed the very sight of each other.'

'That can't have made growing up here very pleasant.'

'No. It made life difficult. It still does.' He folded his arms across his chest. 'After he died, I hoped she might mellow a little, but I suppose some habits are too ingrained to break.'

'How sad.' She looked at him sympathetically. 'Is that why you're angry, too? Because of your father?'

'What do you mean?' His expression sharpened abruptly. 'What makes you think that I'm angry?'

'I...' She hesitated, the steely glint in his eye making her wish she could take the words back. Why *did* she think that? And what on earth had made her say so? It wasn't as if he were obviously outraged like his mother and sister, or indolent or sulky like his brothers. If someone had asked her the day before, she might have said he was almost devoid of emotion, only now she had the sneaking suspicion that his inscrutability was only a veneer, a granite wall holding back something else, a vein of something powerful and raw. And when he'd mentioned anger…the word had just seemed to fit. 'I don't know exactly. You just seem tense. Restrained.'

He unfolded his arms and stalked slowly towards her, his face all hard lines again, without a hint of softness anywhere. 'That hardly makes me angry. I told you in Bath, I control my emotions, not the other way around. You asked me yourself why I *wasn't* angrier with you.'

'Yes, but I'm starting to think I was wrong.' She dug her heels in, refusing to back away. 'Just because a person doesn't wave their arms around and shout doesn't mean they're not feeling anything. You might not *want* strong emotions, but that doesn't mean you don't have them.'

He stopped a foot away from her. 'And you presume to know me so well after three days? You think that I'm hiding my true feelings?'

'No. I think you're denying them!' she retorted and then gasped with recognition. That was it! He hadn't *lied* about not being angry with her. He truly thought that he hadn't been. A person who prided themself on being in control of their emotions might not realise the difference. 'It's not your fault,' she added quickly. 'I can understand why you want to be in control, but maybe it's better to face your emotions than to deny them?'

'I'm not denying anything.'

'Are you sure?' She was increasingly sure that she

ought to stop talking and yet she couldn't seem to keep her mouth closed, her own temper rising at his refusal to even consider the possibility. 'I mean, isn't that better than the alternative?'

'And what exactly would that be?'

'That you're *so* in control of your emotions that you've lost the ability to feel anything at all!'

'Indeed?' His voice was clipped. 'Well, then, I'm sorry to be such a disappointment to you. Now, if you'll excuse me, I'm going to find my sister.'

Chapter Ten

Quinton strode along the woodland path, taking care not to stomp or storm or do anything that might suggest he wasn't completely in control of his temper. He didn't look back to see if Beatrix was following, although he sincerely doubted she would be after the way he'd just behaved. He'd been rude and confrontational and ungentlemanly, but he was feeling shaken to his core. *Not* angry, he assured himself, just shocked at the way her accusation had come so suddenly out of the blue. One moment he'd been trying to work out the best way to tell her about the Roxbury family scandal, trying not to be distracted by the way her hazel eyes and hair blended in perfectly with the foliage around her, even inwardly comparing her to some kind of woodland nymph, the next she'd been accusing him of anger and denial, of wearing a mask of control to conceal a seething mass of emotional turmoil beneath!

How *dared* she? When all he ever did was try to keep the peace within his family! When he'd not only forgiven *her* for humiliating him on their wedding day, but had actually brought her back to Howden as if nothing had happened! When he'd done everything in his power to help her settle in! How many other husbands would have done the same? And in return, she had the temerity to accuse him of being angry! And not just that, but to say that she preferred that idea to the alternative! He had emotions—*of course* he had *some* emotions—but if he *hadn't* been in complete control of them then he would have been furious!

'Helen?' He veered off the path and into the undergrowth at the sight of his younger sister crouching behind an ash tree. 'What is it?'

'Shh…' She lifted a finger to her lips. 'There's a hedgehog. I think he just woke up.'

'So there is.' He came to crouch beside her.

'He's probably hungry. I'm calling him Prickles.'

'You don't think that's a tiny bit obvious?'

'Sometimes it's best to call things what they are.'

'What?' He gave her a sharp look, but her face looked completely innocent as she glanced over his shoulder.

'Where's Beatrix?'

'Waiting with the horses.'

'Do you think she'd like to come and see Prickles, too?'

'She's busy.'

He raked a hand through his hair, relieved that Helen was too preoccupied to notice the trace of bitterness in his voice. Bitterness that sounded alarmingly close to anger. He frowned. *Could* there be a grain of truth in what Beatrix had said? He didn't want there to be, but what were the other words she'd used? Tense. Restrained. They had a horrible ring of familiarity about them. He certainly wasn't relaxed. Hell, he wasn't sure he knew how to relax any more. *Was* he denying his true feelings? *Was* he angry?

Yes. The word entered his head, unbidden. Instinctively, he tried to push it away, but it persisted. Oddly enough, it brought a faint sense of relief, too, as well as something else, a weight pressing at the back of his mind, demanding his attention. A branch snapped in his hand, one he hadn't even known he'd been holding. Maybe he *was* angry, not just at his father, but at all of it. Maybe he had been for years. More than that, maybe he was exhausted, too, at the effort of holding his feelings back, at controlling or denying or whatever the hell he *was* doing to them… He tugged at the top of his cravat, finding it difficult to breathe suddenly, as if someone had wound a steel band around his chest and was squeezing it tight.

'Come on.' He stood up abruptly, forcing the weight back before it overwhelmed him. He couldn't think, not there and then. 'We need to get back to the house.'

'Already?' Helen looked disappointed.

'I've a few matters to attend to before dinner.' He was aware of how weak the words sounded. 'We'll come for a ride another day.'

'Well, that was a small improvement on yesterday. Everyone arrived on time and nobody stormed off to bed early.' Corin blew a ring of cigar smoke across the table. 'Still, it's probably best not to leave your new bride alone with Mother and Antigone for too long.'

'Mmm.' Quinton looked at his own, untouched cigar. Maybe if he didn't make eye contact with his brother then he wouldn't have to acknowledge the irritation his words provoked. Irritation that seemed to get stronger every time anyone, usually Corin, spoke. Much as he hated to admit it, his self-control was under severe duress. Since returning from his ride with Beatrix and Helen that afternoon, he'd been haunted by the mental image of a dam with a crack running straight through its centre, allowing a thin trickle of water to escape. The trickle was manageable, but he felt more and more on edge, with the horrible feeling that the slightest comment might cause the crack to spread uncontrollably and the whole dam to collapse. And then where would he be? He needed to be alone, to have space to think. He just needed to get through dinner first...

'Any plans for tomorrow?' Corin was annoyingly persistent.

'I need to visit a few of the farms. They're trying some different crops this year and I'd like to see how matters are progressing.'

'Sounds fascinating.'

'It is to some of us. I'll probably be gone for most of the day.'

'Neglecting your new wife already?' His brother tutted. 'I thought you'd be out with her for longer this afternoon, to be honest. It was barely an hour.'

'I didn't realise we were being timed.'

'She was quiet at dinner, too.'

'Everyone was quiet at dinner.' He grimaced. It hadn't been quite as dirge-like as luncheon, but an attentive listener could still have heard a pin drop. Perhaps he ought to have invited Helen to regale them with stories about Prickles, the hedgehog. She'd been loquacious with enthusiasm about him all the way home.

'What did you expect after you warned Antigone

and Justin not to argue?' Corin chuckled. 'They don't know how else to communicate.'

'I do!' Justin sat up indignantly.

'In any case, your wife was quieter than usual. I tried to draw her out about that biscuit shop, but she barely responded. She didn't eat much either, I noticed.'

Quinton tightened his grip on the cigar, wondering if his brother was deliberately trying to goad him. 'You seem to be paying an undue amount of attention to *my* wife.'

'No need to be jealous. I'm only trying to help.'

'Don't.'

'Mr Harker says that my Latin has improved a lot,' Justin chimed in with a rare display of tact.

'Really?' Quinton lifted an eyebrow in surprise. That was one piece of good news at least. 'And your mathematics?'

Justin's face fell. 'Not quite so much.'

'You need to apply yourself more.'

'Don't pressure the boy.' Corin rolled his eyes. 'The men in our family have never been good with figures, present company excepted, of course. You're the only Roxbury in the past century to be any good at making money instead of just spending it.'

'Quite.' He felt a scowl settling over his features. It seemed distasteful to describe his marriage as a means of 'making' money, as if he'd actually done some real work for it, instead of simply trading his name for a fortune. Oh, he was a Roxbury all right, the latest in a long line of bad husbands who either didn't have feelings or, apparently, denied them. And now here he was, trying to persuade a woman who'd grown up feeling unloved and worthless to abandon the happiness she'd finally found as an independent woman simply for *his* sake. To save him and his family from any more scandal. Maybe a guilty conscience was part of the reason he'd reacted so badly to her accusation earlier. If he was angry at anyone at that moment, it was himself. And there was only one thing he could do about it, unpleasant as it might be.

He stood up, holding himself together with an effort. 'Please excuse me to the ladies. I'm going to my study.'

'You're working at this hour?' Even Corin looked surprised.

'Not exactly. I have some thinking to do.'

Chapter Eleven

Week Two. Day Ten

Beatrix rubbed her cheek against her pillow, enjoying a few last seconds of slumberous peace before remembering where she was and what she was doing there. She was halfway through her second week at Howden and, at this rate, the remaining four and a half were going to feel like an eternity. She'd barely spoken to anyone except Helen and Corin for days. Her husband, while perfectly 'pleasant and polite', seemed preoccupied with his own thoughts and determined to spend his days either shut up in his study or riding around the estate, and he hadn't invited her to join him again either. On the one hand, she couldn't help but feel spurned. On the other, it was a relief. Their argument by the copse had been a timely reminder that she was there for one reason and one reason only: to get a divorce. There was no need for them to be friends or confidantes, and *definitely* no call for stomach-flutterings or racing heartbeats in the meantime.

She sat up and reached for the bell rope. Breakfast

in bed was one of the few things she'd come to appreciate about being a married woman and it was eminently preferable to her husband's company.

'Good morning, Your Grace.' Mrs Hastings herself arrived with the breakfast tray, arranging it neatly across her lap with a smile. 'I hope you're feeling well this morning?'

'Very well, thank you, Mrs Hastings. And you?'

'The same as ever, thank you for asking, Your Grace. Now, is there anything else I can fetch for you?'

'No, this is perfect.' Beatrix licked her lips enthusiastically. 'I don't know what's in this jam, but it's delicious. Like damsons and apricots and strawberries all mixed together. I must ask Cook for the recipe before I go.'

'Go, Your Grace?' The housekeeper looked taken aback. 'Are you planning a journey somewhere?'

'Oh…no. I meant…' She bit her tongue, resolving to be more careful with her words in future. 'Not at the moment, no.'

'Well, I'll be sure to ask her, Your Grace.' Mrs Hastings gave her a quizzical look before starting towards the door and then hesitating. 'Actually, I wondered if I might have a conversation with you about certain household matters? After breakfast, of course.'

'No need to wait.' Beatrix smeared a generous spoonful of the aforementioned jam across her toast. 'We can talk now.'

'If you're certain? You see, it's about the daily menus, Your Grace. I wondered whether you'd like me to bring them to you for approval from now on…' She dropped her voice as though she was afraid of being overheard. 'Instead of the Dowager, I mean?'

'Oh.' Beatrix swallowed her toast mid-chew. Of course, as she was the new mistress of the household, such decisions ought to be hers, but, since she had no intention of staying beyond the agreed six weeks, she hadn't honestly considered the matter. 'Has the Duke said anything about it?'

'He said that it was up to you, Your Grace.'

Of course he did. 'I see.'

'Usually I see the Dowager in the Duchess's suite every morning to discuss the arrangements.'

'The Duchess's suite?' She dropped the toast back onto its plate. 'You mean there's a suite of rooms reserved for the Duchess?'

'Ye-es.' The housekeeper looked uncomfortable suddenly.

'And these aren't them?'

'No-o.'

'Because my mother-in-law is still occupying them?'

'Ah…yes. There was some discussion about her moving into a different room when you were first married, but…' Mrs Hasting's voice trailed away, her cheeks flaming more and more with each word. 'Perhaps she intends to do it soon, Your Grace?'

'Perhaps.' Beatrix picked up her cup of tea and took a pensive sip. She doubted the idea had even entered the old battleaxe's mind. 'In that case, before we make any other decisions, I believe I'll go and speak to the Dowager myself.'

In retrospect, Beatrix thought, standing outside the door to what was *apparently* the Duchess's suite, she ought to have asked for a drop of brandy in her tea for breakfast. A little Dutch courage wouldn't have gone amiss at that moment. In her just-woken state, speaking to her mother-in-law had seemed like a reasonable idea. A good one even. It wasn't that she *wanted* to take over either the rooms or the household responsibilities, but it had occurred to her that a discussion about them might help to improve their relationship. Not that she particularly wanted a 'relationship' either, but, since they were going to be trapped in the same house together for another thirty-two days, it was surely worth a try.

Unfortunately, now that she was there on the threshold, she had the distinct feeling that she was about to enter a wasps' nest. And there was no way she was going to escape again without getting stung.

Reluctantly, she took a deep breath, lifted a hand and tapped, wondering what Nancy would do in this situation—whatever it was, she doubted she'd have the nerve to emulate her—waiting until she heard a voice answer before entering.

'Good morning.' She closed the door behind her. Her mother-in-law was sitting at an elegant writing desk in one corner of a pretty apricot-and-white-coloured sitting room, a pair of spectacles halfway down her nose and her lips pursed in their customary pout.

'Is there something I can do for you?' The Dowager glanced up briefly before turning her attention back to her writing.

'Yes.' Beatrix lifted her chin. 'I had a conversation with Mrs Hastings regarding the menus this morning. She wondered which of us would be dealing with them from now on and I thought that maybe we could discuss them together?'

The Dowager's quill didn't so much as falter. 'Did you?'

'Yes, and then I thought perhaps we could go through a few other matters, too? Invitations, for example?'

The quill paused. 'What invitations do you imagine we receive?'

'I've no idea, but I presume *some*. Howden Hall must be an important centre for the county…isn't it?'

'He hasn't told you, then?' Her mother-in-law's voice turned smug. 'I thought not.'

Beatrix felt her whole body tense at the implication. Despite her argument with Quinton, she'd still clung to the belief that he was honest and honourable. The very idea that he was capable of deceit sent a cold shiver running down her spine. Or was it something to do with the scandal he'd mentioned, but never explained? 'What do you mean?'

The Dowager twisted slowly in her chair, looking as if she were bestowing a great honour simply by acknowledging Beatrix.

'If my son, your husband, decides not to inform you of certain *family* matters then it is hardly my place to do so. All I *will* say is that despite being a centre for the county, as you put it, we do not receive many invitations. We have occasional callers, or we did immediately after your wedding, but those, too, have stopped. People came out of curiosity, no doubt, but we were forced to tell them that you were indisposed. To *lie* to them, in fact.'

'I see.' Beatrix folded her hands together, wanting to ask more, but reluctant to give her mother-in-law the satisfaction. She doubted that she'd give her any answers anyway. It was becoming increasingly obvious that she was wasting her time there, but she still had one last idea, arguably not a very good one since she was leaving in just over a month, but she wanted to know what the Dowager would say...

'In that case— Oh!' She jumped aside quickly as the door behind her swung open and Antigone charged into the room.

'You?' Her sister-in-law could hardly have looked more surprised to see her if she'd been an actual burglar. 'What are you doing here?'

Beatrix swallowed a retort at the rudeness of the greeting. 'If you must know, I was about to suggest that we pay a few calls around the neighbourhood. You, your mother and I, that is. Or better still, we could invite people to come here, as a way of apologising for my being *indisposed* before.'

'Oh, I'd like that!' To her surprise, Antigone's face underwent a complete transformation, from dour to glowing in under three seconds. It was the first time Beatrix had seen her look anything other than belligerent and the result was quite startlingly pretty.

'Out of the question.' The Dowager's tone was unequivocal. 'If you wish to take over the running of the household then that is, of course, your prerogative. If you wish to make calls then I also cannot stop you. However, you will do so *alone*.'

'But, Mama—'

'You...' the Dowager's gaze speared Antigone '...will remain here at Howden with me. Now, if there are no other matters to discuss?'

Beatrix opened her mouth and then closed it again,

aware of her sister-in-law's face crumpling beside her. Evidently, she'd just been dismissed. 'No, I suppose not.'

'That was a sigh and a half.' Corin was walking along the corridor when she emerged from the wasps' nest. 'The kind that tells me you've been talking to my mother.'

'Yes. I suggested that we pay a few calls together, but apparently I'm out of my mind for even imagining the possibility.' She sighed again for good measure and then looked up hopefully. 'Although before that, she hinted at some kind of family secret.'

'And you want me to spill the beans?' He tapped the side of his nose. 'Sorry, but I'm in Quin's bad books enough these days and if he hasn't told you…'

'You're right, I shouldn't have asked. That's almost exactly what your mother said, by the way, although not quite as nicely. I just thought it might explain a few things, that's all.' She went to stand beside a window, smiling at the sight of Helen playing on the terrace outside, trailing a piece of string for Paws to leap on.

'She looks a lot like Quin, doesn't she?' Corin came to stand beside her.

'Helen? Yes, I suppose so, especially when she smiles.'

'Does that mean you've seen Quin smile, too?' Corin gave a low whistle. 'I didn't know that was still possible.'

'If it was, it isn't any more.'

'Ah. I thought something must have happened. Don't worry, I won't ask.' He rested one arm on the window frame. 'You know, it's funny, how alike they are. Antigone and Justin have a look of each other, too, although they both take more after Mother. Which just leaves me.'

Beatrix glanced sideways quizzically. There was a strange, melancholy note to his voice suddenly, as if he felt left out somehow.

'But you have a faint look of your mother, as well,' she offered, instinctively wanting to console him, though the words seemed to have the opposite effect.

'Yes, but as for blond hair…' A frown settled over his features. 'You know, my father had dark hair and sharp features, just like Quin. Their appearance is the one thing they *do* have in common.'

'Oh.' Beatrix blinked, feeling even more confused. Considering what Quin had told her about their father, it seemed strange that Corin would want to be anything like him and yet his tone was almost jealous. 'Were you close?'

'To my father?' He snorted. 'Not in the least. He was a scoundrel of the first order. He made all of our lives a misery. And a few other people's probably.'

'I'm sorry.' She looked over his face speculatively. Whatever it was that Quin wasn't telling her, she had a sudden strong suspicion it had something to do with Corin. She had a feeling the answer was obvious, too, if she could just concentrate for a few seconds…

'Your Grace?' The butler's stertorous voice interrupted before she could grasp the answer.

'Oh!' She spun around, placing a hand to her chest. 'Dunstan, I didn't hear you coming.'

'Forgive me, Your Grace, but you have a guest.'

'Me?' She moved away from the window in surprise. Who on earth could possibly be calling on her when she didn't *know* anyone in Oxfordshire? 'Are you sure you don't mean the Dowager?'

'No, Your Grace. The lady was very specific and, if I may say so, quite determined. When I said that I would ask if you were at home she insisted you would be. I'm afraid I had no choice but to show her into the drawing room.'

'Did she give a name?'

'Lady Jarrow, Your Grace.'

'*Jarrow...*' She clicked her tongue, thinking. The name was familiar somehow, although she couldn't quite put her finger on why. 'Well, she sounds interesting. Thank you, Dunstan, I'll go down at once.'

'Need any help?' Corin raised an eyebrow.

'No, but thank you.' She smiled, belatedly noticing the black circles around his eyes. 'You look like you could do with some sleep.'

'I usually do.'

'Well, then...' She threw him one last half-sympathetic, half-curious look before hurrying downstairs to the drawing room.

A footman opened the door and she went inside, stopping short at the sight of a white-haired lady swathed from head to toe in black silk standing before her. Although perhaps standing was the wrong word; rather she was leaning heavily on a silver-topped cane while examining a painting of a large white stallion.

'Good morning.' Beatrix fixed a smile onto her face and took a few steps forward. She had no idea who the woman was, but at least it was someone new to talk to, even if she was still feeling slightly bruised from her conversation with the Dowager. 'How kind of you to call, Lady Jarrow. I'm Beatrix Roxbury.'

'I know who you are.' The woman turned her head, drawing herself up to her full and considerable height. 'Or perhaps I ought to call you Belinda? Yes, I'm Lady Jarrow and I'm here in the capacity of spy. My grand-daughter-in-law Anna sent me.'

Chapter Twelve

'**B**ut I've never met Anna!' Beatrix dropped into an armchair as her legs gave way beneath her. 'The Countess of Staunton, I mean.'

'Yes, she told me that, too.' The older woman waved her cane at the painting she'd just been studying. 'D'you know, I like this? With some artists you wonder if they've ever actually seen a horse, let alone ridden one, but this is excellent. Who's it by?'

'I don't know.' Beatrix shook her head in bemusement. 'Why would the Countess of Staunton send you to me?'

'On the instigation of Henrietta and Nancy, I believe. They wanted to make sure you were all right.'

'They did?' Beatrix pressed her lips together tightly, the thought of her friends' concern bringing tears to her eyes. 'That's so…' a small sob escaped '…kind.'

'Oh, dear.' Lady Jarrow hobbled forward, folding her hands on top of her stick as she took a seat opposite. 'Worse than I expected. And I expected things to be bad the moment I heard where you were. I knew Morgana years ago and I don't suppose she's mellowed.

Awful woman. Has her reasons for being that way, I suppose, but doesn't know the first thing about horses.'

'Oh.' Beatrix paused, wondering if she'd just misheard. 'No, I don't think she's ever mentioned them.'

'Of course she hasn't. Probably wouldn't know one end from the other. Barbaric.'

'I think she hates me.'

'Well, I wouldn't worry about that. It's nothing personal. She hates most people, or acts like she does. She always has.'

'That's what Quin said.' Beatrix sniffed. 'He claims it's because of his father.'

'He's right. You know how they say the Prince Regent hates Princess Caroline? Well, times that by a hundred. *Thousand.* Now…' The older woman lifted her cane and rammed it down so violently that a nearby table wobbled '…what about your husband? Does he like horses?'

'I suppose so. He goes for a ride every morning.'

'Does he indeed?' Her expression softened a little. 'Well, that's a good start. And how do *you* like him? From what I hear, he's a bit of a cold fish, but I suppose that's better than endless prattling. I can't bear a man who prattles.'

'He definitely doesn't do that. He's barely spoken to me for the past week.'

'And Morgana's making your life a misery in the meantime? Well, ring for tea and let's see what I can do to help matters.'

'I appreciate the thought.' Beatrix stood up obediently, rubbing the palms of her hands across her cheeks as she went to pull on a bell rope. 'And I'm grateful to you for coming to visit, but I really don't think there's anything anyone can do to help. I just have to bear the situation for another few weeks.'

'Nonsense. There's a way around every difficult situation.' The older woman fixed her with a gimlet stare. 'I would have thought that a person who ran away from her own wedding would know that.'

Beatrix gasped, quickly ordering tea from the maid who'd just entered before turning around again.

'You *know*?'

'Oh, yes.' The older woman smoothed a hand over her white hair with a superior-looking smile. 'Anna didn't intend to tell me that part, of course, but I can recognise half a story when I hear one. Now, don't worry, I've been duly sworn to secrecy, but, from what I can gather, your position is this: you married a man you hardly knew, realised that you'd made a mistake, ran away to Belles, eventually told him where you were in the not unreasonable hope that he'd be *thrilled* to give you a divorce and then discovered he wasn't, not unless you agreed to give your marriage a try for six weeks first. Does that sound about right?'

'I…' Beatrix considered for a moment and then nodded. 'Yes, that's it.'

'And now he's not talking to you. Any particular reason?'

'I said something he didn't like.'

'Pah! He'll get over it. I say things people don't like all the time.'

'Ye-es, but we were getting along before, or starting to. I thought there was even a chance we could be friends, but now it seems like… Wait!' She jerked her head up. 'Do you know anything about a family scandal?'

'Well, of course I do.' Lady Jarrow snorted as if she'd just said something ludicrous. 'Everyone in Society does. It would have been impossible not to hear about it last year. I wasn't even in London and I still heard all the sordid details. I don't recall ever asking either. Gossip can be so dreadfully tedious.'

'But what was it?'

'Oh, it was all the old Duke's fault. Stupid man was always reckless. He'd already lost most of his fortune on gambling, women and who knows what else, but, during the last year of his life, it was as though he was *trying* to lose everything. Which is exactly what someone accused him of one evening. Viscount Scorborough, I think it was, at the Marquess of Dalby's ball last spring. Accused him of trying to ruin his family on purpose.' She glanced at the painting of the stallion, her voice turning distracted as if she'd just lost interest in her own story. 'And that was when he said it.'

'Said what?' Beatrix prompted her.

'Mmm? Oh, that they weren't his family.'

'I don't understand. What do you mean?'

'He disowned them. In the middle of the card room with at least two dozen witnesses, he as good as said that his children weren't his children. Which, given the notorious state of his relationship with Morgana, sounded utterly plausible, I might add. He always liked to make an impact, but to say it in a room full of people was shocking behaviour even for him. He made sure that no one would ever forget it, including the two eldest of his so-called sons.'

'You mean that Quin and Corin were *there*?'

'Standing right beside him, yes. I believe they'd been trying to get him away from the gaming table.'

'Oh.' Beatrix put a hand to her mouth in shock, her imagination envisaging the scene. 'What happened next?'

'Not much. From what I understand, everyone pretended it was all a big joke, but the damage was done. He died not long afterwards, but the rumours persisted.'

'Is that why people don't visit the family? Because of the scandal?'

'Oh, I doubt that. Dukes are never complete social pariahs no matter what they do, but Morgana didn't help matters. Most people were prepared to take her side and agree it was slander, but she's not the kind of woman who appreciates sympathy. I can't say I blame her under the circumstances, but insulting and snubbing everyone in return doesn't help.'

'No. It's not helping her family either.' Beatrix frowned and leaned forward. 'So, was there any truth in what the old Duke said?'

'Who knows? It's hard to believe he would have said something so malicious without any evidence, but then he was a vindictive, self-centred old man, to put it politely. Handsome though, I have to admit, and from what I hear your husband is the spitting image of him. It's the second son people wonder about.'

'Corin...' Beatrix couldn't believe she hadn't guessed at the truth when they'd been standing together earlier. 'Yes, he isn't much like the others. There's a sadness about him, too.'

'Pshaw. Sadness has nothing to do with anything. Officially he's the second son of a duke. The *ton* might gossip for a while, but it'll blow over eventually. He ought to forget it and move on.'

They fell silent as the tea tray arrived and Beatrix

started to pour. At least now she knew the source of all the tension under the large and formerly leaking roof. The whole family must still be reeling from the accusation the late Duke had levelled against them—and surely there was no way Quin *couldn't* be angry about it! They needed to band together and comfort each other, but, judging by appearances, the opposite was happening. Then again, it was hard to imagine them all sitting down to a calm discussion with the Dowager. Honestly, it was easier to imagine a conversation with a rock. But Lady Jarrow was right. Officially, they were all the Duke's legitimate heirs, whether he was their true father or not. Maybe the best thing they could do was put aside what had happened and move on, but unfortunately emotions weren't always so easy. Coming to terms with them was often easier said than done.

'At least now I understand why Quin married me.' She sighed. 'I always wondered why he didn't just find a rich member of the *ton*. There must have been a few heiresses among them.'

'Several, but none of them would have touched him with a hot poker.' Lady Jarrow accepted her cup of tea with a snort. 'Not for a few years anyway. What he *ought* to have done was retreat to the country for a Season or two and then come back when everyone could have pretended they'd forgotten about it.'

'I think he needed the money quickly. That's why he found me. And now he wants to keep me to avoid any more scandal.' Beatrix stirred her tea half-heartedly. 'I can understand his reasoning and I'm truly sorry to make things any worse, but I'm not going to change my mind about a divorce. It's ridiculous my being here at all. I'm just whiling away the time doing nothing.'

'I hardly see how that's possible. You're a duchess, for goodness' sake. You must have duties to attend to.'

'Not really. I asked the Dowager whether we might do them together, but she didn't want my help. She said that it was either her or me.'

'Well, of course she did, but it *ought* to be you.'

'How can it be? I wasn't trained to be a duchess. Or even an aristocrat for that matter. I wouldn't know where to start.'

'Then find out. My dear girl, this is Morgana's territory and I can guarantee that she won't give it up without a fight. Think of a cat with particularly sharp and vindictive claws. And possibly some kind of concealed weapon, too. If you're going to take over the running of Howden then you can't just wait for her to step aside.'

'What's the point when I'll be leaving in just over a month?'

'Well!' Lady Jarrow rolled her eyes. 'I must say I expected better.'

'I'm sorry?'

'You should be. I expected somebody with spirit. After what Anna told me, I thought you sounded rather eccentric. Instead it seems you're simply defeatist.'

'I am *not* defeatist.' Beatrix stiffened her spine in chagrin. 'I just don't want to cause a lot of upheaval that will only need to be undone again in a few weeks' time. Now if that's all you have to say then you may inform Henrietta and Nancy that me and my lack of spirit are doing quite well and will be back in Bath soon.'

'That's more like it.' Lady Jarrow smiled, completely ignoring the dismissal. 'Now, what does your husband say about his mother's behaviour?'

Beatrix paused, thrown by the sudden change of

tone. She was also unwilling to cast Quinton in a positive light, but her conscience compelled her to be honest. 'Actually, he threatened to send her to the dower house if she wasn't polite to me.'

'Excellent. And what has he said about your unwillingness to assume your duties?'

'We haven't discussed it. For all I know, he'd rather that his mother remain in charge.'

'Well, you won't find out until you challenge her. If he objects, he'll *have* to talk to you again.' Lady Jarrow gave her a pointed look. 'Of course, perhaps this apathy is part of the reason he's *not* talking to you. You're hardly fulfilling your side of the bargain.'

'What do you mean?'

'According to Henrietta and Nancy, you agreed to give your marriage a chance.'

'I'm here, aren't I?'

'Only in body. From what I can tell, you've already made up your mind.'

'Because I don't want to be a duchess! I want a divorce.'

'And a reasonable person might ask *why* you're quite so determined. The majority of women would aspire to such a position.'

'Maybe, but I'm not the majority of women and I want my independence. The freedom to make my own decisions is important to me.'

'A woman can have independence in marriage. I'm living proof of that, although I admit it depends on the husband. Yours seems rather more tolerant than most, however.'

'Yes, but he's *still* a husband. Legally, that gives him power over me, just like my uncle had when I was growing up. I don't want to be under the control of any man. I won't live in another kind of prison. I want to be in control of my*self*.'

'And yet you married him?'

'Yes.' Beatrix closed her eyes. 'It was a mistake.'

'Obviously, but you still made a vow. A serious one. And from what I can tell, your husband made his in good faith.'

'So did I. Or at least I thought I did. I was confused. Disillusioned.'

'*Disillusioned?* What a curious choice of word. With what exactly?'

'With myself, with love.'

'Ah.' Lady Jarrow set her teacup aside. 'Now we get to it. Tell me, who was he?'

Beatrix opened her mouth to claim she didn't understand and then changed her mind. 'His name was Alec Beddows. He was a friend of my cousin's and we were…close.'

'Close?'

'Too close. We shared a bed, although we didn't… it didn't go so far…although I told Quin that it did.'

'You told your husband that you'd had relations with another man when you hadn't?' Lady Jarrow arched an eyebrow. 'How original.'

'I thought it might encourage him to divorce me.'

'Ah. Well, there's some logic in that, I suppose.'

'Our relationship still went much further than it should have. I thought Alec loved me, but, as it turned out, all he wanted was my fortune. He thought that if he compromised me then my uncle would be forced to let us marry. Only things didn't quite work out the way he wanted.' She clenched her jaw. 'Ever since my father died, my whole identity has been tied up in my fortune. You know, the only reason my uncle took me in was because he was paid to do it. And then Alec…' She drew in a deep breath to steady herself. 'I might have been worth a fortune on the outside, but he and Alec together made me feel worthless inside. I married Quin because I felt heartbroken and trapped and desperate to get away, but after the ceremony, I realised that it was just the same situation all over again. My husband might have been more honest about it, but he had the same motives as my uncle and Alec underneath. All he wanted was the money.'

'So you ran away?'

'Yes. I ended up in Bath. I was at my wits' end and it was the only place I could think of to go, but I found Belles and they liked me for *me*. My fortune was lost, but I was happy. I felt restored, with a new sense of independence and self-worth.' She leaned forward. '*That's* the life I want. The life still waiting for me in Bath. Why would I give it up just for a title and fortune?'

'You don't necessarily have to. Surely you could have self-worth and happiness here, too?' Lady's Jarrow's gaze seemed very direct suddenly. 'Your marriage might have been based on money, but your feelings—and your husband's—might still change. Or is there no hope of you coming to care for him?'

Beatrix tensed, feeling as if the truth were being drawn slowly out of her. The idea of caring for Quin wasn't completely outlandish any more, though when or why that had changed she had no idea. 'Honestly, I don't know. I don't dislike him. I can even respect him for wanting to protect his family. And as for the money, he offered to pay me back once the estate was profitable again so I know he's not just mercenary, but he says he doesn't care for strong emotions. According to him, he doesn't even allow them.'

'Nonsense. Even *I* have strong emotions occasionally.'

'But what kind of a fool would I be to open my heart to a man who says he *can't* love me in return?' She shook her head. 'I *do* believe true love exists. I see how much Henrietta and Sebastian care for each other, but maybe it's not for everyone. And I won't be made to feel used or worthless ever again, not by any man.'

'Nobody ever wants to get hurt, my dear, although when you put it like that, I do understand.' Lady Jarrow nodded kindly. 'Still, I'm not saying that you *have* to fall in love with him, just to keep an open mind about being a duchess. At the very least, start behaving like one. There are far worse ways to pass the time. You never know, you might like it more than you expect.'

Beatrix took a large mouthful of tea to calm her nerves. Much as she hated to admit it, perhaps Lady Jarrow was right and she *hadn't* been fulfilling her side of the bargain she'd made with Quin. In which case, taking over her duties as the Duchess was the least she could do. And perhaps a good shake-up would be a good thing for everyone. She could hardly make the situation at Howden any worse.

'I don't know. I'm not very good at asserting myself.'

'Says the woman who ran away on her wedding day.' Lady Jarrow stood up. 'Now, I'm currently staying in Faringdon with my friend Mrs Blenkinsop. We're both widows so we can wear black and drink gin as late into the night as we please. If you decide that you want to assert yourself then I shall be standing by to assist.' She tapped Beatrix's skirt with her cane. 'In the meantime, what shall I write to Anna? That you're miserable and bored or that you're grasping the bull by the horns? The bull in this scenario being your mother-in-law, of course.'

'Well…'

'Oh, for goodness' sake.' The old woman tutted loudly. 'I couldn't have framed the question any more clearly.'

Beatrix laughed despite herself. 'In that case, I suppose I'd better grasp.'

'Thank Hades for that. Just bear in mind that divorce is a serious business. You might think that you've already made your decision and for good reasons, too, but don't close your mind because of it. You might stop yourself from seeing other possibilities. Take it from an old woman, you're much too young to give up on love. And so is your husband, for that matter.' She paused. 'Only for goodness' sake, don't ever tell Nancy I said so. Morgana might not frighten me, but that young woman is a younger version of me.' A look of affection mixed with amusement crossed her face. 'One of these days, I really must do something nice for her.'

Chapter Thirteen

'Good morning!' Quinton called out, dismounting beneath the front steps of Howden Hall with a combined sense of surprise and trepidation. He'd spotted his wife standing at the top from half a mile down the drive and she appeared not to have moved a muscle since, her hands clasped firmly at her waist while strands of dark hair billowed around her face like ribbons. There was something different about her, he thought, something he couldn't quite put his finger on except to say that she looked resolute. Purposeful. And quite strikingly attractive.

'Beatrix?' He stopped two steps below her so that they were standing eye to eye. 'Is something the matter?'

'Yes. We need to talk.'

'You're right.' He acknowledged the words sombrely. They were exactly what he'd been thinking for days, only he hadn't known where to begin. He was simply aware that he'd been behaving badly, being distant and cold and generally doing everything possible to convince her she was right to want a divorce. Which was no doubt what she was about to tell him.

'Beatrix, I—'

'I'm tired of doing nothing,' she interrupted before he could apologise. 'And it occurred to me that part of the reason for my coming here was to learn the duties of a duchess.'

'Um…yes.' He tried not to let the relief show on his face. It wasn't exactly what he'd been expecting.

'So that's what I'm going to do. *I'm* the Duchess and I want to start acting like it. In fact, I already have.'

'Good.'

'Good?' she repeated, catching a lock of hair before it blew into her eyes. 'Really?'

'Yes.' He moved towards the front door, gesturing for her to precede him into the house. 'I just didn't want to be the one to suggest it.'

'Well, then…' She threw him a suspicious look as they entered the hall. 'In that case, maybe you could take a look at—'

'What is *this?'* His mother appeared at the top of the main staircase suddenly, waving a piece of paper in the air.

'Good morning, Mother.' Out of the corner of his eye, he saw his wife's chin lift up a notch. 'It looks like a letter to me.'

'It's an invitation!'

'From?'

'From *us!*'

'It's an invitation I wrote this morning.' In contrast to his mother, Beatrix's voice was completely calm. 'I intend to send it to all of our closest neighbours and anyone else you'd care to invite. I also asked Mrs Hastings to give a copy to your mother in case there were any changes she wished to make.'

'Yes!' The lady in question came storming down the staircase. 'I want you to tear it up!'

'Wait!' Quin lifted a hand in his mother's direction, keeping his eyes fixed upon Beatrix. 'What is it that we're inviting people to exactly?'

'A dinner party. I thought that now I was here, I ought to introduce myself. This way people will know that I'm not fictitious or an invalid.'

'What on earth does it matter—?'

'*And* I think it will be good for Antigone, too.' She spoke over his mother. 'It will give her an opportunity to practise her social skills before making her debut in Society.'

His mother's indrawn breath was audible. 'Antigone is not your concern.'

'But she is mine,' Quinton countered, 'and I think it's an excellent idea. I'd be more than happy to help with that invitation list.'

'You can't be serious!' Every part of his mother, from the top of her head to the tips of her toes, appeared to be seething.

'I am. It's about time we started entertaining again.'

'Half of the neighbours probably won't come!'

'Then we'll make do with the half that will.'

'This is outrageous!' His mother's voice was shaking now. 'I for one have no intention of attending.'

'That's your choice. However, Antigone *will* be attending, no matter what you say.'

'We'll see about that!' She made a low, snarling sound before storming off in the direction of the drawing room. 'You'll regret this, mark my words!'

'Oh, dear.' Beatrix watched her go with wide eyes.

'I knew she wouldn't like the idea, but I didn't expect her to be quite so upset.'

'It's not your fault.' Quinton clasped his hands behind his back. 'You've every right to send out invitations.'

'I'm afraid it's going to get even worse. I also told Mrs Hastings that I'll be discussing the menus and household arrangements with her from now on.' A faint crease appeared between her brows. 'Only, judging by the lack of bloodshed, I don't think she's mentioned that part to your mother just yet.'

'Perhaps not.' He studied her face. 'Might I ask what's brought about this change of heart?'

'Yes. I had a visitor while you were out. The Dowager Baroness Lady Jarrow.'

'You've had a busy morning. I didn't realise you were acquainted with her.'

'I wasn't, only it turns out that she's the grandmother-in-law of the Countess of Staunton. Anna,' she clarified when he looked at her blankly. 'Formerly Anna Fortini. She used to run Belles.'

'Ah, I see. And she sent Lady Jarrow here to check on you?'

'Something like that. Nancy and Henrietta were worried. Anyway, we talked and she made me realise that it's high time I started to assert myself.'

'I'm glad. Although I'm also sorry it took someone else to make you feel better. I haven't been a very good husband for the past week, have I?'

'No.' She didn't hesitate.

'I apologise. Truly. I had some things I needed to think about, but that's no excuse. Perhaps you'd allow me to make it up to you and explain?'

'How?' She folded her arms across her chest.

'How about a picnic?' He had a sudden burst of inspiration. 'I was going to visit the site for some new cottages after luncheon, but perhaps you'd like to come with me now? We could take something to eat and discuss the invitation list on the way.' He glanced towards the drawing room. 'Then at least we'll be at a safe distance when my mother discovers the rest.'

For a moment he thought she was about to refuse, her hazel eyes narrowing before he noticed the sparkle behind them.

'Ask me nicely.'

'Wasn't that nice?'

'Not enough.' She tipped her head towards the cold marble floor. 'Grovel.'

'Ahem.' He threw a quick look around, checking that no one else was in sight before crouching down on one knee. 'Beatrix Roxbury, *Bea*, in exchange for my most abject apologies, would you do me the great honour of accompanying me on a picnic?'

'Will there be cake?'

'I'll insist upon it.'

'Mmm.' She let him wait on the floor for almost a full minute before breaking into a smile that seemed to warm the very insides of his chest and left him feeling oddly breathless. 'That sounds acceptable.'

Chapter Fourteen

The sky was more overcast than it had been for the previous few weeks, a pale shade of oyster grey streaked with occasional ribbons of blue as Beatrix spurred her horse across wide, open parkland towards the still-unexplored, winding expanse of river in the distance.

Quinton's offer of a picnic had come as something of a surprise, but a convenient one. Frankly, she was relieved to be getting out of the house. Her conversation with Lady Jarrow had given her a lot—*too much*—to think about, and, after taking her first stand against her mother-in-law, some fresh air had sounded like an excellent idea. As for his apology…well, that had been a surprise, too, one she wasn't entirely sure how she felt about. She wasn't prepared to forgive his reclusive behaviour over the past week quite so easily, but after what she'd recently discovered about his father it was impossible not to feel slightly sympathetic.

'Hungry?' he asked, drawing on his reins as they approached an ancient-looking oak tree.

'Ravenous. It feels like a long time since breakfast.' She drew to a halt, too, dismounting quickly before he could come and help her. The last thing she needed at that moment was any more confusion.

'Well, then, let's see what we have.' He pulled a blanket from his pack and spread it out beneath the branches. 'Make yourself comfortable.'

Beatrix crouched down, curling her legs up beneath her and smiling at the sight of a cob of bread, a block of cheese, two apples, a few small cakes and a bottle of lemonade.

'This should keep the hunger pangs at bay.' Quin sat down beside her, stretching one leg out before him and bending the other at the knee.

'It looks delicious.' She took a deep breath and exhaled slowly, letting the sound of running water in the distance calm her senses. 'What a beautiful spot.'

'It's one of my favourite places on the estate.' He rested one arm on his knee. 'Bea, I want to apologise properly for my behaviour the last time we went for a ride. You made a perfectly reasonable observation and I overreacted. It was unpardonable of me.'

'I appreciate that. Although I shouldn't have said what I did either. It was none of my business.'

'But it was. It *is*. You're my wife and...now that I've had a chance to think, perhaps some of what you said was true. Perhaps I'm not as in control of my feelings as I thought. Perhaps I *have* been denying the existence of certain...emotions.' He cleared his throat as if the subject were difficult for him. 'I just didn't like hearing it.'

'I understand. It must be very hard, considering...' She hesitated, wondering whether or not to say any more. After the last time, she didn't want to risk another argument, but then, what was the point of talking without honesty?

She shuffled her body around to look straight at him. 'Considering your father. I know what he said at the Marquess of Dalby's ball. Your mother mentioned a secret so I asked Lady Jarrow to tell me.'

'Ah. I'm sorry.'

'*You're* sorry? Why?'

'Because I ought to have told you myself. In my defence, I presumed that your uncle would have mentioned it before our wedding and when I realised he hadn't…well, part of me didn't want to talk about it and the other part didn't want to put you off coming here.' He handed her a chunk of bread and cheese. 'For what it's worth, I was going to tell you the other day.'

'It's all right. I'm sure it's not easy to talk about. It must have been awful.'

'My father often was.'

She took a bite of bread, chewing in silence for a few moments before continuing. 'Lady Jarrow also said that you look like him.'

'Oh, yes. No matter what he said, I've no doubts at all about who my father was. I sometimes wish that I did.'

'But Corin *does* have doubts, doesn't he?'

He seemed to freeze for a moment before answering. 'Yes.'

'Have the two of you talked about it?'

'Not since that night, no. We were both furious, but I tried to persuade him to ignore the whole thing. I told him it didn't matter a damn to me who his father was and that he was still my brother.' A muscle clenched in his jaw. 'Unfortunately, I was never very good at talking about feelings. I'm afraid I only made things worse. Then father died not long afterwards and there were so

many things to do, so many duties, all of them accompanied by whispers and stares and even more rumours.
Not thinking or talking about how I felt seemed like
the best thing to do. I prided myself on being calm, on
having dealt with my emotions so effectively, but perhaps I was deluding myself.'

He ran a hand around the back of his neck. 'When
you accused me of being angry, I didn't want to believe
that I wasn't in control, that it was all still bubbling
away underneath. But it is and it affects everything.
I've worked so hard to restore our family's reputation
and fortune, but, if anything, we've all drifted further apart. Now it's like we're all trapped here licking
our wounds and hiding from the world. And when my
mother isn't crying about all the things my father did
and said then Antigone's arguing with Justin, Justin's
trying to goad her, Helen's hiding under a table and
Corin thinks the best way to prove he's our father's
son is to act like him. It's exhausting.'

'It sounds it.'

'Then they all come to me, expecting me to fix all
of their arguments and problems, and sometimes…' He
paused, his expression stricken. 'Sometimes, I *know*
that I love them, but I can't feel it. It makes me wonder whether you were right and I really have lost the
ability to feel. I'm afraid that when I buried my anger,
I buried every other emotion, as well. Good and bad.'

'I think if that were true then you wouldn't care either way.' She placed a hand on his arm, unable to stop
herself when there was something so despairing about
his posture. 'Do Antigone and Justin know what your
father said?'

'They know that something happened in London,

but not the specifics. I'll have to tell them before Justin leaves for Eton, but it's not an easy subject to broach.'

'Maybe you need to come to terms with it first?'

'I've been trying for this past week and, believe me, it's not a pretty sight.' He grimaced. 'I broke a chair.'

'Oh… Did the chair deserve it?'

His gaze sparked with amusement. 'I never liked the design. Stripes.'

'Well, then, if it helped you to move on, maybe it was a worthwhile sacrifice.' She squeezed his arm reassuringly before releasing him again. 'I'd like to help you move on, too, if you'll let me? Start with your father. Tell me how you really feel about him.'

'I've thought about that all this past week and, if anything, I'm even more furious now than when it happened. I can forgive him for the gambling and women, but what he said, what he did to Corin…' He shook his head. 'You know, my brother wasn't always the way he is now. He used to sleep, for a start, but ever since… How could I not be angry at my father for that?'

'You can't. Have you asked your mother if there was any truth in it?'

He gave her an incredulous look. 'You mean ask my mother if she cuckolded my father?'

'Yes. I'm not saying it would be easy, but perhaps Corin needs to know the truth. Maybe you both do or you'll stay angry. Not at each other, but at the whole situation.'

'The whole situation…' He ran a hand over his chin, staring out at the river. 'Some days I feel like there's no escape. That's why I *do* understand what it's like to want to run away and start all over again somewhere new. I'm a little jealous that you actually succeeded.'

She nudged a shoulder gently against his. 'Maybe we ought to run away together next time?'

'Not a bad idea. How does Antarctica sound?'

'A little chilly. How about you come to Bath and bake biscuits, too?'

'Do you think your friend Miss MacQueen would teach me?'

Beatrix let out a guffaw of laughter before she could stop herself. '*That* might be more of a problem.'

'Indeed.' He chuckled and then sobered again. 'Unfortunately, there *is* no escape. I'm Howden. I was born Howden and I'll die Howden.'

'That doesn't mean you have to be the strong one all the time.'

'Yes, it does. Otherwise all of this would collapse. Literally.'

'Maybe at one time, but not any more... The estate won't fail now.'

'Thanks to you.' He caught her eye with an intense look. 'However, I was wrong to marry you for the money. It seemed like the practical thing to do at the time, but I never wanted that kind of marriage. I had my own parents as a warning, but I chose not to think about that either. When I look back to the way I behaved before our wedding, I feel ashamed. It bothers me that I made an agreement with a man like your uncle. It bothers me that I never made the effort to put my own burdens aside and talk to you. Most of all, it bothers me that you felt you had no choice but to run away from me.'

She dropped her gaze, reaching for one of the cakes as if the sincerity in his voice hadn't made her throat feel tight suddenly. 'Then how did you really feel when I ran away? Surely you weren't as calm as you claimed?'

'I don't know. I just remember it as another burden on top of all the others. If I felt anything it was numbness.'

'Oh.'

'I didn't mean…' He started to reach a hand out and then pulled it back again. 'Maybe there was more. I don't know yet. I'm still trying to understand all of it.'

'That's all right.' She took a bite of cake. 'I appreciate the honesty.'

'I don't believe anyone's ever accused me of being charming.' He lay back with a sigh, propping himself up on his elbows. 'Do you know what this picnic lacks? Belles.'

'*My* Belles?'

'The very same. My morning coffee isn't the same without one.'

'Maybe I'll go down to the kitchens one of these days and scandalise your staff by baking.'

'I wouldn't have any objections. On a scale of one to ten, I do believe it would be one of the least scandalous things my family has ever done.'

She finished the last mouthful of cake and lay down beside him, stretching her legs out and gazing up at the leafy canopy overhead.

'Bea… I really am sorry for my behaviour this past week. I needed time to think, not just about how I felt, but about what you said about growing up with your uncle and aunt and how their house felt like a prison. If there were a way for me to give you a divorce without hurting my family then I'd take it. I don't want to be your gaoler and I don't want you to be unhappy. I

want you to know that if I could go back and do things
differently then I would.'

'Thank you.' Oddly enough, the words made her
feel better. 'So would I.'

'But this is where we are now. I know that we've
had a rough start and I'm probably deluding myself
all over again, but I still hope that you'll come to like
it here.' He made a face. 'It may be a lot to hope for in
four and a half weeks, but what I'm trying to say is,
could we start again? *Again?*'

'Yes.' She nodded. 'Yes, we can.' And she would *try*
to like it there, she decided. As much as she wanted
to return to Bath, Lady Jarrow was right, she'd made
a vow and she owed him that much. And maybe she
would come to like it—and him, too. She was already
halfway there. He wasn't trying to deceive or control
her and he certainly wasn't as cold and hard-hearted
as he'd first appeared. He obviously cared for his family even if he, and they, had a strange way of showing
it. So maybe he *was* capable of love, after all. And if
he was, then maybe *she* could risk opening her heart
again, too. Just so long as she was careful...

'Thank you.' His smile was warmer than she'd ever
seen it before. 'I'll speak to my family about their behaviour again tonight.'

'You know, Antigone was actually excited by the
idea of making some calls. Maybe she's lonely. Or
bored. That might partly explain why she behaves so
badly. I think this dinner party might be good for her.'

'It's worth a try. So...company for Antigone, a
proper conversation with Corin...any advice about
Justin?'

'Yes, since you asked. I think that you ought to encourage him a bit more.'

'Encourage him? At what?'

'Anything. Everything. He looks up to you. Have you noticed how he reports anything positive his tutor has said at dinner? He wants your approval.'

'I give it.' He frowned. 'Don't I?'

'Yes, but usually with a sting in the tail. You tell him to keep it up or not to be complacent or to work harder in a different subject. Maybe some unconditional approval would be helpful?'

'Perhaps you're right. I'll give it a try.'

'Good.' She smiled, pleased by his willingness to listen.

'What about you? What else can I do to help you?'

'Well…there is *one* thing.' She took a deep breath. 'Lady Jarrow thinks that I ought to demand the Duchess's suite. She says the only way to fight fire is with fire, but I think… I don't know…would it be going too far?'

'Not necessarily.' He looked thoughtful. 'It's about time I moved into the Duke's rooms and I'd rather not have my mother on the other side of the dressing-room door.'

'Oh.' She felt a tremulous sensation at the idea of it being *her* on the other side of the door instead. 'So… are you saying that my moving rooms would help you?'

'Yes. I think Lady Jarrow has a point. My mother's never been good at compromise. She just digs herself into holes and refuses to budge. So maybe it's time we made her. It might help her change her views on a few other things.'

'But I don't want to be cruel. She doesn't have to go as far as the dower house.'

'That's up to her.' He folded an arm behind his head. 'I'll tell her later.'

'Today?' She glanced sideways at the bulk of his arm muscles through his jacket. 'I think I've done enough to enrage her for one day.'

'We might as well take advantage of an already bad mood.'

'Good point, but *I'll* tell her. It's my decision so I ought to be the one to do it.'

'Are you certain?'

'Yes, but I appreciate your offering.'

'You're my wife.' He twisted his head towards her so quickly she didn't have a chance to move hers away. 'What kind of a husband would I be if I didn't?'

She didn't answer, transfixed by the sight of his mouth so close to hers. She could hear his breathing, hers as well—both of them sounding far too loud above the babbling of the river. And there was her heartbeat, too, thudding like a drum in her ear. His gaze had dropped to her lips, she noticed, as if he were thinking about kissing her. Was he? Did she want him to? The idea of it made her heart skip and then thump even faster. It wasn't part of their agreement. It wasn't part of the duties she'd discussed with Lady Jarrow either. Only at that moment, agreements and duties didn't seem to matter so much any more.

'Beatrix?' He lifted a hand to her cheek, skimming the line of her jaw with the backs of his fingers and then stroking them downwards over her throat, his touch feather-light and yet so compelling that her whole body seemed to sag beneath it. She'd never been so close to him before and now the scent of his cologne in her nostrils made her limbs feel strangely heavy. She had a feeling she wouldn't be able to get up even if she wanted to, which she didn't. Strangely enough, she wanted him to keep on touching her. Even more strangely, she wanted to touch him, too, as if time and reality had been suspended for a few minutes.

And then he kissed her. Or she kissed him. She wasn't sure which one of them moved first, only that one moment she was looking into his eyes and the next their lips were touching, gently at first, as if each of them expected the other to pull away, then with a growing intensity as neither of them did. The fluttering sensation was back in her abdomen, although this time she recognised it for what it was: desire, unfurling like a bud in the springtime. And then one of his hands was cupping the back of her neck and one of hers had found its way around his shoulders and into the soft, silky locks of his hair, and they were clinging to each other, each of them deepening the kiss as if they were both too hungry to let go.

He gave a low moan and she moved closer, sliding her body towards his until her breasts were pressed up against his chest, so close that she could feel every thud of his heartbeat. She gasped with the pleasure of it, every vibration sending ripples of feeling out through her body, like pulses of electricity through her veins. The feeling was vital and heady and intoxicating, as if her blood were bubbling with excitement even as her limbs were growing heavier by the second; so heavy that she felt as though her body were sinking into the undergrowth. Which it was, she realised, suddenly aware of Quin moving on top of her.

'Bea?' He lifted his mouth away, holding her gaze for a long moment, his own filled with searing intensity, before lowering his head again and trailing a line of open-mouthed kisses over her neck, as if he were determined to kiss and caress every inch of exposed skin. She gasped, arching her back as a hand found her right breast, teasing the peak of her nipple through the cotton fabric of her dress. It seemed so strange to be out in the open, with the branches of the tree waving overhead, where anyone might see, and yet natural somehow, honest and real, not furtive in the way her relationship with Alec had been. Quin's kisses were different, too, a hundred times more intense, but giving rather than demanding, as if he wanted to give her pleasure as much as he wanted to take it.

But it was all too soon, a voice in the back of her head argued. Just a couple of hours ago, they hadn't even been talking. She might have learned more about him since and he might have apologised, but this was still much too fast.

'Wait.' She stiffened, lifting her hands to grasp hold of his shoulders.

'I'm sorry.' He moved away at once, rolling to one side as if she'd pushed him.

'No, there's no need to be sorry.' She shook her head, feeling as if her thoughts were all spinning away from her. 'It was just...unexpected.'

'Of course. We ought to be moving on anyway. You just have a...' He reached around the back of her bonnet and plucked off what appeared to be a small bundle of leaves.

'Oh...thank you.' She clambered to her feet and

moved away quickly, brushing her skirts down as if nothing had happened when inside she felt as if everything just had.

Chapter Fifteen

'Excellent work.' Quinton stood in the doorway of the library, clapping his hands approvingly as Justin came to the end of a long and particularly tricky-sounding piece of Latin translation, a speech by Cicero, if he wasn't mistaken.

'*Quin?*'

'Forgive the intrusion. I thought I'd just look in and see how your lessons were going.' He threw a quick look at Harker, who appeared to be even more startled than his brother. 'Justin appears to be making good progress.'

'He is, Your Grace. He's a very determined pupil.'

'I'm still having problems with mathematics.' Justin looked sheepish.

'Well, no one can be good at everything.' He came to lean against his brother's desk, trying to appear casual despite the curious stares being levelled at him. 'I was always terrible at Greek.'

'Really? You?'

'I'm not perfect.'

'No, but…' Justin's eyes lit up with a look of glee. 'I'm *good* at Greek. It's my best subject.'

'I'm delighted to hear it.' He lifted his shoulders in what he hoped passed for a nonchalant shrug.

'Quin?' His younger brother lowered his voice. 'Are you all right?'

'Never better. Why?'

'You're behaving oddly. Did you know that you're smiling?'

'I'm in a good mood, that's all.' As he had been all afternoon, he thought with an even bigger smile, co-incidentally ever since the oak tree… 'I just wondered if you'd care to join me for a game of billiards when you're finished?'

'Really?' Justin's chin almost hit his chest.

'Really. How soon until my brother's finished for the day?' He glanced at Harker enquiringly.

'We can be done in half an hour.'

'Perfect. In that case, I'll meet you in the billiards room afterwards. We can have a quick game before dinner and you can tell me how you're feeling about going to Eton.' He patted his brother on the shoulder. 'By the way, Harker, I don't believe I've ever thanked you properly for tutoring him. Justin would never have achieved so much without your help.'

'Thank you, Your Grace.' His secretary's chest visibly swelled with pride.

'In fact, you've earned a holiday. Take next week off. Full pay, of course, and I'll see to Justin's lessons.' He lifted an eyebrow at his brother. 'Except for Greek, obviously.'

'Ah, there you are.' He found his sister alone in the second drawing room, lying on a chaise longue with a novel in one hand and a cup of hot chocolate in the other.

'Quin?' If he'd found her in a tryst with one of the footmen, she couldn't have moved any faster, almost spilling her drink as she shoved the book under a cushion.

'Dare I ask?' He looked pointedly at the cushion.

'Oh, all right.' She pulled it out again. 'It's called *The Castle of Otranto* and Mama would never approve and now I suppose you won't either.'

He took the slender volume from her fingers and skimmed a few pages. 'Might a concerned elder brother ask how you were able to get hold of a copy?'

'You can *ask*.'

'Corin, I presume?'

'Yes, but *please* don't be angry. I have to read something and our library is abysmal! Why do we have so many books on land management and no novels?'

'That's a good question.'

'Quin?' Antigone looked faintly worried. 'What are you doing with your face?'

'Mmm?'

'Your face. You're smiling.'

'Yes, Justin told me.' He sat down on the end of the chaise longue. 'You're quite right though, we ought to have a bit more variety in the library. Perhaps you'd like to come into Faringdon and select a few books tomorrow?'

'Wh-what?' Antigone gaped at him.

'It would make sense, seeing as you're the one who wants to read them.'

'But you know that Mama doesn't approve of me reading, especially novels.'

'I do, but I also know that they make you happy and I've decided we all need a bit more happiness from now on. For the record, I also intend to hire you a governess. I know you've been listening in on Justin's lessons for the past year.'

'How?' Antigone's expression turned almost comically guilty. 'How did you know?'

'Harker's suspicions were alerted when the library door kept opening itself. He asked me if I objected and I decided that I didn't. If it's helped you then I'm glad.'

'It *has* helped me.' To his horror, Antigone's eyes welled with tears. 'I'm much better at mathematics than Justin.'

'I'm sure you are.' He put his hands on his knees and pushed himself back to his feet. 'And doubtless you're both brilliant at Greek. So, Faringdon tomorrow, then? For books and a dress.'

'A dress?'

'For the dinner party in two weeks, yes.'

'But Mama said—'

'*I* say that you can.'

'Even though I'm not out?'

'It'll be good practice for when you are.'

'So…you mean…' she looked almost afraid to ask '… I'm going to have a Season one day?'

'If you want one. Only not yet. In a couple of years' time when you've read enough novels to know what a villain looks like.'

'Oh, Quin!' Antigone leapt to her feet and threw her arms around his neck. 'Thank you! I thought I was going to be stuck here as Mama's companion for the rest of my life, reading the same old books over and over again and… Wait!' She froze and took a step back, pursed lips giving her an uncanny resemblance to their mother. 'This is all so I'll be nice to *her*, isn't it?'

'If by "her" you mean Beatrix and by "this" you're asking whether I'm placing conditions on your future happiness, then no. I'll buy you as many books as you want and give you a Season no matter how you behave, but I would *ask* that you try to be a little nicer.'

'After what she did—'

'What she did is frankly none of your business. And since I've drawn a line under it, I expect my family to, as well.'

Antigone's expression wavered. 'Do you *like* her, then?'

'She's my wife.'

'Yes, but we all know you only married her for the money.'

'I did.' He clenched his jaw, resenting the words, no matter how true they were. He *had* married Beatrix for money, only the idea sounded so dishonourable now, so tawdry and contemptible and completely unworthy of her. 'However, now that I've got to know her, I like her, too. A good deal, in fact. And I would prefer that my wife and sister were friends.'

'Oh, all right.' The rebellious gleam in her eye faded. 'I'll be good.'

His final stop before billiards was the second floor and the Duke's bedchamber, although he had to stop with his hand on the door handle for a few seconds, summoning the nerve to go in. Recognising and accepting feelings of anger was one thing. Actually entering his father's old room, where every object would be a visceral reminder of the man he'd grown up with, was quite another.

He took a steadying breath, opened the door and waited. There was a pang in his chest, yes, but to his surprise it was more muted than anger, more like regret. Sorrow. A sort of mourning for the kind of father he'd wanted and never had. As for the room itself… Whatever else he could criticise his father for, he couldn't find fault with his style. The bedchamber was spacious and uncluttered, with blue-grey silk wallpaper, a few solitary pieces of mahogany furniture and two floor-length windows that gave impressive views of the main, oak-lined drive and parkland beyond.

'Is that you, Mrs Hastings?'

The door to his dressing room, which appeared to have been left slightly ajar, burst open suddenly.

'Oh!' Beatrix stopped short, her cheeks flushing at the sight of him. 'I heard a sound and I thought you were…well, never mind.' She gestured over her shoulder. 'Maybe I should—'

'Wait!' He put a hand out to deter her from leaving. She looked even warier than she had after their kiss and during the rest of their ride, as if she wasn't sure how to react to being alone with him again. Which was unfortunate when all he wanted to do was pull her into his arms and kiss her senseless. The memory of what had happened during their picnic was still vivid in his mind, but he would have been more than happy to make a few more memories just then. One kiss hadn't been nearly enough… 'You don't have to go. I'm just taking a look around.' He cleared his throat, trying not to look at her mouth. 'Are you moving into your new room now?'

'Yes. I told your mother there was no hurry, but

she went straightaway so…' she lifted her shoulders, her gaze darting briefly towards the bed '… I thought there's no time like the present.'

'Good idea. Perhaps I'll do the same after dinner.'

'This is a lovely room.'

'Yes. I like it. I didn't think that I would, but I do.'

'No ghosts?'

'Not yet, but perhaps they only come out at night.'

'Well, I'll be close by if you need me.' She bit her lip, seeming to realise the other implications of that statement as her cheeks flushed an even deeper shade of pink. 'Not that you'll need me, I'm sure.'

'It's still good to know. And vice versa, in case of bad dreams.'

'Thank you.' She dropped her eyes to the floor, nudging the oriental rug with one of her slippers.

'What about you?' He resisted the urge to step closer to her. 'How do *you* like your new rooms?'

'They're beautiful. I can see why your mother didn't want to leave.' She peered up through her lashes, her expression pensive. 'She didn't say a word when I told her, just got up and walked out. Then a few minutes later Mrs Hastings arrived with some maids to move her things.'

'That sounds about right. We probably won't see her at dinner. Or possibly for a few days. She likes to make sure everyone knows how she's feeling.'

'You don't think she's busy plotting revenge, then?'

'If she is, we'll deal with it together.'

Another blush. 'I really didn't want to upset her.'

'I know. Believe me, it's almost impossible not to sometimes, but perhaps we can have some conversation at dinner now?'

'Maybe if we ate in the breakfast room instead?'

'Dinner in the breakfast room?'

'Is that too much like revolution?' Her lips twitched. 'All right, how about we just gather around one end of the dining table so that we don't all have to shout? Some of us don't find it easy to raise our voices.'

'Not a problem that's ever afflicted my family, but you're right. I'll inform Mrs Hastings.'

She nodded and looked at the rug again. 'Well, I'd better—'

'I spoke to Antigone,' he interrupted, still unwilling to let her leave. 'Justin, too. I've promised him a game of billiards in about five minutes.'

'That sounds pleasant.'

'And I volunteered to take Antigone shopping for some books and a new dress tomorrow. I was hoping you might want to join us, too?'

'With Antigone?' She looked doubtful.

'She's promised to behave. I think she means it.'

'Well...maybe.' She slid her tongue along the seam of her lips in a way that made his pulse quicken all over again.

'Unless you'd rather not?' He swallowed, his gaze drawn to the thin layer of moisture her tongue left behind.

'Mmm.'

'Or is something else the matter?'

'It's just...about earlier. When we kissed...'

'Ah.' He felt a distinct sinking feeling. Judging by her tone, she wasn't savouring the memory quite as much as he was. 'Forgive me. I overstepped the boundaries of our agreement. We ought to have discussed it first.'

'It's not that. I admit, it caught me by surprise, but it was both of us. I just want to be clear that it doesn't mean I've changed my mind. In terms of our agreement, I mean.'

'I see.'

'Not that I didn't enjoy it, but it was just one kiss. We still have four and a half weeks to go.'

'Understood.' He inclined his head.

'Good.' She sounded relieved. 'In that case, I'd be delighted to join you in Faringdon tomorrow.'

Chapter Sixteen

Week Two. Day Eleven

'Here we are.' Quinton climbed down from the carriage first. 'This is Faringdon.'

'It looks very nice.' Beatrix took his proffered hand, her eyes meeting his in a way that made his blood stir and then sizzle a little hotter in his veins. And it had felt hot enough on the journey. Unfortunately, they weren't alone today…

'So…*how many* books am I allowed exactly?'

He chuckled at his sister's blatantly avaricious expression as she jumped down behind them. 'That depends. How many books do you want?'

'A whole shelfful.' Antigone's eyes gleamed. 'Have *you* seen the selection in our library?'

'Me?' Beatrix, who was busy surveying the main street, looked surprised to be spoken to. 'No. Mrs Hastings showed me where the library was, but I haven't been inside yet. I didn't want to disturb Justin.'

'Mmph. Mama insists that he has his lessons in there to stop me going in. She says that ladies shouldn't damage their eyes and addle their brains with reading.'

'Oh, dear. In that case, my brain must be horribly addled already.'

'You like reading? Novels?'

'Yes, among other things. Whatever I can lay my hands on, usually.'

'Are there any you recommend?' His sister looked reluctantly impressed. 'Quin says that I can buy a few novels, but I don't want anything educational or instructive. I want as many fog-shrouded castles and mountain lairs as possible.'

'Naturally.' Beatrix smiled. 'Have you read anything by Rachel Hunter?'

'No. Is she good?'

'She's very dramatic. *Lady Maclairn, the Victim of Villany* is her latest, but I enjoyed *Letitia* a great deal, too.'

'Victim of Villany...' Antigone repeated dreamily. 'That sounds perfect. Who else?'

All things considered, Quinton thought, escorting his wife and sister, one on each arm, along the main street, the day was going much better than he'd expected. Conversation had been somewhat limited on the journey, but Antigone's face had finally lost its tightly clenched look and Beatrix appeared to be in a good mood, too. She looked fresh and pretty, as if she'd had a restful night's sleep in her new bedroom. Which was a good thing, obviously. Not at all a disappointment. Because really, what kind of a man harboured hopes of his wife having a nightmare just so he could rush to comfort her?

They went straight to a bookshop, the clerk inside looking as if his eyes might burst clean out of his head at the sight of them.

'Good morning.' Quinton nodded as the man practically ran around the edge of the counter. 'My sister here is interested in purchasing a few novels. As many as you have in stock, I believe.'

'As many…' The clerk's expression became almost as excited as Antigone's. 'Of course. This way, my lady.'

'I wouldn't have taken you for a lover of gothic fiction,' Quinton murmured to Beatrix as the clerk led his sister towards a tall bookcase in the corner.

'There's a lot you don't know about me.' She gave him an arch look. 'I thought we'd already established that.'

'I'd like to learn. For example, are there any books you'd like to purchase today?'

'Mmm.' She tapped a finger against her chin. 'A guide to dinner parties perhaps?'

'I'm sure we could find something with an awful title about etiquette, although I'm equally sure you don't need it.'

'Based on what evidence exactly?' She gave a sceptical-sounding laugh. 'I'm starting to wonder what I was thinking by even suggesting the idea. I've never even been to a dinner party, let alone given one.'

'There's nothing to worry about. It's essentially just dinner with more courses and better jewellery.'

'And a lot of new people I don't know, all asking questions about us.'

'Then we'll just have to get our stories straight.' He moved a step closer, lowering his mouth to her ear. 'Personally, I'm looking forward to it. I can't remember the last time we held any kind of social event at Howden. You're like a breath of fresh air, Beatrix.'

She looked up at him through her lashes, a half-flattered, half-suspicious look that made him want to gather her into his arms right then and there in the middle of the bookshop. Or better still, to abandon the shopping trip, return to the carriage and spend an hour or two in semi-darkness exploring the perfect bow shape of her lips. How was it possible that he'd never noticed how perfectly shaped they were before? Surely that ought to have been one of the first things he noticed about her?

'This is my favourite place in the world!' Antigone came hurrying back across the room, her whole manner exhilarated.

'Really?' Beatrix smiled. 'Have you found something you like?'

'*Somethings.* At least a dozen books.'

'Will that be enough?' Quin tore his eyes reluctantly away from his wife and towards his sister.

'For now, but Mr Thompson promises to send word to the hall as soon as he gets a new delivery.'

'Excellent. I'll send my man to collect your purchases later, but first we have some more shopping to do.' He rubbed his hands together briskly. 'So... dresses next?'

'I'm exhausted.' Antigone flung herself onto the chaise longue where he'd found her the day before with a contented-sounding sigh. 'Choosing dresses is hard work.'

'So it would seem.' Quinton deposited a pile of books onto an elm-wood table beside her. 'But then you did demand to see every scrap of material in the shop.'

'The right fabric and colour is important. It's not every day I get a new dress.'

'I know. That's why I said you could order three.'

'Which of course meant I had to see everything again!' Antigone grinned. 'I can't wait for them to be ready. A week seems like for ever!'

'You'll just have to pass the time with one of your new books. Here.' He picked up a small leather-bound volume and winced. 'I refuse to repeat that title.'

'Don't be so stuffy. You might enjoy a bit of swooning in castles.'

'I think not.'

'You might if it were Beatrix doing the swooning…' Antigone's expression turned coy. 'I saw the way you were looking at her in the bookshop. And the dressmaker's. And the carriage. You really *do* like her.'

Quinton gave a pointed cough. Not that he objected to the idea of his wife swooning into his arms. On the contrary, it sounded rather tempting, but he was hardly going to discuss it with his little sister. 'I've no idea what you're talking about. Now, if you don't want me to confiscate your new purchases…'

'Then I won't say another word until dinner.' Antigone flung open the book cover. 'In fact, I won't move from this spot until the bell goes for dressing.'

'Fine, only no books at the dinner table.' He glanced towards the door, wondering where Beatrix had got to. She'd been quiet again on the journey home, though every time he'd looked in her direction he'd had the distinct impression that her eyes had just moved away. And he'd been looking in her direction a *lot*.

'I think she went to her room.' Antigone answered his unspoken question. 'Maybe she's tired. On the verge of swooning perhaps.' She chuckled. 'You know, she isn't so bad, after all.'

'I know.'

'I might even be persuaded to like her one of these days.' She lifted her gaze from the book again. 'I suppose she had a good reason, for running away on your wedding day?'

'She did.'

'Well, then, if *you* can forgive her... All right, I admit it, I like her already. Happy now?'

Quinton considered for a moment and then nodded. *Yes.* Yes, he'd enjoyed his day out more than he'd expected. He *was* happy. The emotion was just so unfamiliar, it had taken him a while to recognise it.

Beatrix stood in front of a large gilt mirror, twisting her head from one side to the other as she admired her new green silk bonnet. It was, in fact, one of four new bonnets, three more than she technically needed, but Antigone's enthusiasm for shopping had been infectious. That, combined with the novelty of shopping at all. Her aunt had always been in charge of her wardrobe and she'd never chosen her anything remotely attractive or colourful, even as part of her wedding trousseau. Most of her life seemed to have been spent in assorted shades of dull grey. And then when she'd arrived at Belles and been given a yellow shop dress... well, suddenly she'd felt nostalgic for dullness. Yellow might have been a perfect match for the golden-haired Henrietta, not to mention a surprisingly complementary shade on Nancy, but it had made *her* look positively ill. As a result, the thought of buying a few new clothes in colours that actually suited her had been too tempting to resist. Somehow she'd ended up ordering two new day dresses, an evening gown for the dinner party, a pelisse, cape, five pairs of gloves, a silk shawl, three pairs of stockings and two pairs of shoes. Not to mention the bonnets. In retrospect, perhaps she'd gone a little bit crazy…

'Pretty.'

She gave a start, looking past her reflection in the mirror to see Quinton standing a few feet behind her.

'Thank you.' She turned around, feeling her cheeks warm at the way his eyes travelled up and down as if he were appreciating more than the bonnet. 'What about this one?' Quickly she replaced the green with a blue velvet.

He narrowed his gaze a little, appearing to take the question seriously. 'No, I prefer the green. Although…' He moved closer, reaching for the ribbons and tying them in a loose bow beneath her chin. 'There. That's better.'

'Thank you.' She licked her lips, unnerved by the way his fingers hovered against her cheek for a few seconds. The fact that they were standing in her bedroom didn't help. She'd felt far too aware of him all day. And the previous night. And the day before. Ever since their kiss under the oak tree, in fact. He hadn't tried to kiss her again, but she'd found herself thinking about it all too frequently. After everything she'd said to Lady Jarrow, she could hardly believe that she'd allowed it to happen, but since it had…she couldn't honestly say that she regretted it either. It had been a moment of connection, of shared sympathy for the situation in which they found themselves. And it had been…pleasant. *Very* pleasant. Stirring in a way that she'd never imagined or experienced before, making her wonder whether their marriage could be about *more* than money and reputation, after all. Quinton had seemed like a different man since, too: thoughtful and courteous, not quite relaxed, but definitely less tense, the kind of man it would be all too easy to fall in love with. Not that she'd changed her mind about leaving—her independence was still far more important, but he was making it harder to be quite so definite…

'I got a little carried away, didn't I?' She gestured towards the collection of parcels on the bed.

'Not at all. I'm pleased you enjoyed yourself.' Even his smile felt like a caress.

'What about you?' Standing so close, she was aware of an almost overpowering urge to lift her hands to his chest the way she had the day before. She could remember what it felt like… 'I didn't see you buy anything.'

'I have all the clothes I need.'

'You didn't buy any books either.'

'True, but, unlike my sister, I'm perfectly happy with what's available in the library.'

'But what *would* you like? If I were to buy you a present, for example?'

'Me?' He looked genuinely surprised and then pleased to be asked. 'You want to buy me a present?'

'Maybe… Oh, all right, Helen mentioned that it's your birthday next month.'

'Yes, but there's no need to buy me anything.'

'I disagree. No matter what happens with…*us*, I'd like to think that we're friends now, and friends buy each other gifts. Now, what are your hobbies? What do you do to relax?' She tilted her head to one side when he didn't answer. 'You must relax somehow.'

'I suppose I did when I was younger. Only I haven't had time for hobbies recently. Riding, I suppose, not that I need you to buy me a horse.'

'No, I was thinking of something a little smaller. Maybe a set of spurs? Or a riding crop?'

'A crop?' His voice sounded oddly strangled.

'Yes, or—'

'Bea,' he interrupted abruptly, lifting a hand to adjust his cravat. '*Thoughtful* as those ideas are, you ought to know that my birthday is in thirty-one days.'

'Thirty-one?' She blinked. 'But that's…?'

'The end of six weeks. Yes, I've already appreciated the irony. In my defence, I didn't anticipate the date when we made our agreement, but I think, all things considered, we might have other things on our minds when we get to it.'

'Yes, I suppose so.'

'In the meantime…' He cleared his throat. 'Is there anything else you think we might need for the dinner party?'

'I don't think so. I've discussed the menu with Mrs Hastings and she has most of the preparations in hand. As for the invitations, I've decided to deliver them to your neighbours in person. That way I can introduce myself and it'll be much harder for anyone to say no, especially if they have reservations about coming.'

'Good idea. I'll accompany you, if you wish?'

'Oh…' She felt a stab of disappointment. 'I'm afraid I already asked Lady Jarrow to accompany me. She's staying with a friend in Faringdon, but she offered to help.' She made an apologetic face. 'I assumed that you'd be busy so I sent her a note this morning.'

'That's quite all right. From what I know of Lady

Jarrow, she'll be much more persuasive than I could ever be.'

'That was another consideration. I thought I might ask Antigone, too, if I can lure her away from her new books.'

'I'm sure she'll be thrilled to accompany you. I do believe your *Victim of Villany* has won her over.' He held onto her gaze a few seconds longer than necessary before stepping away. 'Until dinner, then.'

Chapter Seventeen

Week Two. Day Twelve

'*That* was fun,' Antigone whispered to Beatrix as they made their way down the front steps of Coverly Manor, home of Lord and Lady Coverly and their son, the Right Honourable Stephen Coverly. 'I always thought that Mama was intimidating, but Lady Jarrow is just…' her eyes gleamed with admiration '…*magnificent*. I want to be just like her when I grow up.'

'Really?' Beatrix threw her a dubious look. As role models went, Lady Jarrow probably wasn't quite what Antigone needed. The words frying pan and fire sprang to mind.

'Yes! She just says exactly what she thinks and she doesn't let anyone bother her. She actually likes it when they try and argue, not that many of them do. Has *any-one* refused to come to the dinner party?'

'No, although I suppose they could always send some excuse later.'

'I doubt it if they know she's still in the area.' Antigone took a seat in the open carriage. 'And you were very good too, you know. Mrs Padgett said you were *perfectly charming.*'

'Was I?'

'Yes, actually.' Lady Jarrow, overhearing the last piece of the conversation as she swept magisterially into the seat opposite, nodded her head in vigorous agreement. 'I believe that everyone was most impressed. So, everything seems to be in order. You have a dining room, a good cook, new gowns and now a sufficient number of guests, too. Which just leaves your mother-in-law to deal with. Is she planning on attending the dinner party?'

'She says not.'

'Mmm. It would still be just like her to play the bad fairy and ruin things.' Lady Jarrow threw a cursory glance at Antigone. 'No offence, my dear.'

'None taken.' Antigone shrugged as the carriage rolled away. 'Corin says that Mama can stifle all the joy in a room just by walking past the door.'

'That's awful.' Beatrix put a hand to her mouth as Lady Jarrow chuckled.

'True enough though. Perhaps *I* ought to speak with her.'

'No.' Beatrix shook her head quickly. 'We should let Quin do it.'

'Quin speak to Mama?' Antigone gave an unladylike snort. 'Trust me, that won't make any difference. All she ever does is cry and accuse him of being like Father.'

'Oh, dear.' Beatrix twisted her hands in her lap. In that case, maybe *she* ought to be the one to speak to her mother-in-law, no matter how awful the prospect. After all, she was friends with Helen and Corin and Justin now, and she was making good progress with Antigone. Maybe it was time to confront the most forbidding family member of all. And if things went badly, well, she'd probably be leaving in a month's time anyway.

'Speaking of your husband…' Lady Jarrow lifted her cane suddenly, pointing further along the road. 'I do believe this is him now.'

'What?' Beatrix turned her head to find Quinton approaching on horseback, dressed in a sleek-fitting black riding coat and tan breeches that accentuated the muscular physique of his thighs. Her heart gave a strange little jump of excitement at the same moment as her stomach clenched with something stronger.

'Good seat,' Lady Jarrow murmured. 'Excellent posture.'

'Quin?' Beatrix felt ridiculously aware of her breathing as he approached the carriage, doffing his hat and turning his mount around to keep pace. 'I didn't expect to see you.'

'I assumed that you'd be almost done with your calls so I thought I'd come and escort you home.' He gave her a warm smile, his tousled hair making him look almost boyish for a moment, before shifting his gaze sideways. 'Lady Jarrow, an honour to see you again.'

'How many hands?' The older woman didn't waste time with pleasantries, gesturing at his horse instead. 'Sixteen?'

'Sixteen exactly.'

'A fine-looking beast.' She nodded approvingly. 'I believe that I'd like to visit to your stables, Howden.'

'Please do. You're welcome at any time.'

'Good. I have time now, although I shan't stay long. My hostess is expecting me back before dinner, but I'd like to satisfy myself on a few points first. I've always thought you can judge a man by the quality of the stables he keeps.'

'Indeed?' Quinton raised an eyebrow, his expression amused. 'Am I being judged, Lady Jarrow?'

She gave him a look that suggested the answer was obvious. 'Well, of course you are. What on earth did you think I was doing here?'

'Aren't you coming with us?' Lady Jarrow barked as Beatrix turned towards the house instead of the stables.

'No. There's something I need to do,' she answered. *Before her nerve failed her,* she added silently.

'Very well. I'm sure your husband will take good care of me.'

'I'm certain he will.' She threw Quinton an encouraging look and then hurried inside, almost ripping her cloak off in her haste. 'Oh, Dunstan…' She found the butler in the hallway. 'Do you happen to know where my mother-in-law is?'

'I believe that she's in her own room, Your Grace.' The butler lowered his voice. 'Although if I may be so bold as to say so, it might be better not to disturb her.'

'You're probably right. Unfortunately, I don't think I have a choice.' Beatrix took a deep breath and made for the staircase, rushing along the upstairs gallery and tapping gently on the door of the Dowager's new chamber before she could change her mind. After several seconds with no answer, she opened the door anyway.

'Your Grace?' She peered inside. The room was dark, the curtains drawn tightly across the windows to keep out even the tiniest sliver of daylight. From what she could tell, the only source of illumination was the fire, which was roaring fiercely enough to make her break into a sweat from almost ten feet away.

'It's generally the custom to wait for an invitation to enter. I'd expect even a woman like *you* to know that.'

'Oh!' Beatrix almost leapt into the air as the Dowager's voice scraped through the gloom. She was sitting in a winged chair in one corner of the chamber, to all appearances doing nothing, her spine as stiff and ramrod straight as ever. 'I'm sorry, Your Grace, you're right, I do know that.'

'In that case—'

'*But* I need to talk to you. It's important.'

'We have nothing to talk about. You may leave.'

Beatrix gritted her teeth, any hope that the Dowager might be in a receptive mood evaporating into thin air. In truth, she'd only come to talk about the dinner party, but now she was there…maybe she was the only one who *could* broach the rest. It wasn't as if the Dowager could hate her any more. She opened her mouth, already regretting what she was about to say.

'Corin.'

There was a moment of utter stillness, followed by what felt like a lightning bolt as the Dowager sprang out of her chair. *'What?'*

Beatrix took another step forward despite an urge to turn tail and run. 'We need to talk about Corin.'

'How dare you?'

'I dare because somebody needs to. He's obviously miserable and I think you are, too.'

'What do you mean?' The Dowager's eyes flickered as if there were small fires burning behind them. 'What do you know of it?'

'I *know* of it.' Beatrix lifted her chin stubbornly. 'I

know what your husband said in London and from what I can tell, it's tearing this family apart.'

'And you think I'll talk to *you* about it?' The flickers were building into substantial flames now...

'Not necessarily, but I think you should talk to someone. You might not like or approve of me, but I'm not here to judge or condemn. I only want to help.'

'You shameless, unprincipled, brazen—'

'You can call me as many names as you like, but I'm not going anywhere.'

'*Get out!*'

'No. This has gone on long enough. Now you can either talk to me or you can talk to Lady Jarrow. She's in the stables right now, but I'd rather you spoke to me.' She waited for the threat to sink in and then took another step closer. 'Please?'

The fires in the Dowager's eyes gave one last furious flare and then suddenly, surprisingly, went out. 'There shouldn't be any need to talk. It was all nonsense. My husband only said it to hurt me.'

'But he hurt your sons, too. Corin especially.'

'And that's *my* fault?'

'Yes, if you don't help him to feel any better. You're the only one who can do it because you're the only one who can tell him whether what his father said was true or not. All he knows is that he doesn't look like the rest of his siblings.'

'I shouldn't have to dignify such slurs with an answer. Corin should know me better.'

'He knows that you had an unhappy marriage. Maybe he thinks you took comfort elsewhere. Maybe he doesn't care whether you did or didn't. He just needs to know the truth.'

The Dowager turned her face away with a jerk, staring intently at the wall.

'Very well, that's all I wanted to say.' Beatrix sighed and then clenched her fists. 'Actually, no, it isn't. What I *should* say is that you're making everyone's lives here a misery with your behaviour and it's not fair. It's like there's a black cloud hanging over the whole house. You don't *have* to be angry and unhappy any more and you don't have to make your family feel the same way, too. They could all move on if you'd let them!' She reached for the door handle and then froze, wondering if her ears were deceiving her at the sound of a small sob.

'Your Grace?' Beatrix spun around, giving a startled gasp before hurrying across the room. One sob had already degenerated into several sobs, accompanied by a high-pitched wailing as the Dowager's whole body shook with tremors.

'Get away from me!'

'No.' Beatrix wrapped her arms firmly around the Dowager's shoulders. 'I'm not leaving you.'

'I want to be alone!'

'No! I'm not letting you push me away like you push everyone else. You need to stop this!'

'*I know!*' The words released a fresh burst of tears. 'But you have no idea what it was like, being married to that man. I've been angry for thirty years, not just at him, but at my parents for making me marry him. They knew what he was like, they knew his reputation, but he was a duke and that was all they cared about.'

'Did he hurt you?'

'Not with his fists. Most of the time he was just casually cruel, never caring about anyone except himself. He was a liar and a cheat and a terrible father. Do you know *why* he almost bankrupted the estate during that last year? Why he said what he did, too? It was because he was jealous of Quinton. His own son! Oh, it was partly to get some kind of twisted, pre-emptive revenge on me. He knew he was dying and that I wouldn't mourn him, but he also knew that Quinton was a better man than he'd ever been or could ever be. He knew what he thought of him, too, and he resented him for it. It was *him* he was trying to hurt with those rumours, not Corin. He might have succeeded, too, if they hadn't looked so much alike.'

'How despicable.'

'He tried to ruin us all out of spite, but I *never* once betrayed him with another man, no matter how much I wanted to. I swear it.' The Dowager clutched at her shoulder. 'You believe me, don't you?'

'I do.' Beatrix nodded as the wailing started again. It was strange to realise what she and the Dowager had in common. Both of their marriages had been arranged by their families and yet what had happened afterwards was completely different. She was coming to like Quinton more, not less. She'd been luckier than she'd realised.

'I'm sorry.' She tightened her arms around her mother-in-law, letting her cry herself out. 'I really am, but I'm not the one you should be telling all this to.'

'I can't.' The Dowager shook her head violently from side to side. 'I wouldn't know what to say.'

'Just tell them what you've told me. Clear the air. It's for the best, I promise.'

'Do you really think so?' A loud sniff. 'Very well, then, send them to me.'

* * *

'Has Lady Jarrow left?' She met Quin on the landing halfway down the staircase.

'Just now. She said not to worry about saying goodbye and that she'd visit in a couple of days.' He raised a hand to his forehead. 'I feel like I've just gone ten rounds in a boxing ring.'

'Who won?'

'I'm not entirely sure, but I've to tell you that she approves of my stables.'

'High praise.'

'I do feel strangely proud of myself. She's quite a character, isn't she?' He laughed and then peered closer at her expression. 'Bea? Is everything all right?'

'I think so. I just left Corin talking with your mother.'

'Corin and my mother?' He looked up the staircase in alarm.

'She's telling him about your father. Your *shared* father, in case you were wondering.'

'You mean you've talked to her about that?' His expression shifted to one of amazement.

'Yes. I hope you don't mind. I went to discuss the dinner party and somehow…well, I thought it might be easier for her to talk to a comparative stranger. It still took a bit of persuasion and I had to threaten her with Lady Jarrow, but it turns out that Corin inherited his looks from your paternal great-uncle. Apparently there's a dusty old portrait of him somewhere that proves it.'

'And she never thought to show Corin that *before*?'

'I think she didn't want to dignify your father's accusation with a response.'

'Bea…' He let out a long breath and then reached for her hands, almost crushing her fingers against his lips. 'Thank you. I don't know how you've done it, but thank you. Not just for Corin, but for all of it. For helping me. Us.'

'I haven't done much.' Her voice seemed to snag in her throat, emerging several notes higher than she'd ever heard it before.

'Yes, you have. It's more than I could ever have expected from any wife, but especially…'

'One who ran away?' She finished for him, her lips curving. 'Or one who isn't tall and blonde?'

He winced. 'They're hardly the only qualities I find attractive in a woman.'

'It doesn't matter.'

'It does if you think I still feel the same way. For the record, I want you to know that my feelings on the subject have changed a great deal over the past two weeks.'

Something in his voice made her insides clench. 'You don't have to say that.'

'But I mean it. I admit, the first time I saw your friend Mrs Fortini I thought she was the most beautiful woman I'd ever set eyes on. Now I wonder how I ever noticed her in the same room as you.'

'That's ridiculous.'

'No, it's not.' His gaze intensified over the backs of her knuckles. 'Whatever happens, I'll always be grateful that you came to Howden. You've changed my life.'

'Oh…' She swallowed at the look of sincerity on his face. 'Then I'll always be glad that I came, too.'

'Beatrix…' he murmured as he lowered her hands from his lips and held them against his chest instead, between both of their hearts, his mouth finding hers in a kiss that was soft and searching and so tender she thought she might never want it to end…

The sound of raised voices, Justin and Antigone's, in fact, jolted them apart. By the sound of it, they were arguing.

'Some things, on the other hand, never change…' Quinton smiled ruefully.

'I'll go and see what it's about.' She pressed her lips together, trying to imprint the memory of his kiss. She wanted to keep it there, to remember and savour again later. 'You go on up to your mother and don't worry about dinner. I'll tell Mrs Hastings that things might be a little different this evening.'

'Thank you.' He gave her that slightly amazed look again. 'I'm grateful, Beatrix. Truly.'

It was three hours before Quinton leaned his head back against the door of his bedchamber with an exhausted sigh. Talking to his mother and Corin had taken longer and been far harder than he'd expected. There had been tears, arguments, recriminations, explanations and finally embraces, leaving him feeling wrung out, emotionally bruised and better than he'd felt in months.

He looked at the bed, wondering if he could summon the energy to reach it, then noticed the door to his dressing room was open and started towards that instead, unfastening his cravat as he went. To his surprise, the door on the other side was slightly ajar, too, revealing a faint glow that suggested at least one candle was still burning in the bedroom beyond.

'Beatrix?' he whispered, nudging the door open a

bit further and peering around the edge, willing her to still be awake.

'Quin?' She sat up at once. 'What happened?'

'A lot of talking and crying.' Despite the words, his heart leapt at the sight of her. She was dressed in a white cotton nightgown, the ripples of her hazel-brown hair hanging loose around her shoulders. 'I've never seen my mother cry before.'

'I think she had a lot to cry about.'

'Yes. She says she never wants to speak of it again, but she wanted to get it all out, once and for all. Then she apologised for the way she's behaved.' He rubbed a hand over his jaw and laughed. 'I thought I was dreaming.'

'What about Corin? How's he?'

'I'm not sure yet, but I think… I hope it's helped. We'll see.'

'And you? Has it helped you?'

'More than I can say. I feel reconciled, not just to my family, but to who I am, too.' He looked around at the walls of the bedchamber. 'I'm Howden. I need to stop resisting that just because my father was, too.'

Beatrix peered at his face in the candlelight. 'You look like you're about to collapse.'

'I feel like it. All this emotion is a lot more draining than I realised.'

She hesitated briefly and then beckoned him forward, patting the space on the mattress beside her. 'Here. Lie down.'

Even exhausted, he felt a flare of heat in his chest. 'Are you certain?'

'I'm certain that you need some sleep.' She shuffled sideways. 'And I've already warmed this side of the bed for you.'

'Then how can I refuse?' He reached down to pull off his boots, then wriggled out of his jacket and waistcoat and slid under the covers, sighing with contentment as the scent of her hair floated out of the pillow and into his nostrils. 'This reminds me of that inn we stopped at on our journey here. You were horrified by the idea of sharing a room with me then.'

'I wasn't horrified.' Her voice sounded smaller. 'I was just afraid it was a trick.'

'What kind of a trick?' He turned his head towards her, the contented feeling evaporating. 'Did you think I intended to seduce you?'

'Not exactly.' A shadow passed over her face. 'I thought you were honourable, only it reminded me of another time. One I'd rather forget.'

'Ah. You mean…?'

'Alec,' she whispered softly. 'His name was Alec.'

'Did *he* trick you?' Quinton went very still, half afraid to hear the answer.

'He told me he loved me.' A note of bitterness entered her voice. 'And I was so grateful for any kind of affection that I believed him. It sounds so pathetic now.'

'It's not pathetic to want to be loved.'

'I know, but that's how it made me feel when I realised the truth. Pathetic and foolish and used.'

'I'm sorry.' He cupped a hand against the side of her face, smoothing his thumb gently across the soft skin of her cheek. 'I would never deceive you like that, Beatrix, I swear it. I would never say anything I didn't truly mean.'

'I know. I trust you.' She huddled closer, her shoulder touching lightly against his. 'That's why I'm here.'

That's why I'm here. The words echoed around his head as he closed his eyes, savouring the feeling of her body tucked up against his, more determined than ever to convince her to stay.

Chapter Eighteen

Week Two. Day Thirteen

Beatrix opened one eye and listened. She was lying on her left side, facing away from Quinton, if he was still there… She strained her ears. *Was* he still there? There was no sound of breathing, no telltale movement of the mattress either that she could tell. At last she summoned the courage to roll onto her back and look across the bed only to find…nothing. The space beside her was completely empty.

She rubbed a hand over the sheet where he'd been, already cool to the touch, wrestling a combination of relief, regret and disappointment. But it was probably better this way. She would have had no idea what to say if he *had* still been there and yet…she missed his presence. She'd wanted to wake up beside him, she realised with a jolt, as if they were a real married couple and not a soon-to-be-divorced one. Which was what they were…weren't they?

Yes! She pushed the question aside along with the covers and jumped out of bed in a hurry, deciding to dress herself and go downstairs for breakfast rather than ring for her maid. It was much too dangerous to stay there and remember how cosy she'd felt, curled up against Quin in the night. If she were completely honest with herself, she hadn't invited him to stay just to offer comfort. Part of it had been curiosity, too, to find out how it would feel to lie beside him now compared to the first time. And it had felt good. So much that she'd even confided in him about Alec. Not *all* of the truth— after his ordeal with his mother she hadn't wanted to start another long discussion—but some of it…

She threw one last confused glance at the bed, realising that it was the first day since her arrival that she'd woken up and *not* thought she was still in Bath, then slipped into her new slippers and hurried downstairs, surprised to find Corin sitting at the table beside his brother.

'Good morning.' Quin saw her first, his eyes lighting up as he pushed his chair back and stood to greet her.

'Good morning.' She tried her best not to look too happy to see him, though she had a feeling the attempt wasn't very successful.

'Sleep well?'

'Very well. And you?'

'Incomparably.' His mouth twitched in a way she might almost have called flirtatious. 'I believe it was the best night's sleep I've had in months.'

'Is this a competition?' Corin looked between them both curiously. 'Because if it is then I win. I can honestly say it's the first *night's* sleep I've had in the past year.'

'Does this mean you're feeling better?' Beatrix smiled at her brother-in-law as she slid into a seat.

'Like a new man. Or the same man with a better idea of himself now. Thanks in part, I believe, to you.'

'You know, there'll still be rumours.' Quinton gave him a concerned look. 'About all of us probably.'

'To hell with rumours. *We* know the truth. That's what matters.' Corin reached for a piece of toast and grinned. 'It's almost enough for me to hope you have daughters.'

'What?' Beatrix spluttered on a mouthful of coffee.

'Daughters,' Corin repeated. 'You see, one of the things that bothered me most this past year was the idea that I was Quin's heir when I maybe shouldn't have been. Ergo, once you married, I hoped you'd start having sons as soon as possible. Dozens of them. Whereas now...' another grin '...feel free to have as many daughters as you like. Little Corinnes, perhaps?'

'We'll bear the name in mind.' Quinton gave her a look that was both ironic and heated at the same time. If she wasn't mistaken, his foot nudged lightly against hers beneath the table, too.

Fortunately, she was saved from any further discussion of children's names by the arrival of Antigone and Justin, both of them gasping at the sight of a smiling and wide-awake-looking Corin.

'New man.' He shrugged by way of explanation.

'So, what are everyone's plans for today?' Quinton asked, glancing around the table.

'Reading.' Antigone gave a happy-sounding sigh.

'Maybe some more billiards?' Justin looked hopeful. 'Or I could come out for a ride with you before my lessons?'

'Why not come out with me instead?' Corin suggested, chuckling as the table vibrated with a loud thud.

'And Helen, too, apparently. We really ought to give the newly-weds some time alone together.'

'There's no need if you want to go out riding.' Beatrix felt her stomach flutter treacherously. 'I have some correspondence to attend to.'

'Then why don't you join me in my study? We can work together.' Quinton paused with his coffee cup in mid-air as every head turned in his direction. 'Is there a problem?'

'Just that you never let anyone except Harker into your study.' Antigone answered for them. '*I'm* not even sure what it looks like in there.'

'My wife is not *anyone*.' Quinton gave his sister a superior look. 'I'm more than happy to share my study with her.'

'Well...' Corin leaned back in his chair with a whistle. 'All we need now is for Mother to come down to breakfast. Then I'll have seen and heard everything.'

'Sorry about that.' Quinton looked at her apologetically as he held open the door to his study. 'Sometimes it would be useful if I could gag the whole lot of them.'

'I didn't mind. Breakfast was fun.'

'Fun?' He looked quizzical. 'Yes, I suppose it was in a way.'

'I thought that Corin's jaw was actually going to hit the table when your mother appeared.'

'I have to admit, mine felt a little loose, too. She even smiled at one point.'

'You mean when Helen poked her head out? Yes, I noticed that.'

'I would never have believed it if I hadn't seen it with my own eyes. She looked like...'

'What?'

He looked slightly embarrassed. 'Happy. The way she used to look sometimes, when we were boys, Corin and I. It wasn't often, but she wasn't quite so angry back then.'

'Then hopefully she'll rediscover who she is now.' Beatrix stepped into the study and caught her breath, looking around at the red carpet, floor-to-ceiling bookcases and brown leather armchairs. It was the first time she'd been inside and she felt instantly, instinctively, at home. 'Quin, this is lovely! Now I understand why you spend so much time in here.'

'It helps that my father rarely used it, but consider it yours now, too.' He gestured towards a large walnut desk. 'I thought that perhaps we could take a side each?'

'Thank you.' She accepted the chair he pulled out for her. 'Although now that I'm here, I'm afraid I need to beg for some writing supplies. I'd like to write to Henrietta.'

'Help yourself.' He pushed an inkwell and sheaf of paper towards her as he sat down opposite. 'Did you really sleep well? I was afraid I might have disturbed you when I got up.'

'Not at all. I didn't even know you were gone.'

'I didn't want to give you an unpleasant surprise when you woke.'

'I don't think it would have been unpleasant.' She bit her lip and then couldn't seem to stop herself from adding, 'I think it might actually have been quite pleasant.'

'I thought the same thing, but I didn't want to presume…' The pupils of his eyes seemed to swell. 'In any case, I appreciated your letting me stay.'

'You needed to talk.'

'No. I was tired of talking. I just wanted to see you.'

'Oh.' She glanced down at her sheet of paper in confusion. When he looked at her like that, it was harder than ever to think straight.

'Good morning, Your Grace… Ah.' A dark-haired man emerged through a side door and then stopped abruptly at the sight of them. 'My apologies, I didn't realise…'

'It's quite all right.' Quinton waved for the man to come closer. 'Harker, forgive my lack of manners in not introducing you to my wife sooner. Beatrix, this is Frank Harker, my secretary and Justin's tutor. Harker, this is my wife.'

'An honour to meet you, Your Grace.' The secretary made a low bow as she got up and held out her hand.

'Please, call me Beatrix. I'm delighted to meet you. From what Quin's told me, you've helped work wonders with both Justin and the estate.'

'I've done my best.' The man's colour rose. 'In fact, I was just bringing a list of possible sites for the new mill, as His Grace requested.'

'Excellent.' Quin took the list with a nod. 'I'll take a look and we can discuss them later over coffee.'

'In that case, I'll hurry up with my correspondence and get out of your way.' Beatrix moved back to her chair again.

'No, I meant all three of us.' Quin placed a hand on her arm, staying her.

'You mean, you want my opinion?'

'Of course. It's your estate now, too.' He paused significantly. 'For as long as you want it.'

'Oh…' She gazed back at him in surprise, feeling slightly breathless. Was this how it would be if she stayed, she wondered, working intimately yet equally alongside him, sharing his desk, his work, his bed? Because if it was then maybe Lady Jarrow was right. Maybe it *was* possible to retain her sense of independence and self-worth within marriage.

She blinked, suddenly realising that both men were still looking at her, expecting an answer. 'I'd be delighted.'

Chapter Nineteen

Week Four. Day Twenty-Eight

'How do I look?' Beatrix twirled around, her diaphanous blue satin gown billowing outwards at the hem. The short, slightly puffed sleeves were light and comfortable, but the fashionable neckline was lower than she was accustomed to, making the tops of her breasts visible in a way that made her more than a little self-conscious. It had seemed so sophisticated in principle, but now she was tempted to stick a handkerchief down the front.

'Much better than I do.' Antigone pouted from where she was sitting dejectedly on the bed. 'I think I was wrong about pink being my colour.'

'You weren't wrong at all. Trust me, you look lovely.'

'You're just saying that.'

'No, I'm not.' Beatrix smiled affectionately. Antigone's half-anxious, half-combative manner reminded her in a funny way of Nancy, although the thought of her friend caused her a pang of guilt, too. Nancy was back in Bath, holding the fort at Belles and waiting for her to come back. And she wanted to go back, she truly did. Only just recently, she'd found herself wishing that she could be in two different places at once…

'Do you really and truly think so? Because I don't want anyone laughing at me.'

'If anyone laughs, they'll have me to deal with,' a male voice answered. 'Better still, Lady Jarrow. However, I can promise you they won't. You both look beautiful.'

Beatrix twirled around one final time to find Quin standing in the dressing-room doorway, arms folded and one shoulder propped against the door jamb, looking so dazzlingly handsome in formal black and white evening clothes that she felt her stomach flip over and then perform some kind of vigorous, gravity-defying jig. Which was the last thing she needed when she already felt jittery enough to be sick. She had no idea how she was going to eat so much as a mouthful at her own dinner party.

'Are the guests arriving?' Thankfully Antigone spoke up when her own lips refused to work.

'They will be soon. You'd better go downstairs and sit with Mother. She hasn't said anything, but I can tell she's nervous.'

'Oh, no!' Antigone's eyes widened.

'Don't worry, she understands how important this is for all of us.' He inclined his head. '*And* I've seated her close to me just in case.'

'Good idea. All right, then…here goes!' Antigone got to her feet with unexpected poise. 'You're absolutely, completely positive that pink suits me?'

'On my honour.' He laid a hand over his heart, waiting for her to depart before walking towards Beatrix with a smile. 'I thought that she'd never leave. She's become like your shadow recently.'

'Shh.' Beatrix lifted a finger to her lips, looking pointedly towards the curtains. 'It's time for bed!'

'Can't I watch everyone arrive?' Helen's face appeared around the edge. *'Please?'*

'Only if your nurse agrees. So you'd better hurry on up to the nursery and ask her.'

'I'm sure she will.' Helen came skipping happily across the room. 'It's all so exciting. Goodnight.'

'Goodnight.' Beatrix bent down to kiss her cheek. 'See you under the table at breakfast?'

'I stand corrected.' Quinton chuckled as his youngest sister ran out of the door. 'You have *two* shadows. It's just harder to spot the smaller one.'

'It won't be for much longer, I expect. Their new governess is arriving next week.'

'Thank goodness.' His gaze travelled down to her feet and then slowly back up again, lingering briefly, but noticeably, at the top of her gown. 'It's hard not to be jealous when I want you all to myself.'

Beatrix dug her teeth into her bottom lip, feeling her stomach tremble again at the words. She wasn't entirely sure that she understood them either. Ever since the night she'd invited him into her bed, Quin had behaved like a perfect gentleman. There had been a certain look in his eyes on occasion, as if she meant more to him than a means of upholding his family fortune and reputation, but he hadn't visited her room at night or even *tried* to kiss her again. Only something about his voice at that moment set her pulse racing. Suddenly dinner-party jitters seemed quite insignificant.

'Is that what you want?' The question was out before she could think twice about it. 'To have me all to yourself?'

'Very much. In fact…' his voice turned husky as he slid his fingers slowly along the ribbon tied in a bow beneath her breasts '… I had an idea. I haven't been up to London since our wedding and I have several business matters to attend to. I wondered if perhaps we might take a trip there together? I remember you once said you hadn't seen much of the city.' He tugged gently on the ribbon. 'So why don't we go and explore, just the two of us? We can walk by the Serpentine, go shopping on Bond Street, maybe visit Vauxhall Gardens?' He cleared his throat as if he felt uncertain suddenly. 'Think about it anyway. There's no need to give me an answer now.'

'I don't need to think about it,' she answered impulsively. 'It sounds wonderful.'

'Good. In that case, I'll send word for the town house to be made ready.'

He smiled, looking young and happy and so unlike the severe, careworn Duke she'd first met that for a moment she felt utterly breathless.

'Bea?' His smile faltered. 'Are you all right?'

'Yes.' She forced herself to act normally. 'I'm just a little anxious about all of this. Actually, a lot anxious. I hope the weather won't put people off.'

'It'll take more than a bit of rain to do that, trust me. Now, don't worry, you'll be perfect. You *are* perfect.' He tucked her hand inside his elbow, leading them both towards the door. 'We're going to do this together.'

Quinton stood contentedly beside the fireplace, gazing at his wife across the drawing room. She was like a candle, he thought, shining brightly and vibrantly enough to dazzle him. A whole candelabrum, in fact. Had anyone else noticed, he wondered, or was it just him? He hoped the latter. Somehow the thought of other people looking at her in the same way made his chest contract with a feeling he thought must be jealousy. He couldn't be sure, having never experienced jealousy before, but he suspected it might be.

The dinner party had been an undisputed success. One perfect hostess, one well-behaved family, and twenty-two guests, more than the house had seen in the past decade, each of them clearly determined to enjoy themselves. Contrary to his mother's expectations, there had been no whispering behind hands, no barbed comments or cutting looks, just laughter, conversation and several loud toasts that had resulted in even more laughter. Even the formidable Lady Jarrow had refrained from intimidating anyone, regaling the table instead with stories about horses as well as her Trafalgar hero grandson, the Earl of Staunton.

'Your new Duchess is charming, Howden.' Mr Aloysius Fox, an elderly and, judging by the way he was swaying dangerously from side to side, somewhat inebriated gentleman, waved a monocle in front of him.

'She is,' Quinton agreed, unable to stop himself from smiling agreement.

'Now I understand why you've been hiding her away from us all.' Mr Fox laughed at his own witticism. 'Invalid, eh? She doesn't look very sickly to me. Still, I don't blame you. I remember being a newly-wed myself.'

'Aloysius!' *Mrs* Fox, arriving to steady her husband before he fell over, obviously didn't appreciate the comment.

'It was a brief illness after the wedding.' His mother, overhearing the exchange, spoke loudly from a few feet away. 'Since then, my new daughter has been taking the time to settle in. It's a considerable task, running a house like Howden Hall. Fortunately, I have no doubts that my legacy is in good hands. I heartily endorse my son's choice of bride.'

It was as if a large blanket had fallen over the room suddenly, swathing them all in silence. Quinton looked towards the spot where Beatrix was staring at his mother with an expression of wonderment, Corin and Antigone beside her looking similarly stunned. Words of approval from his mother were like gold dust, but so many at once were unprecedented.

'Eh? Oh, absolutely, hear, hear!' Mr Fox lifted his glass. 'To the new Duchess of Howden! Long may she reign!'

Quinton raised his glass along with the others, struck with a strange sense of disquiet. His mother's praise was all very well, but she had no idea about the agreement he'd made with Beatrix and how it might end. Admittedly, they were spending more and more time together—breakfasting together, working in his study together, going for rides and trips about the estate together, dining together and then sitting in the drawing room together afterwards, often long into the night—but he had no idea how she felt about him. She appeared to enjoy his company, and she was certainly happier now than when she'd first arrived, but as to whether she was having second thoughts about a divorce, he had no idea. All he knew was that *he* enjoyed every moment he spent with her. And he was running out of time. There were only fourteen days to go.

'Why don't we have some dancing?' Lady Jarrow's voice brought him back to the present. 'There must be somebody here who can play a few reels.'

'I'd be happy to.' Mrs Banks, the diminutive wife of the local doctor, made her way to the pianoforte.

'And I'd be happy to dance!' Corin made a bow in front of her even more diminutive daughter. 'If you'd do me the honour, Miss Banks?'

'And if Lady Howden would do me a similar honour?' Stephen Coverly approached Antigone.

'My lady?' Quinton walked slowly across the room, the other guests parting to let him through as he held a hand out to Beatrix. 'Would you care to?'

'I'd be delighted, Your Grace.' She dipped into a curtsy and smiled, keeping her eyes fixed on his as they went to join the two lines of dancers. Once there, they broke apart to stand at arm's length and yet their eyes still held, each of them gazing into the other's face as if there were nobody else in the room, or the hall, or the world even.

His blood surged as he looked at her. She looked animated and beautiful and…what was the word he'd used before? It had come to him spontaneously because it was true: *perfect*. That was it, she was perfect. For Howden, for his family, but most of all, for him. If she would only stay…

Was this what love felt like? he wondered, this all-consuming combination of need and longing and desire to just *be* with the object of your affections? His mind shied away from the idea. Falling in love had never been part of the plan. Four weeks ago, he would never even have acknowledged the possibility, but now he knew better. Thanks to Beatrix, he could no longer deny or control his emotions, even if, at that moment, he wished he still could. Because if he loved her and she chose to return to Bath then he had a feeling the pain would be overwhelming, stronger even than the anger he'd felt towards his father, stronger than anything he'd ever felt before, a pain that would shatter his heart and reach down into his very bones. And it would have nothing to do with money or scandal or reputation. It would all be because of *her*.

A feeling like panic took hold of him. No, he couldn't allow that to happen. His family were happy for the first time in as long as he could remember; he wouldn't allow the atmosphere at Howden to become tainted by misery again, not for any reason. He'd bottled up his feelings once and he could do it again, starting now. Love was the one emotion he wouldn't allow himself, at least not for another two weeks. If she decided to stay then maybe he could surrender that last tiny shred of control. In the meantime, he could desire her, but that was all, nothing deeper.

The music started, bringing their fingers and footsteps together again. He had the feeling the next two weeks were going to be torture.

Chapter Twenty

'Why are you sitting in the dark?' Beatrix peered around the edge of the study door, lifting a candle into the shadows. Judging by the grey shape on the other side of the room, Quinton was sitting behind his vast walnut desk, staring into nothingness.

'It's not completely dark.' He gestured to one of the large bay windows. 'There's a full moon tonight.'

'So there is. The rain must have stopped.' She walked slowly towards him, surprised by the stern tone of his voice after such a lively and successful evening. 'Why did you run away so soon after the guests had left? Corin's been teaching Antigone, Justin and me to waltz. We all felt too buoyant to go to bed.'

'Indeed? What did my mother say to that?'

'Who do you think played the piano? You would hardly have recognised her.'

'Apparently.'

'Is something wrong?' She left the candle on a tripod table and came around the front of the desk to join him. 'I've told the servants to go to bed. We can tidy up tomorrow, but I thought it went well.'

'It did.' He pushed his chair back slightly. 'You were a triumph.'

'You did wonderfully, too. I've never seen anyone more Ducal.'

'How many dukes have you seen?' His lips curved slightly, drawing the sting from the words. 'For what it's worth, you were also very Duchessy.'

'Thank you.' She slid herself backwards, perching on the edge of the desk in front of him. The atmosphere in the room felt charged with something, some powerful emotion that made her nerves prickle despite her exhaustion. 'Are you coming upstairs?'

'No.'

'Why not?'

His brows contracted. 'Because I need to think for a while. Goodnight, Beatrix.'

'Oh.' She slipped back off the desk, trying not to feel hurt. 'All right, but if you want to talk—?'

'No.' He shook his head before she could finish the offer. 'Go to bed. I'll sleep down here.'

'Down here? Why?'

He groaned. 'Because I *can't* sleep so close to you.'

'You…?' The words froze her where she was. They sounded cold and yet the look on his face was anything but. 'What do you mean?'

'I mean that adjoining rooms was a mistake.' He lifted a hand and placed it lightly on the side of her hip. 'I want you in my bed.'

'Oh…' Her breath hitched as she tried to speak. 'So you want us to sleep in the same bedroom…like before?'

'Yes and no.' His fingers trailed a path slowly up to her waist and then across her stomach, a frown puckering his brow as his gaze followed. 'I want you in my bed every night, but not like before. I want more. More than our agreement.'

'Quin...'

'I know.' His fingers stilled. 'Which is why you should leave now and I should sleep down here.'

She curled her fingers around the edge of the desk as a shiver of desire raced down her spine. He was right, she ought to leave and go to bed, only she didn't want to. Her thoughts were reeling, her imagination running wild, fantasising about how it would feel to lie in his arms without inhibitions, to kiss and touch and hold him. But it was madness. She still hadn't made up her mind about the future. She'd only come to his study to find out where he was. She'd felt so close to him during the dance that she hadn't been able to bear the thought of *not* ending the evening with him. Because she liked him, she cared about him, she loved him...

The realisation almost made her exclaim out loud. She loved him. It had crept up on her unawares, but now it seemed so obvious. So blindingly, dazzling, *obviously* obvious! She loved him. Which meant that she had to tell him the truth about Alec before anything else happened between them.

'Bea?' His voice sounded deeper, huskier, almost pained. It seemed to vibrate over her skin, raising goosebumps on her flesh even though she felt far too hot all of a sudden.

'I don't want to go right now.'

She heard his indrawn breath, though he didn't speak for a few seconds, simply lifting his gaze to hers with a look that felt scorching. And then both of his hands were around her waist, holding her still as he leaned forward and pressed his forehead against her chest, touching his lips gently into the hollow between her breasts.

She gasped and threaded her fingers into his hair, letting the glossy tresses slide over her fingers as she tried to control her breathing. It was no use. She was already panting helplessly, her overheated body betraying the depth of her desire. Instinctively, she tipped her head back, running her hands over his shoulders and back, trying to get more air to the exposed skin of her throat, but, if anything, it made her feel hotter still.

'Beatrix?' He stood up, sliding one hand around the back of her neck and drawing her mouth up to his, his tongue parting her lips and sliding between them, kissing her so deeply she felt as if her mind were spinning.

'Quin...' She forced herself to break the kiss before she forgot what else her mouth was intended for. She needed to find the words to explain about Alec. More than that, she needed to tell him that she didn't know what she was doing, not exactly anyway. Alec had made certain aspects clear, but the specifics themselves were still vague. 'Wait.'

He lifted his head, his eyes glazed as if he were struggling to focus. 'If it's that you'd rather I didn't manhandle you on my desk, then I understand.'

'No, it's not that.' She caught her bottom lip between her teeth, repressing a giggle. 'I think that I might actually like to be manhandled.'

Her heart fluttered as he laughed. The sound was so rare and unexpected, it made her feel weak at the knees. Which made it another good reason not to try and get off the desk. She doubted her legs would hold her.

'Then it would be my pleasure.' His voice was almost a growl.

'There's just something I need to… Oh!' She gasped as his lips found the side of her neck, sending an arrow of desire shooting straight to her core. When he kissed her like that, it was downright impossible to think straight.

'If you're worried about one of my family coming in, then don't be.' He murmured the words between kisses. 'They all know not to.'

'I know. I just…' She didn't finish the sentence, moaning as he covered every inch of exposed skin with hot, open-mouthed kisses. Maybe she didn't need to tell him about Alec after all, she thought helplessly. It would only ruin the moment. And maybe it didn't matter that she didn't know what she was doing either, since her body seemed to have a mind of its own. All it wanted was for her to slide out of her gown, or, more accurately, to have *him* slide her out of her gown, which to her immense relief appeared to be his aim, too. Her breasts were already exposed and his hands were making their way down her to her hips, tugging the fabric up while she wrestled with his cravat and jacket, tossing them both to the floor.

'You feel so good.' He closed his arms about her, drawing the lower half of her body tightly against him while lowering the upper half backwards.

'Mmm.' It was a good thing his desk was so tidy, she thought as her back touched the wood. There were no piles of paper to be swept aside, no ink wells for her to be impaled upon. It was a perfect desk for debauching women, although something told her she was the first. Somehow that idea made her want to do it even more.

'Maybe we should go upstairs?' he suggested, his actions belying the words as his lips found one of her breasts, drawing her nipple into his mouth.

'No.' She shook her head, writhing and arching her body with anticipation as she felt him position himself between her legs.

'Are you certain?'

'Yes. Quin...' She whimpered his name as he nudged forward, his body hot and hard against hers. And then he pushed harder and she had to clench her teeth to stop herself from tensing at the intrusion.

'Beatrix?' He paused mid-thrust, his voice tight with concern.

'Don't stop.' She blew air between her teeth, forcing herself to relax.

'Tell me if it hurts.' He pushed again, all the way inside her this time, so deeply that she felt almost afraid to breathe, let alone move. For a moment, she panicked, caught off guard by the pain, but then she looked at him and both panic and pain subsided and excitement and curiosity took over. It seemed impossible that he could be embedded inside her so deeply and yet there was a feeling of rightness about it, too, of belonging, as if they were meant to be together.

She nudged gently against him and he moaned aloud, one of his hands cradling her back while another slid beneath her bottom, cushioning her against the desk as he moved, too. And then they were both moving, writhing and pushing and bucking against each other, their rhythms mismatched at first, until finally they were moving together, completely in time, faster and harder until she felt a coil of heat low in her abdomen, one that intensified the more she lifted her hips and arched her back, until at last the heat exploded in one hot burst of sensation that left her whole body shaking.

'Quin!' She cried out his name at the same moment as he shouted hers, a split second before they both collapsed, breathless, onto the desk.

'Here.' Quin pulled her into his lap, wrapping his arms around her waist as they sat on the floor against the desk, both of their chests still heaving. 'Is that more comfortable?'

'A little.' She laughed breathlessly. 'You might have been right about using a bed.'

'I'm not sure I could have made it that far.' He laid his cheek against the top of her head. 'Now, what was it you wanted to tell me?'

'Mmm?' she murmured evasively. The candle was almost burnt down to its wick, threatening to leave them in total darkness, but she felt as though all her other senses were enhanced somehow. When she burrowed her head against his chest, she could hear the force of his heartbeat, feel the warmth of his skin, even smell the musky scent of cologne and sweat on his skin. She didn't want to talk, not yet, and she *definitely* didn't want to start thinking, to comprehend what they'd just done and all the ways their relationship had now changed.

She didn't regret it, but she was aware of a growing sense of disquiet at the back of her mind, as if she'd just lost some of her independence. She'd only *just* realised that she was in love with him. She hadn't had a chance to think about what that might mean for the future. If she loved him then surely that meant giving up the idea of divorce and staying at Howden? Or did it? She didn't want to rush into a decision, even if she'd just rushed into other things. And now she thought of it, intense as their lovemaking had been, Quinton hadn't said a single word about love. Neither had she, but she knew how *she* felt. He'd been looking at her intently all evening and he'd said that he wanted her, but wanting was different. If he was in love with her, too, then wouldn't he have said so? Except that he'd promised never to deceive her, which surely meant...

'What's the matter?' He trailed a hand from her shoulder all the way down to her elbow, caressing the bare skin as if he were trying to soothe her. 'You just tensed.'

'Did I?'

'Yes.'

'It's nothing.' She glanced towards the door. There didn't seem to be enough air in the room suddenly.

'Did I hurt you?' He took hold of her shoulders, twisting her around so that she couldn't help but look at him, his own expression concerned.

'No. Well... Only a little.' Her thighs were aching, but with soreness rather than pain.

'Forgive me. I should have insisted on going upstairs. Come.' He pressed his lips against her forehead. 'Let's go to bed.'

'No!' She pushed her hands against his chest, wriggling out of his lap and onto her feet, afraid of being alone with him any longer. If he took her to bed, behaving so tenderly and looking so ridiculously handsome with his shirt hanging open and a lock of dark hair trailing across his forehead, then she wasn't sure she'd be able to resist him again. And she *had* to, at least until she got her thoughts in order. If he didn't love

her then she'd just made another terrible mistake with
a man—even *more* of a mistake since she'd never actually slept with Alec! It was the exact situation she'd
been determined to avoid, the one she'd described to
Lady Jarrow: falling in love with a man who didn't
love her back!

'You stay here and do…' she waved a hand '…what-
ever you were doing before.'

'What I was doing was thinking about you.' He got
to his feet, too, adjusting his clothes. 'And how much
I wanted you. You've no idea how much I've wanted
to do this over the past few weeks.'

'Oh…' She closed her eyes. The words made her insides quiver again, and yet there was still no mention
of love. Instead, the disquiet was building into panic,
as if she'd been sleepwalking and woken up to find
herself in some kind of trap. Now that they'd slept together, he might simply presume that she would stay,
whether he cared about her or not. And what if she was
carrying his child? She glanced nervously down at her
stomach. If she was, then there would be no question
of leaving. She'd lose her freedom and be trapped as
the Duchess of Howden for ever. Which she'd known
and accepted as a possibility beforehand, until she'd
noticed what he *hadn't* said.

'Beatrix?' He put a finger under her chin, nudging
it upwards. 'What's wrong?'

'I just… I think…this was a mistake.'

'What?' His face seemed to go very still. 'What do
you mean?'

'I have to go.' She wrenched herself away, fleeing
towards the door. She had to get out of there, had to
run away and think…

'Wait!'

He slammed the door shut again just as she opened it.

'What?' She spun partway round, shocked by the change in his voice. He sounded shocked, horrified even, but he wasn't looking at her. He was looking at the back of her dress, at a point she couldn't see, but could suddenly, horribly, imagine.

'Beatrix…' He seemed to be forcing the words out. *'What* the hell is that?'

Chapter Twenty-One

Quinton stared at the back of his wife's dress in horror. *Blood.* A small, but distinct patch of it on the back of her gown. Blood. As if she were...as if she'd been... even after she'd told him... He staggered backwards and pushed a hand through his hair, searching his brain for any other explanation and failing to come up with anything remotely plausible. He hadn't intended to make love to her, not unless and until she decided to stay, but when she'd come and stood so close to him, when she'd said that she didn't want to go, when she'd slid her hands over his back and moaned his name when he'd kissed her, all his resolve had crumbled away. But he would *never* have done it if he'd thought for one moment...if she hadn't told him... His throat worked silently. Damn it, he'd just deflowered an innocent— his own wife!—on a desk, and he hadn't been remotely gentle about it.

'Why did you tell me—? No.' He shook his head. 'Why did you lie to me?'

She looked over her shoulder and blanched. 'Oh.'

'*Oh?* You told me you'd had a lover!'

'No.' She folded her arms defensively. 'I said that I was promiscuous.'

'What's the difference?'

She met his gaze and then looked away again quickly. 'I don't know exactly, but I shared a bed with a man. We didn't do...what *we* just did, but I didn't think you'd care about the technicalities.'

'Of course I bloody care!'

She jerked her chin up. 'My aunt always said that suspicion was as bad as the act itself, especially to the *ton.*'

'I'm not the damned *ton!*' He gritted his teeth, taking a moment to calm himself. 'Beatrix, if I'd known, I would have been gentle. I damn well wouldn't have used a desk.'

'It *was* quite hard.'

He bit back an oath. 'Explain it to me. *Why* did you say you were promiscuous? What happened?'

She didn't answer for a few seconds, gripping her arms so tightly that he could see her fingernails digging into the skin of her biceps. 'Alec was a friend of my cousin, Jaspar. They were at university together and he came to stay for part of the holidays last summer. He was nice to me, or at least I thought he was. He asked me about myself and talked to me about books and art and music. He even found excuses for us to spend time together. I really thought he liked me as much as I liked him.' She paused, turning her face to one side so he could only see her profile. 'Then one night, after a couple of weeks, he came to my bedroom. It was late, after midnight, I think, because I remember waking up when he scratched at the door. He must have bribed my maid because she let him in and then left us alone. I asked him to leave, but he said he only wanted to talk. Then he said that he loved me, that he couldn't stop thinking about me and then…then he climbed into my bed and kissed me.'

'Wha—?' He started towards her, but she thrust a hand out, holding him back.

'I didn't invite him into my bed, but the truth is I kissed him back at first. You can't imagine what it's like, to hear someone say they love you when you've been lonely for so long. It stops you thinking clearly.' She swallowed. 'But then he started doing other things, touching me in other places, and I got scared. I asked him to stop, but he didn't, so I pushed him away and that was when he got angry. He said that I'd led him on, led him to expect certain rewards for being kind to me. He said that I ought to be grateful for his attention.'

'Bastard.'

'I thought so, too, but then he changed again, saying that sleeping together was the only way to convince my uncle to let us marry since he didn't have a job yet. And for a few moments, maybe ten whole seconds, I thought that he was genuine, that he really did care for me and want to marry me. I was so happy. I said that I'd run away with him that day if he wanted, but he refused. He said that if I wouldn't allow myself to be properly compromised then we'd have to wait the three years until I came into my fortune.' She gave a ragged sounding laugh. 'Stupidly, I'd thought he didn't know about my inheritance, but obviously someone had told him. *That* was when I knew he didn't love me. Everything he'd said and done…it was only ever about the money.'

Slowly, she turned her head back towards him. 'I told you I was promiscuous because I thought it would encourage you to divorce me, but also because I was ashamed.'

'No. Bea, listen to me. You have nothing to be ashamed of.'

'I know. Deep down I know, but it doesn't make it any less humiliating. Alec made me feel worthless and unlovable and like a fool for thinking anyone would ever care about me for *me* and not just my money.' She looked him straight in the eye before reaching for the door handle again. 'And now I've made the same stupid mistake all over again!'

Beatrix slammed the door of her chamber even harder than the one to Quinton's study, hot tears scalding her eyes and cheeks as she stumbled inside. How could she have been so stupid, so witless and delusional? Not just falling in love with a man who'd deliberately married her for her money, but to have slept with him, too? She squeezed her eyes shut at the memory. How could something that had felt so incredible at the time now feel so terrible? And after such a wonderful evening? She wanted to accuse him, to tell herself that he'd taken advantage of her, but she couldn't. *She* was the one who'd gone to him, to talk, just to talk…until talking had turned into something else entirely. Something that had obviously detached her brain from her body because she'd actually encouraged him to keep going when he would have stopped. She'd as good as flung herself over a desk and offered herself to him. And all without so much as a word of love…

She wrenched her evening gown over her head, glad that she'd told her maid not to wait up, battled out of her stays, petticoat and chemise, then poured cold water over herself from the basin. Unfortunately, as it turned out, not even standing naked and dripping wet in the middle of her bedroom could cool her down when so many painful emotions were still gushing through her in a succession of hot torrents. She didn't bother with a nightgown, sliding into bed and pressing her face into her pillow instead.

She woke up in the early hours, surprised to have slept at all. One of her bedroom curtains was slightly open and pale silver light was filtering through, enough to illuminate the figure of her husband sitting in an armchair. He was still wearing his clothes from the previous night, looking even more dishevelled than when she'd left him in his study, but his eyes were open, his forearms draped across his knees as he stared at her from across the room.

'Quin?' She sat up with a jolt, pulling the sheet with her. 'What are you doing here?'

'What happened last night had nothing to do with money.' His voice was heavy and sombre. 'What you said before, if that's what you meant, I want you to know, nothing about it had anything to do with money. It happened because...' He stopped and rubbed a hand across his jaw. 'You know, it's not easy talking about emotions when you've avoided them for so long. Maybe I need to go back to the start. I was angry.'

'What?' She blinked. 'You mean last night?'

'No, when you ran away on our wedding day. You asked me once how I felt about it and I told you I was too numb to feel anything, but underneath...' His brow knotted as if he were thinking. 'I'm not saying that I was blameless, but I want to be honest and now I know

I *was* angry when you ran away. At you *and* myself, for getting us into that situation in the first place.'

'Oh…' She swung her legs sideways, sitting up on the edge of the bed.

'But then you wrote to me and you came here and we spent time together and now I'm not angry any more. Not at you, or my father or anything. I feel as if a weight has been lifted. *You've* lifted it. I've actually felt happy during the past few weeks. Happy and scared.'

'Scared?'

'Terrified. Because I love you. I only realised it last night, when we were about to dance, but I told myself it was only desire. I didn't dare admit the truth to myself because I was so terrified you might still want a divorce.'

'Quin—'

'I'm not telling you this to make you stay. I don't want you to feel guilty or bound or compelled in any way. I just want you to know. What happened between us…it wasn't a mistake, not for me. It never will be.'

She got up and crossed the room at a run, falling to her haunches in front of him. His eyes looked almost too bright in the darkness, glowing like blue coals. It seemed impossible now that she could ever have thought him cold. Whatever was visible on the outside, his inner core was molten lava.

'I *should* have told you how I felt last night.' He reached for her hands, drawing her up against him, his voice a growl in her ear. 'I know that now. I love you. With all of my heart and soul, and if I hurt you—'

'You didn't.' She lifted her hands to his face, cradling his jaw between her fingers, the sheet already slipping down between them. 'I realised how I felt about you last night, as well.'

'You did?'

'Yes.' Her heart wrenched at his hopeful expression. 'I love you, too.'

'Bea.' He rested his forehead against hers, rubbing gently. 'Do you remember the first day we met? If I'd known who you really were back then, I would have dropped to one knee and started quoting poetry.'

'Poetry?' A burble of laughter passed her lips. 'I'm not sure I can imagine that.'

'Something short. A couplet maybe.' He pushed a few whispery tendrils back from her eyes. 'I love you for *you*, I swear it. You're priceless to me. I never imagined it was possible to feel this way about anyone.'

'Me neither.' She pulled back before he could capture her mouth. 'But I'm not ready to decide about staying just yet. I was so certain about what I wanted before and now… I know what I feel in my heart, but I need time to think. I need my full six weeks.'

'Then you'll have them. I won't renege on our agreement, I promise.'

'Thank you.' She let out a shaky breath. 'Come to bed?'

'I thought you'd never ask.' He started to stand and then dropped back into his seat, pulling her against him as a light tap on the door preceded the entrance of a housemaid.

'You can leave the fire.' He wrapped an arm around her shoulders to keep the sheet up.

'Oh! Yes, Your Grace.'

'And please tell my maid I won't need her for a few hours.' Beatrix half turned her head, giggling as the door closed again. 'I probably didn't need to add that part, did I?'

'Probably not.' He gave a low chuckle of his own. 'But it's good to know we won't have any interruptions.'

'You need some sleep.'

'We both do.'

'Stay with me?'

She smiled, feeling her heart lift and then soar. 'There's nothing I want more.'

She loved him. Quinton opened his eyes at the sound of a bird chirruping loudly on the windowsill, a robin by the sound of it. He didn't know how long he'd slept, only that he'd gone to sleep and woken up in her bed with the exact same thought in his mind. He loved Beatrix and Beatrix loved him. Surely that meant she would stay? Surely she would choose him—*them*—over her friends and their biscuit shop in Bath? He just had to wait another two weeks to find out.

He let out a sigh of contentment. For that moment at least, she was his, tucked up in front of him, their bodies spooning with their feet entwined beneath the coverlet. They were also both naked. He'd been emotionally wrung out enough to fall asleep despite that fact earlier, but now he was awake again, with the round curve of her bottom touching his groin, the smell of her hair in his nostrils, not to mention the silky, smooth warmth of her skin pressed against the whole length of his body… The combination was starting to have an irresistible effect on his senses. An effect that was becoming increasingly potent and impossible to suppress.

'Quin?'

He bit back a groan. Even her murmur sounded seductive.

'Sleep well?' He tried to keep his voice normal.

'Mmmm.'

'I should go.' He pressed a kiss to her neck and started to pull away.

'Not yet.' She lifted an arm and clamped it over his, pulling him back again.

'I think I have to.'

'Why?' She rolled over this time, her eyes sleepy and not remotely innocent. 'Do you know, this is the first time we've lain together naked?'

'I'd noticed.'

'I like it.' She smiled languidly, trailing a finger over his chest.

'So do I.' A raw ache of desire shot straight to his groin. 'But you must still be sore from last night.'

'I'm not.'

'We should wait.' He was acutely aware of the strain in his voice.

'Why?'

'Because…' He stopped talking, groaning aloud this time as she pushed him onto his back and slid on top.

'Because?' She straddled his hips with her thighs and then reached for his hands, lacing their fingers together.

'This isn't fair.'

'I know. But you said you love me and I love you and we've been married for almost five months already. We have a lot of lost time to make up for.'

'Starting now?'

'Unless you want to wait for another two weeks?' She lowered herself over him slowly. 'On the other hand, maybe we should find out just how well suited we are beforehand…?'

And then she kissed him in a way that prevented any further discussion for the next hour. As it turned out, they were even better suited that morning than they had been the previous night.

Chapter Twenty-Two

~~~~~~~~~~

Week Five. Day Thirty-Nine,
Berkeley Square, London

'Saffron, please.' Helen licked her lips, her blue eyes sparkling with excitement.

'Bergamot for me.' Beatrix's eyes were almost equally bright.

'You're certain this time?' Quinton made a pretence of looking stern. 'Because you've both named every flavour from parmesan to elderberry to lavender in the past ten minutes. I don't want you changing your minds again.'

His two female companions exchanged a glance and then nodded at the same moment. 'We're certain.'

'Well, thank goodness for that.' He beckoned a waiter over to their open carriage and gave the order.

'Aren't you having anything?' Helen looked shocked.

'Oh, all right, and a chocolate ice, too.' He leaned back, draping an arm along the top of the carriage seat behind Beatrix as they waited for their treats to arrive. 'So what do you think of Gunter's?'

She peered thoughtfully at the grey stone building beside them. 'It's no Belles *obviously*, but it's still quite impressive. I like that we can sit out here under the trees. It would be such a shame to be trapped inside on a day like this.'

'It would,' he agreed, glancing up at a perfectly aquamarine sky through the branches of a plane tree. As it turned out, coming to London had been one of his better ideas. Naturally, Antigone and Justin had wanted to come too, but the arrival of the new governess, combined with Corin's sudden and surprisingly helpful offer to take his younger brother on a trip to one of the northern estates, had saved him from having to think up excuses. Only Helen had managed to inveigle her way into accompanying them, not that he particularly minded. Despite his desire to be alone with Beatrix, it was good to see his youngest sister finally emerging from her shell. She'd eaten her breakfast *on* instead of *under* the table for the past three days.

He looked down again, meeting Beatrix's smile with one of his own. She seemed happy. He hoped that was a good sign. In a matter of days, their six weeks was up and they would be leaving London, hopefully *both* in the direction of Howden. He daredn't let himself consider the alternative.

'What are you thinking?' she asked quizzically.

'Just about how my life has changed over the past five and a half weeks.' He grinned. 'Although for the life of me, I can't work out why.'

'Very funny.'

'*And* about whether we might take a drive through Hyde Park after this.'

'Perhaps. Although…' She pursed her lips in an

expression of mock concern. 'It's only three o'clock. Won't we be unfashionably early?'

'Terribly, but there may be a few other carriages about. The *ton* should be starting to get out of their beds roundabout now.'

'I can't believe so many people only go to bed at the same time I get up.'

'Not many of them are bakers. Still, you'd better start getting used to it, temporarily at least. We're going to the theatre tonight, remember?'

'Ye-es.'

'Don't you want to?'

'It's not that.' She folded her hands together, the way she always did when she was nervous. 'I've just heard that a lot of people go to the theatre to watch the audience, not the play. I'm not sure how I feel about being stared at.'

'I'm afraid that may be unavoidable.' He glanced at Helen, but her attention was distracted by a squirrel jumping between the branches overhead. 'You're a Roxbury now.'

'I *like* being a Roxbury. It's funny, I was happy as Belinda Carr, but now I wonder if I was still in the process of becoming me—the real me, I mean—the me I would have been if my parents had survived, if that makes any sense? Beatrix Roxbury feels real. I know who I am now.' She smiled. 'And I like who I am.'

'You should. Beatrix Roxbury is one of my favourite people in the world. Although I should warn you, there are a few rumours about us. Quite lurid ones apparently.'

Her mouth dropped open. 'Like what?'

'It seems the fact that I whisked you off to the countryside, *allegedly*, so soon after our mysterious wedding and then refused to let anyone else set eyes on you for the next three months has given us a somewhat…' he paused, searching for a suitable word '…*gothic* reputation.'

'Oh, dear.'

'Me in particular. I believe that my reputation is now somewhat similar to one of Antigone's villains.'

'Goodness.' Her eyes danced. 'Well, that might not be such a bad thing. I've read a couple of her novels and I rather liked the villains. There was one in particular who reminded me of you. The Dastardly Duke of Deverel, I think it was.'

'And was he also dashingly handsome and suave?'

'Yes, but, more importantly, his cold exterior hid a ferociously passionate nature underneath. Although, for some reason, the heroine preferred the ever-so-boringly-bland hero.'

'Silly woman.'

'Extremely. So should I live up to our gothic reputation and look languishing this evening?'

He laughed, moving his hand from the seat to the back of her neck as he leaned closer. 'That really would start tongues wagging.'

'They might not be so far from the truth.' Her breath caught as he trailed his fingers down her spine. 'We may be having unfashionably early nights, but we aren't doing a huge amount of sleeping.'

'True. Maybe I *am* a little dastardly.'

She gave him an arch look. 'You know the first time I told Nancy about you, she was afraid you'd chain me up in a dungeon.'

He started coughing, throwing a quick look at Helen

before moving his lips to her ear. 'One cravat hardly counts as a chain.'

'You weren't the one tied to the bedpost.'

'Next time perhaps.' He sat up again and discreetly crossed his legs. Just thinking about all the positions they'd explored the previous night made sitting uncomfortable. 'So, there was the Tower of London yesterday, Gunter's today, the theatre tonight and then the Earl and Countess of Illingworth's ball on Friday evening. Is there anywhere else you'd like to visit before we head home?'

'Not to any more dress fittings, for a start. I still feel bad for that poor seamstress you commissioned to make me a ball gown in four days.'

'We'll pay her double, don't worry.'

'At least double.' She drew her brows together. 'Actually, now you mention it, there *is* somewhere else I'd like to visit, although I'm not sure—'

'Here they come!'

They both gave a start as Helen leapt to her feet suddenly, clapping her hands with enthusiasm.

'Oh!' Beatrix's eyes widened as a waiter bearing a tray laden with glass dishes approached the carriage. 'They look delicious. I'm not sure one is going to be enough, after all.'

'Why do you really think I ordered the chocolate?'

She laughed as he winked at her. 'Dastardly or not, I do believe those words make you the perfect man.'

'Cook will be handing in her resignation tomorrow.' Quinton leaned back against the kitchen table, watching with amusement as Beatrix slid a rolling pin back and forth through the dough.

'Why? I'm not making a mess and it's not like we're disturbing anyone. It's the middle of the night.'

'It's the principle. This is her domain.'

'Where else am I supposed to bake? You said you wanted some Belles!'

'I meant that you could give Cook the recipe in the morning.'

'I can't just *give* somebody else the recipe! Nancy would never forgive me.' She tossed her head and then sighed wistfully. The recipe was a closely guarded secret, shared only by a small group of people, the same people who'd helped her when she'd needed help the most. If she didn't go back to Belles, then she'd probably never bake with any of them again. On the other hand, as much as she missed her friends now, if she left Howden, she had a feeling she might miss Quin even more.

She pushed the thought aside along with the rolling pin and started dividing the dough into equal segments. 'There's no way I'd be able to sleep yet anyway. The theatre was so incredible, I feel like my mind is still buzzing.'

'It was quite good.'

'Quite good?' She gave him a disbelieving look as she rolled the segments into balls and then flattened them out between her palms. 'The acrobatics were amazing! I've never seen anyone walk on a rope before, let alone do it with their hands. And the operetta was sublime. I can't believe so few people paid any attention.'

'Personally, I liked the comedy.'

She threw him a mischievous look. 'It wasn't a little too close to home?'

'Just because it featured an aristocratic villain chasing a maiden around the stage? I'll have you know he was a mere baron.'

'Is that *all*?' She began to lay the shapes out on a tray. 'How disappointing.'

'But you enjoyed it? Despite all the staring and whispering behind fans?'

'Most people didn't bother to use fans. I never realised the *ton* were quite so blatant. But yes, I enjoyed it despite that. Even when all those hundreds of people came to the box wanting to be introduced in the interval.'

'I counted ten.'

'Close enough. Although, I will say that Colonel Wentworth and his wife were very pleasant.'

'They are. Gordon has been a close friend for years. I thought we might call on them tomorrow, if you don't mind?'

'I wouldn't mind at all, except there's something else I think I ought to do instead. I was going to mention it earlier, but I got distracted by ices.'

'Really? I'm intrigued.'

'Well...' She took a deep breath. 'Now that I'm in London, I should probably pay a visit to my uncle and aunt. I haven't had any communication with them since I ran away and they're bound to have heard rumours about us being in town together.'

'Are you sure?' He frowned. 'Do you *want* to see them?'

'No, but I want to put the past behind me and prove that I'm not the timid, obedient girl they thought they could control any more. I want them to see that I've moved on.'

'All right.' He looked unconvinced. 'If that's what you want.'

'It is.' She put the last piece of dough down and wrapped her arms around his neck. 'But let's talk about it some more in the morning. At the moment, you're not being nearly dastardly enough for my liking.'

'Indeed? Because if you want me to chase you around the kitchen then you only have to say so.'

'That depends…' She chewed on her bottom lip, inner muscles clenching with anticipation at the thought. 'What would happen when you caught me?'

'Something about having my wicked way, if I recall the play correctly.'

'Interesting. And I suppose a kitchen table is a *little* like a desk.'

A genuinely villainous grin spread across his face. 'Well, when you put it like that… *One…*'

'But we can't. I'm sure half the servants are waiting up even though we told them to go to bed.'

'I'm wicked, remember? *Two…*'

'Cook really would hand in her notice!'

'Three!'

'Quin!'

She let go of his neck and darted across the kitchen, only to find herself caught before she reached the opposite end of the table.

'You wouldn't!' She gasped as he scooped her up in his arms.

'Actually, you're right, I wouldn't. At least not until those biscuits are ready. But after that, I'm taking you to bed and, for once, we're keeping *ton* hours and sleeping in.'

Chapter Twenty-Three

Day Forty

Mr and Mrs Benedict Thatcher lived in a five-storey, red-brick town house in a square on the edge of Hammersmith. It was a respectable address in a genteel area, a place that Beatrix both dreaded and yet felt compelled to visit.

'Are you certain about this?' Quinton squeezed her hand as the carriage rolled to a halt. 'We can still turn around if you want?'

'I'm certain.' She curled her fingers around his in return. 'It's important for me to do it.'

'I won't leave your side, I promise.'

'Thank you. I don't need a guard, but I do appreciate the offer.'

'Come on, then.' He made a face as the door opened. 'The sooner we get this over with, the sooner we can get on with our plans for the rest of the day.'

'I thought we didn't have any plans for the rest of the day?'

'Exactly.' He lifted their hands together, caressing

her chin with the backs of his knuckles. 'After last night, I need a nap.'

Despite their surroundings, she felt her lips tug upwards. 'And whose fault is that?'

'Yours for being so irresistible. I just can't help but be dastardly around you.'

She stepped down from the carriage, pressing a hand to her stomach to calm her nerves. For a moment, she wondered if she might be calming someone else, too, though if she was it would be far too early to tell. If she and Quin wanted a child, however, then they were certainly going the right way to get one. Curiously enough, the thought didn't alarm her any more.

They climbed the front steps together and were admitted into a familiar and yet somehow alien-looking hallway. Beatrix looked around, feeling as if it belonged to a dream rather than her own past. It was a strange sensation. Twelve years of her life had been spent in this house and yet nothing about it felt remotely like home. How ironic that she now found herself faced with a choice between two possible homes, both of them warm and loving. *If only* she'd ever felt that way about this place. Even the ancient butler, Jenkins, seemed hardly to recognise her, shuffling ahead of them to the drawing room where her uncle, aunt and cousins, Jasper and Cordelia, all stood stiffly waiting to greet them.

'Their Graces the Duke and Duchess of Howden,' the butler intoned, as if they were arriving at court rather than making a social call.

'It's an honour to see you again, Your Grace…and Beatrix.' Her aunt's smile was so rigid it looked painful. 'Please, do take a seat.'

'Thank you.' She sat down in a chair by the fireplace while Quinton came to stand behind her.

'Would you care for some refreshments?'

'No, thank you. We only came to tell you that we were in town for a few days.' She looked at the other members of her family in turn. Cordelia and Jasper both looked overawed and awkward while her uncle was scowling openly. 'As you can see, the Duke and I have reconciled.'

'That's excellent news.' Her aunt shifted forward in her own chair, though her eyes, Beatrix noticed, kept straying nervously towards Quinton. 'Although you gave us quite a scare. We were beside ourselves with worry.'

'Were you?'

'Why, of course. We had no idea where you'd gone!'

'Then I apologise for alarming you. Perhaps I ought to have written.' She was careful to maintain a composed expression. 'Please forgive me, Aunt.'

'I… Well, naturally, but where *have* you been?'

'With friends and then…family.'

'Family?' Her aunt blinked with a look of confusion. 'Well, perhaps the less said about it all, the better. So long as things have worked out for the best.'

'They have.' Beatrix twisted around, smiling up at Quinton behind her. 'All things considered, they've worked out very well.' She held onto his gaze for a long moment, feeling her heart lurch at the concern in his blue eyes. It was true, she *had* been with friends and then family, friends who'd become as close as sisters, and then a new family, a strange, belligerent group of people who'd wound their way into her heart almost without her noticing, a family held together by the stern, honourable, secretly warm-blooded man she'd fallen in love with. Something clicked into place in her mind and the way forward seemed obvious suddenly.

'And now everything's settled, I hope we'll be seeing a lot more of you.' Her aunt continued, 'We're family, too, after all.'

'I don't think so.' Beatrix stood and held a hand out. 'I'm grateful to you for putting a roof over my head for so many years, but I have a new family, people who really care about me. I'll be spending my time with them from now on, but let's part on good terms, for my father's sake.'

A flash of something like guilt flashed over her aunt's face, followed by another nervous glance towards Quinton. 'Why, I can't imagine what you mean. Why wouldn't we be on good terms?'

'Perhaps before you go we might discuss those business matters we agreed on, Your Grace?' Her uncle's expression was more pointed.

'What plans were those?' Quinton's voice practically dripped ice.

'The ones we discussed prior to your wedding.'

'Ah, my wedding. To your *beloved* niece. I believe those were the words you used.'

'Meaning?' Her uncle's expression turned ugly.

'I believe that you understand my meaning, sir. Naturally I cannot stop you from referring to our family connection in public, but I consider all other communication between us to be at an end.'

'We should go.' Beatrix placed a hand on his wrist. 'Goodbye, Uncle, Aunt, Jaspar, Cordelia. I wish you all well.'

* * *

'You were wonderful.' Quinton wrapped an arm around her shoulders as they settled back into the carriage.

'Really?' Beatrix placed her hands over her face. 'I didn't realise how upsetting it would be, seeing them again. I thought it would make me feel liberated, but now I just feel sad.'

'I know, but you don't have to face them ever again if you don't want to. They're in the past now.'

'Yes.' She let out a long shuddering breath. 'But I want you to keep your word, too. Whatever you promised my uncle before our wedding, I want you to do it.'

He stiffened. 'I promised to recommend his business to some of my contacts in Parliament. Which is going to be somewhat hard to swallow when I'd rather flatten the bastard.'

'Quin!'

'Sorry.'

'Not that I don't appreciate the sentiment, but it's important to me that we do things properly. I don't want to hold grudges or feel bitter. I just want to move on.'

'All right.' He tugged her tighter against him. 'I hope this proves how much I love you.'

'It does. And I love you even more for doing it.' She tucked her face into his neck, savouring the soft, steady warmth of his skin. 'I'm sure I'll feel better in a few days.'

'We don't have to go to the ball tomorrow if you don't want to.'

'Yes, we do. We have to show the world just how respectable and *un*-scandalous we are.'

'Un-scandalous? Is that a word?'

'Normal, then. I'm going to wear my new ball gown and we're going to waltz. I can't let all Corin's lessons go to waste.'

'Good point.' He laughed, although his body tensed slightly. 'So…about this "new family" you mentioned? The one you're going to spend your time with from now on? Does this mean…?'

'It might.' She smiled at the question. 'You'll just have to wait for your birthday to find out.'

'One more day?'

'One more day,' she agreed. She'd made her decision. One day, one ball, one waltz, one dastardly duke and then happily-ever-after…

Chapter Twenty-Four

Day Forty-One

'Last chance to come for a stroll.' Quinton came to stand behind her in the window bay, sliding his arms around her waist as he pressed his lips to the slope of her neck. 'And a visit to my solicitor, but that won't take long.'

'Tempting though a visit to your solicitor sounds, I think I'll stay here.' Beatrix tipped her head to the side, encouraging his mouth down to her shoulder. 'It's a beautiful morning, but I don't feel in the mood for going out.'

'Are you still upset about yesterday?' He moved around slightly to look at her, one eyebrow raised. 'You were tossing and turning all night.'

'A little, but I'm fine. You go and enjoy the sunshine.'

'I won't enjoy it if I know you're upset.'

'Go! I have a letter to write anyway.'

'All right, but if this—' he touched the pad of a finger against the furrow between her brows '—is still here when I get back then I'm taking you back to Gunter's for more ice cream.'

'What a terrible thing to say...'

'I know.' He stroked a hand tenderly across her hair before kissing her nose and heading for the door. 'I won't be long.'

'Take as long as you need. Helen and I will be fine here. She's still eating breakfast.'

She smiled and waved as he went down the front steps. It was true that she was still feeling shaken from the interview with her uncle and aunt, but she was glad it was over, too. Now that part of her life was behind her and she and Quin could move on together. Tonight they would go to a ball and tomorrow they would celebrate his birthday and the end of six weeks by returning to Howden together. She would put Belinda Carr behind her, albeit not without some regret, and become Beatrix Roxbury, Duchess, daughter, sister and wife. Which meant that today she needed to write and tell Henrietta and Nancy her decision... She only hoped that Nancy would understand and forgive her.

She'd just turned away from the window, heading towards her writing desk, when there was a knock on the front door. She hadn't seen anyone approaching the house, but perhaps they'd come from another direction. Whoever it was, it seemed unusually early in the day for callers.

'Your Grace?' The butler appeared in the doorway a few moments later. 'There's a Mr Thatcher waiting in the hall.'

'My uncle's here? Now?'

'Yes, Your Grace. He's requesting a private interview.'

'Oh…' She put a hand to her throat reflexively. The last thing she wanted was a private anything with her uncle. It was unlikely to be another social call so soon, especially after the way their interview had ended the day before, and it was definitely too much of a coincidence that he'd arrived just moments after her husband's departure. The idea that he'd been watching the house, possibly observing her and Quinton standing together in the window, made her shudder, but she wasn't going to hide either. If she'd made up her mind about anything, it was that she wasn't going to be cowed or told what to do by any man ever again.

'Please send him in. Only perhaps I might have some kind of appointment in ten minutes?'

'Of course.' The butler nodded discreetly. 'I'll be sure to remind you of it, Your Grace.'

'Thank you.' She folded her hands together, taking deep breaths to calm herself until the familiar lean figure of her uncle stalked into the room.

'Uncle?' She inclined her head politely. 'This is a surprise.'

'I'm sure it is.' His expression was anything but polite. 'Since you seem to think you can simply put your family behind you and forget about us. *Us*, who raised you, who gave you a home for twelve years.'

'It was never a home. You barely tolerated my existence and confined me to a room for most of my years with you. For which *generosity*, incidentally, you were paid.'

'Not enough.'

'Plenty. One hundred pounds a year when I can't have cost you even half that amount. You certainly never spent it on things for me.' She lifted her chin.

'If you think that I'm indebted to you now, then you're very much mistaken.'

'Your husband made promises.'

'Which I've asked him to keep. He'll provide the contacts you want.'

'That's not enough. Not any more.'

'But it's all you're going to get. Now if that's everything, then I'd like for you to leave.'

'I think not.' Her uncle's mouth twisted into a sneer. 'In fact, I think you're about to change your mind and give me a *lot* more.'

'Then you're mad. Why would I want to give you anything?'

'Because I know things about you that your husband doesn't. About you and Alec Beddows, for example.'

Beatrix felt a cold shiver, like a block of ice at the base of her neck, melting down her spine. 'I've no idea what you're talking about.'

'Don't play games. He came home with Jasper for a visit last summer. You took quite a shine to him, as I recall.'

'We were friends.'

'So it was a *friendly* liaison in your bedroom that night, was it? Tsk-tsk.' Her uncle wagged a finger mockingly. 'I thought I raised you better.'

'You didn't raise me at all!' She took a step forward, aware that her hands were shaking now. 'How did you know about that?'

'The boy wasn't half as clever as he thought. One of the servants saw him leaving your room and reported it to me the next morning.' The sneer widened. 'He was only ever toying with you.'

'I know. I found that out for myself. I just wouldn't have expected you to care.'

'I didn't, but I had bigger plans for you. That's why I suggested he and Jasper take a trip to the coast. I had to get him out of the house before you made a complete fool of yourself.'

Beatrix gritted her teeth. She remembered her cousin and Alec leaving the following morning. Alec had looked happy and carefree, as if nothing had happened between them, as if he hadn't cared a fig about seeing her again... 'If you're threatening me then there's no point. My husband already knows about Alec.'

'Does he?' Her uncle's crowing expression faltered and then returned again. 'How disappointing. I would have enjoyed being the one to tell him about it after yesterday, but not to worry. Perhaps he'll be interested in paying for this instead?'

'What is it?' She had to make a concerted effort not to stagger backwards as he pulled a folded piece of paper from the inside of his coat.

'*This* would be one of the notes you wrote to him. He was far too careless leaving them lying around his room. It makes quite touching reading, in a pitiful kind of way.'

She felt her mouth turn dry. She'd forgotten all about the notes she'd written to Alec. He'd written first, telling her how much he admired her and she'd responded in a similar vein, telling him of her growing affection. Just the thought of those words made her cringe now, though surely she hadn't said anything *too* incriminating?

'And then there's this...' He reached into his pocket again and pulled out a small framed portrait. 'You painted this of him, didn't you? It's a charming like-ness. Easy to forge, of course, although I also have your former maid's testimony about the night he visited your room. She was quite distraught when I challenged her about it. She even tried to defend you.'

'Defend me? *She* was the one who let him in!'

'Nonetheless, she told me everything. About how he was in your room for almost an hour… Quite long enough to ruin you.'

Beatrix stiffened. There was no point in telling her uncle the truth. Even if he believed it, he wouldn't care. He only cared about how incriminating it all looked and how much she would give him to keep it a secret. There was no doubt in her mind about that.

She wrenched her shoulders back, trying to bluff. 'My husband won't pay for your silence. Blackmail is a crime.'

'A serious one, yes, although it might look somewhat embarrassing if he were to have his wife's own uncle arrested. And then when the contents of your little let-ter got out, along with your maid's testimony… Think of the scandal. The humiliation for your *new* family, on top of everything else people already say about them. *The new Duchess of Howden enjoying private trysts before she was married.* They'll wonder what you're up to now. And when you have a son…well, *who knows* who they'll think the father is? It strikes me as rather ironic under the circumstances. I wonder, will your hus-band still think you're worth the fortune you brought him then?'

Somehow Beatrix kept her head up despite the sound of blood rushing in her ears, so loudly it seemed to echo and bounce around the walls of the room. Considering how Quinton felt about her uncle, she knew he'd never pay, and if she asked him to give her a large amount of money without any questions then he'd guess something was wrong. But if they didn't pay then it would cause even more disgrace and scandal, for his—*their*—family. And it would all be her fault. Because of her past stupidity.

'Perhaps the best way would be for *you* to pay me?' her uncle continued, examining his fingernails as if the conversation had started to bore him. 'You can afford it. Five hundred pounds would be nothing to you.'

'Five *hundred*?' She gasped. 'That's impossible. Quin would be bound to notice such a large sum going missing!'

'I'm sure you'll think of some explanation. From the look of things, you seem to have him wrapped around your little finger already.' He looked over her dismissively. 'Although I honestly can't imagine how.'

'*Why?*' She ignored the insult, staring at him in disgust instead. 'Why are you doing this? I'm your niece. Doesn't that mean anything to you?'

'No.' Her uncle didn't even pause to consider. 'Now, you can meet me in the gardens in Cavendish Square this afternoon. One o'clock.'

'You can't expect me to raise that much money so quickly!'

'No, but I'd like something.' He waved a hand. 'Let's call it a gesture of goodwill, shall we? Ten pounds ought to do it. As for the rest, I'll be generous and give you a month. Just remember that if you don't pay, there are plenty of gossip sheets that would love to.'

'Sorry to intrude, Your Grace.' The butler opened the door at that moment. 'But your appointment—'

'I'm just leaving.' Her uncle flipped his hat onto his head. 'Delightful to see you again, *Your Grace.*'

'What are you doing?'

Beatrix froze halfway across her bedroom at the sound of Quinton's voice. 'Packing.'

'Why?' He sounded confused. 'We're not in any rush to leave tomorrow.'

'I've changed my mind.' She shoved three pairs of stockings into her bag without looking around. 'I've decided to return to Bath.'

'Bath?' The word hung in the air for so long that eventually there was nothing she could do but turn and face him.

'Yes.' She didn't know what to do with her expression so she tried to keep it blank.

'But I thought…' All the blood seemed to drain from his face in a second. 'You were perfectly happy an hour ago.'

'Not perfectly. I took some time to think and… despite what I might have implied, I've decided that I choose Belles.'

'What?'

She curled her fingernails into her palms, her stomach clenching at the look of hurt on his face, but she had no choice. Paying her uncle was the only way to stop him from ruining the family she loved. And the only way to raise that much money was to leave. No matter how much it hurt her to do so.

'I don't believe you.' He crossed the room in three strides. 'What's happened?'

'Nothing.' She hesitated, wondering whether to tell him about her uncle's visit and deciding it was for the best. He was bound to ask the servants if anything unusual had happened and it gave her the perfect excuse… 'Except that I had a visitor. My uncle.'

His eyes narrowed suspiciously. 'What did he want?'

'Just to complain about yesterday, but it made me realise that if we stay together then I'll always be bound to him. Our marriage will always have been his idea. Tainted. I'll feel like he's won and I can't bear the thought of that.'

He looked disbelieving. 'So you'll throw our marriage away just to spite your uncle?'

'Yes. I'm sorry, but that's how I feel.'

'You can't go. It hasn't been six weeks.'

'Five weeks and six days. That's close enough.'

'The hell it is. You said you loved me!'

'I do.' She swallowed. 'That's why I'm not asking for a divorce. I don't want to cause you any more scandal than you've already been through, but no matter what I feel, I want my independence. You said it yourself, Howden can feel a prison and…' she felt her throat tighten around the words '… I don't want to go back there.'

'I see.' He took a few steps away from her, turning towards the window and staring down into the street.

'I'm sorry.' She saw him flinch at the word. 'Truly. I wish it were otherwise, but—'

'But we had an agreement.' He turned around again, his expression as hard and cold as it had been when he'd found her in Bath. 'Very well. I presume by your packing that you intend on leaving today?'

'Yes. As soon as possible.'

'I'll order the carriage.'

'There's no need. I'll take the stagecoach.'

'You will not. You're under my protection until you get back to Belles.'

She bit her lip, wanting to argue some more, but unable to think of a convincing reason to refuse. She'd just have to find a reason for the carriage to stop at Cavendish Square on the way.

'There's just one other matter.' She closed her eyes briefly, hating the words. 'About money. You said that you'd give me part of my fortune back in the case of a divorce. I presume that applies for a separation, too?'

His expression didn't so much as flicker. 'Of course.'

'I don't need half, just—'

'You'll get your half,' he interrupted her. 'I'll make the arrangements.'

'And if it's not too much trouble, I'd like some now. Five pounds. For the journey.'

'Five?' For a moment, he looked as if he were about to ask something else before reaching into his waistcoat and drawing out several notes.

'Thank you.' She took the money and then turned her back so that she wouldn't have to meet his eyes. 'You can give all my new clothes to Antigone. I won't have many opportunities for wearing them in Bath.'

'As you wish. Goodbye, Beatrix. Or is it Belinda already?'

'*Quin...*' She looked over her shoulder at the sound of the door. The space where he'd been standing was already empty. He was gone.

Chapter Twenty-Five

Quinton staggered into the library, his thoughts in turmoil. He felt hot and cold at the same time, as if his mind were overheating while his body was frozen. What had happened? Everything had been going so well. When he'd gone out that morning Beatrix had been happy...hadn't she? She'd *seemed* to be. A little pensive, perhaps, but that was all. There had been no strange looks, no sharp words, not even the vaguest hint that would have led him to expect anything like this. And now one visit from her uncle, the same uncle she'd seen just yesterday, and she'd decided that her independence meant more to her than him—than *them*.

Their marriage was over.

He sank down into an armchair and placed his head in his hands. Every word she'd uttered had felt like a physical blow, causing an aching sensation in his chest as if his heart were actually beaten and bruised. He tried to ignore the feeling, to push it away, but it was no use. It was just as he'd feared. The woman who'd taught him to feel again, the woman he'd fallen in love with, had broken his heart, and now he was incapable of holding his emotions back any longer.

If only he'd kept on controlling his feelings until the six weeks were up! Then *this* might have seemed like a good result. She wasn't insisting on a divorce, after all. They could live in different places and remain married without any scandal. His family's reputation would survive and his life could go on as before.

Before... The word made him want to weep.

He lifted his head at the sound of the carriage arriving at the front door, followed by footsteps on the stairs and in the hall, a thud like a trunk being put down, voices—Beatrix's first, then Helen's—interspersed with crying, then the front door opening and closing again and then...quiet.

He raked a hand through his hair, waiting for the carriage to roll past the window. He ought to get up and go to his sister. She'd be in need of comfort. An explanation, too, not that he had any to give her. A rush of anger replaced misery. Never mind how Beatrix had treated him, how could she have done this to Helen? And what could *he* possibly say to make his sister feel any better?

He stood up and made for the writing desk, reaching for a quill and writing a short letter to his lawyer instructing him to make enquiries about a divorce. Even if it couldn't go through Parliament at once, he could make his stance clear. He didn't want to go back to *before*. Reputation be damned. If it was freedom Beatrix wanted then he would give it to her, no matter what the scandal.

'Stop here!' Beatrix called up to the driver, opening the door and clambering out onto the pavement almost before the carriage came to a halt in Cavendish Square.

'Your Grace?' The groom riding at the back leapt down after her. 'Is something the matter?'

She could almost have cried at the question, but there were so *many* things the matter that if she started, she didn't know if she'd be able to stop. 'I thought I'd just take a quick walk in the park.'

'A walk, Your Grace?'

'Yes. It's a long way to Bath and I'd like to stretch my legs first.' She shrugged, trying to look as if there were nothing remotely eccentric about the idea. 'There's no need for you to accompany me.'

'With respect, Your Grace, I think the Duke would prefer it.'

'The Duke isn't here.' She looked down her nose, doing her best impression of her mother-in-law. 'And I'm *ordering* you to wait here. I'll be back shortly.'

'Quin?'

A small voice made him drop his quill and jump up from the desk at once. Helen was peering around the edge of the library door, her eyes red-rimmed and her expression so miserable that he berated himself for not having gone straight to comfort her.

'Beatrix has left.'

'I know.' He crouched down on one knee.

'We were going to play bowls in the park later. She promised. I don't know what I did wrong.'

'Nothing.' He put his hands on her shoulders, trying to think of a way to explain. 'It's not your fault. She just realised she had to leave.'

'That's what she said. She said she was sorry and that she loved me, but she had no choice.'

'I know.' He clenched his jaw. 'I can play bowls with

you if you like?' Not that playing games was on his list of priorities at that moment, but if it made Helen feel better…and throwing things didn't sound like *such* a bad idea.

'No.' She shook her head tragically. 'I just wish she hadn't left.'

'Me too.'

'All because of that horrible man.'

He froze. 'What man?'

'The one who called here earlier.'

'You mean her uncle? Tall, thin, grey hair?'

'I don't know.' She made an apologetic face. 'I was behind the door to the breakfast room and I didn't dare peek. He sounded angry.'

'Angry? You mean, he wasn't just complaining?' His heart stopped as a new idea struck him. 'Do you know what he was angry about?'

'I'm not sure. I didn't hear all of it, but they were arguing.'

'Did you hear anything Beatrix said?'

'Well…she asked him to leave and he said no.'

'Anything else?'

Helen pressed her brows together as if she were trying very hard to remember. 'She said that she wouldn't give him anything, but then he said something about a letter and a painting and humiliating our family in public.' She shook her head. 'But I don't *care* about being humiliated. I just want Beatrix to come back.'

'So do I.' His heart started beating again, harder than ever before. 'Did he mention money, by any chance?'

'Oh, yes!' Her brow cleared. 'He said he wanted five hundred pounds, but only some of it this afternoon.'

'Five pounds, by any chance?'

'No…ten…but he said to give it to him in Cavendish Square gardens at one o'clock.' She started as he jumped to his feet. 'Where are you going?'

'Cavendish Square!' Quinton was already running towards the door.

'Wait!' Helen's voice sounded tremulous. 'Are *you* coming back?'

He stopped at the question, spinning around and rushing back to embrace her. 'I'm coming back, I promise. And with any luck, Beatrix is, too.'

'I was starting to think you weren't coming.' Her uncle looked like the cat who'd got the cream, Beatrix thought with revulsion, basking in sunshine with his arms spread wide on the bench behind him.

'I had some packing to do.'

'You're leaving your Duke?' He laughed. 'How dramatic. There was no need to do that.'

She didn't dignify the words with an answer, holding the five pounds out instead. 'Here. It's not ten, but it was all I could ask for at short notice without it seeming suspicious.'

'Why should I care how suspicious it seems? If you think I'll hold my tongue for five pounds—'

'I don't.' She interrupted him tersely. 'I think you'll hold your tongue because you know you can get more if you wait.'

'True.' He stood up, tucking the money inside his jacket pocket with a shrug. 'In that case, we'd better make it a thousand.'

'A thousand what?'

'A thousand pounds. In total. For the delay.'

'We agreed on five hundred.'

'You're hardly in a position to argue.'

'Yes, I am, and I'll only be blackmailed so far. No gossip sheet will give you that much.'

Her uncle's eyes glinted with something like appreciation. 'Maybe you're smarter than I realised.'

'I am. I always was and you can't make me feel bad about myself any more, Uncle. I hope it gave you pleasure, taking your sense of failure out on a young girl for all those years, but it's over.'

'Keep talking and I'll go to the papers out of spite.'

'Try it and I'll set the law on you myself. Now I'll send word when I have the rest of the money, but you'll have to come to Bath with the letter and portrait so that I can see both of them destroyed.'

'I think I can manage that.' Her uncle's voice was unbearably smug, making her flesh creep with dislike.

'*And* I want a note from my old maid saying that she was coerced into making accusations against me.'

'As you wish.'

'Good. Then I think that concludes our business.'

'You know it's probably for the best, your leaving him,' he called after her as she turned away. 'I never liked him much. So cold, so clinical. He was only ever after your money.'

She turned around again. 'You're wrong. I admit, that's why he married me, but things are different now. He's not cold and he loves me, money or not.'

'Ha! Think so if it gives you comfort.'

'I will. Now if that's everything, I—' She stopped talking mid-sentence, her attention drawn by a commotion at one of the square's gates. A man was running towards them, his undignified pace drawing shocked and disapproving stares from the other pedestrians. There was something familiar about him, too, she thought, something about his tall figure and black hair...

'What is this?' Her uncle's expression turned panicked. 'Is that your—? You tricked me!' He glared at her accusingly before turning on his heel and sprinting towards the opposite entrance. Unfortunately for him, Quinton changed direction, too, hurtling across the lawn like a deerhound and tackling him into a flowerbed when he was almost in reach of a hackney cab.

'*Quin!*' Beatrix raced towards them. 'Don't! He's not worth it.'

'Bea?' Quinton staggered back to his feet, dragging her dishevelled-looking uncle along with him. 'Why didn't you tell me he was blackmailing you?'

'What?' She stopped dead in surprise. 'How did you know?'

'Helen. She was behind the door.'

'Oh...' She put a hand to her mouth. 'Oh, no.'

'Thank goodness she was.' He clamped a hand around the back of her neck, pulling her towards him and kissing her breathless while still holding onto her uncle. 'You should have told me. I don't care about blackmail.'

'You don't understand. He has proof that Alec came to my room that night. He could start rumours, cause a terrible scandal...' She looked around the square. *More* scandal, she ought to say, since they were causing enough of a scene as it was. Running across lawns, fighting in flowerbeds and now kissing in broad daylight.

'I don't care. Remember the other day when you said you know who you are now? Well, so do I, and I'm somebody who doesn't give a damn about what other people think any more. Maybe I'm more like my father than I realised, because I genuinely don't care. And neither will my family because we *are* a family. We even know how to behave as one now, thanks to you.'

'Quin, I…' She started to protest and then stopped. 'Do you really mean it?'

'Of course, I do. We can be the most scandalous couple in England for all I care. I love you. I love you so much I was going to give you that damned divorce you wanted anyway.'

'I *don't* want it! I want you!'

'More than Belles?'

'More than anything.'

'Bea.' He kissed her again, even more passionately. 'But as for you…' He swung around, catching her uncle by his coat lapels.

'I don't know what she's told you, but—'

'I ought to horsewhip you.'

'If you do, I'll—'

'*What?* I'd like to find out.'

'Here.' Her uncle reached into his jacket and pulled out the letter and portrait. 'Take them. It was all just a joke, a misunderstanding. I would never have gone through with it.'

'I'm glad to hear it, but if you ever come near my wife again, I won't hesitate to bring charges. Understood?' Quinton shoved him away. 'Now get out of my sight.'

'I'm going.'

'Oh, no, you're not getting away that easily.' Beatrix stepped forward, swinging her fist into her uncle's jaw so hard that he crumpled into a heap on the ground.

'I thought you just told me *not* to hit him?' Quinton gaped at her with a combination of approval and surprise.

'Only because I wanted to do it myself.' She tossed her head. 'I've thought about it and I'm quite sure it's what my father would have wanted me to do.'

Chapter Twenty-Six

'I never thought I'd say this about an event that be-
gins *after* dark, but we're going to be late.' Quinton
stood in the hallway, smiling as Beatrix finally came
hurrying down the staircase, a vision of loveliness in
a sage-green ball gown, its bodice decorated with row
upon row of tiny white pearls.

'Sorry. I was reading a story to Helen.'

'She's still awake?' He glanced at the grandfather
clock in the corner. 'At this hour?'

'Almost asleep, but I wanted to be sure she's all
right. She was so upset earlier. I feel terrible for being
the cause of it.'

'It wasn't your fault, and we'll make it up to her.
Now what about you?' He peered at her with concern.
'Are *you* all right? We don't have to go to this ball if
you don't want to.'

'But I do. I told you, I want the whole of Society
to see there's no cause for any more gossip about us.'

'And I told you, I don't care what they think any
more. Didn't I prove that today?'

'You did, but I've decided that our family reputation

matters to me for Corin and Justin and Antigone and Helen's sake. Even for your mother's. So we're going and that's final.'

'Yes, Your Grace.' He bowed over her hand. 'In that case, your carriage awaits.'

'Carriage? I thought you said it's only around the corner.'

'It is.'

'Then why on earth are we travelling in a carriage? We'll arrive even later if we have to sit in a queue first.'

'And she says she doesn't want to cause any more scandal. You know, common sense is all very well, but it's not very *ton*.' He chuckled and nodded at the butler. 'Could you please inform the coachman that we won't be needing him after all? We'll make our own way there and back. On foot, apparently.'

'Yes, Your Grace.' The butler looked somewhat startled. 'Perhaps you'd like a footman to escort you?'

'No, I think we'll manage on our own.' He took Beatrix's cloak and draped it around her shoulders, leaning close to murmur in her ear. 'I have my wife's right hook to protect me, after all.'

'Shhh.' Her cheeks reddened. 'Don't tell anyone or there'll be even more gossip. I'm sure duchesses aren't supposed to know how to hit people.'

'That's why most of them are so dull. Out of interest, where *did* you learn to punch like that?'

'Do you really need to ask?'

He thought about it for a second and then snapped his fingers. 'Miss MacQueen?'

'She didn't just teach me baking. She says a woman ought to know how to look after herself.'

'Do you know, I think we've finally found something your best friend and I agree on.'

'By the way…' Beatrix nudged her shoulder against Quinton's as they made their way, arm in arm, along the street. 'Helen told me something tonight.'

'Oh, yes?'

'She says that she's ready to be an aunt.'

'Good grief.'

'Don't worry. Apparently there's no rush. She just wants us to know that she's ready.'

'Well, so long as *she* is.' He squeezed her arm. 'Although, when it happens, *if* it happens, I believe that I might be ready, too.'

'I'll bear that in mind.' She gave him a tender smile as they approached the porticoed town house of the Earl and Countess of Illingworth, weaving their way through at least two dozen carriages all fighting their way to the front door.

Beatrix held her breath as they walked up a marble staircase and into a vast golden ballroom, glittering with so many chandeliers, it looked as if the roof had been removed from the house and the stars brought down from the sky. Despite the size of the room, it was filled to bursting, too. Everywhere she looked there were men in evening clothes and women in brightly coloured ball gowns ornamented with sparkling jewellery—sapphires, rubies and emeralds, all the colours she could think of—heightening the starlight effect. It would have been impossible not to be dazzled.

'The Duke and Duchess of Howden,' a man in full, formal livery announced as they entered, drawing what seemed like a thousand curious pairs of eyes towards them.

'Is it normal to feel quite so sick at these events?' Beatrix whispered out of the corner of her mouth.

'For a debutante, I should imagine it might be.' He looked perfectly unperturbed, leading her forward into the room.

'I'm not sure I count as a debutante. I'm an old, married lady these days.'

'But it's still your first ball, isn't it?'

'Yes, it is. And it's spectacular.' She sighed and then cocked her head, smiling at the sound of the orchestra. 'What perfect timing! A waltz? Can we dance?'

'A dance with my own wife? How singular.' His blue eyes glinted, brighter than any of the sapphires around them, as he bowed over her hand. 'I'd be honoured to take the floor with you, Duchess.'

She dipped into a curtsy. 'As would I, Duke.'

It was very different, she discovered a few minutes later, waltzing with the man you loved rather than the brother of the man you loved. With Quinton, the waltz felt like the most wonderful combination of melody and movement in the world, the music filling her body as well as her head, her very soul even, until she felt as though she were flying above the ballroom in his arms. She wouldn't have been surprised to find that her feet had left the floor. She felt breathless and happy and as if she could keep dancing all night. She *wished* she could keep dancing all night. It was pure, perfect, breathtaking, blissful bliss.

'You know, it's not long until midnight.' Quinton's voice sounded husky as they finally came to a halt.

'Which means it's almost your birthday.' She wobbled slightly in his arms, still feeling giddy. 'Although you never told me what you wanted for a present.'

'You know exactly what I want.' He tightened his grip on her waist. 'Your six weeks are up, Duchess. I want to hear you say it.'

'Say what?' She batted her eyelashes.

'That you're staying with me, that you've given up any idea of a divorce, but most of all, that you love me as much as I love you.'

'That's an awful lot of things to say all at once...' She took a deep breath, held it for a moment and then let it all out in a rush. 'I love you, Quinton Roxbury, I'm staying with you, and I forbid either of us from mentioning the word divorce ever again. I want us to grow old and be ridiculously happy together.'

If she wasn't mistaken, there was a hint of moisture in his eyes. 'In that case, perhaps we ought to throw some kind of belated wedding celebration? A house party perhaps? We could invite all of your friends from Bath.'

'Do you mean it?' Her heart jumped with excitement. 'You don't mind that they're all in trade?'

'I don't mind if they have tentacles. They're your friends.' He lifted an eyebrow. 'And I'd rather they didn't hate me quite so much from now on.'

'They won't hate you at all once I explain things. Nancy might need a bit of talking round, but I'd love to invite them all.'

'Good. In the meantime, I want the rest of the world to know how much I love you, too.'

'We're showing them right now, aren't we?' She tugged on his arm. 'Although much as I'd like to dance

with you all night, we'd better get off the dance floor
before we start another scandal.'

He didn't budge. 'Maybe it's in the blood, but I'm
getting quite a taste for scandal.'

'What do you—?'

She didn't get any further as he kissed her. Right
then and there in the middle of the ballroom. And after
a couple of stunned seconds, she kissed him back.

It caused quite the scandal.

Epilogue

'So that's it, then.' Nancy spoke heavily. 'She's not coming back.'

'No.' Henrietta folded the letter and placed it on the table between them. The tea shop had closed for the evening and they were all alone, with only the sound of Sebastian singing in the kitchen to disturb the heavy silence that followed. 'But she sounds happy.'

'Yes.' Nancy turned her head to look out of the window. 'She didn't use the code.'

'What code?'

'We agreed on a word, one she promised to use if she was being coerced into writing anything against her will.'

'That's clever. What was the word?'

'Oranges.'

'Oranges?'

'It's a long story.'

'Oh.' Henrietta looked genuinely sympathetic. 'At least, we'll be seeing her again soon. She's invited us to stay at Howden Hall for a couple of weeks.'

'Some of us have to work.'

'We can close for a while.'

You've only just opened!'

'Yes, but this is a special occasion. Bel— *Beatrix* is happy. We ought to try and be happy for her.' Henrietta touched her hand gently. 'Are you all right?'

'Yes. It's just…' Nancy screwed up her mouth, trying to hold back the words and failing '…*marriage*! First Anna, then you and now Beatrix. It's like you're all just surrendering!'

'We all fell in love. It's not a war and men aren't the enemy.'

'They are where I come from.'

'But you're *here* now.'

'That doesn't mean I've forgotten.' Nancy scowled and stood up. 'You go to Howden if you want. I'll be happy for her from a distance.'

Henrietta looked as if there was more she wanted to say. 'Will you stay for dinner tonight? Sebastian's cooking.'

'No. If you don't mind, I think I'd rather go home.'

'I'll come and help with the baking in the morning. We'll have to start looking for a new assistant for you, too.'

'I suppose so. Goodnight.' Nancy smiled weakly as she gathered her bonnet and cloak and went outside, looking aimlessly up and down the street as if she didn't know Belles was only five hundred paces around the corner. Part of her wanted solitude, another part already felt lonely. All of her friends seemed determined to pair off, live happily ever after and leave her behind. While Beatrix had been there, it had been two against two, the pair of them against the lovestruck Anna and Henrietta, but now it was three against one and she was left all alone. The odd one out, just as she'd always been. Why couldn't they see how much trouble men were? Why couldn't they see the heartache in store for them? Hadn't she warned them often enough? Or was it possible that, after all these years, *she* was the one in the wrong?

The sound of voices made her look round. The shop workers were coming out of Redbourne's General Store for the day. Which meant that James would be coming out to close the shutters up soon. Unlike most managers, he always did it himself. He did a lot of things himself. It was one of the things that annoyed her most about him, that refusal to put on airs and graces like most men who owned their own businesses and employed others beneath them. It would have been so much easier to dislike him if he did, or if he were a bad manager, but no one ever left his employ unless they had to. He treated his employees like equals, not subordinates. He was decent, kind and understanding. As if *he* were determined to prove her wrong about men, too.

She turned away, dragging her feet slowly along the pavement. It was annoying how often her thoughts turned towards James Redbourne these days. More and more since that night in his office just before Beatrix had left. It didn't help that he lived next door to Henrietta and Sebastian and she couldn't help but see him on a regular basis, making it impossible to forget what had happened. What had almost happened anyway, if he hadn't been so damned decent!

She stopped on the corner, looking back over her shoulder, but her pace must have been even slower than she'd thought because the shutters outside Redbourne's were already closed. She'd missed him. He must have

come and gone behind her back while she'd been thinking about him. Somehow the realisation made her throat
swell and feel tight. She never cried, but at that precise
moment she felt as though she could collapse in the
street and start sobbing.

And what good would that do? she scolded herself.
What good had crying ever done anyone? How had it
ever helped her mother? No, if you wanted something,
then you needed to *do* something about it. The question was: did she want it?

She started walking back in the direction she'd
come from, faster and faster until she was almost running by the time she reached the shop. Now it all de-
pended on the door. If it was locked then she would
turn around again and go home to Belles by herself,
but if it wasn't…

It wasn't.

'We're closed, I'm afraid.' James came out of his
office at the sound of the bell, stopping abruptly at the
sight of her. 'Nancy?'

'James.' She tossed a curl out of her eye, feeling uncharacteristically nervous at the sight of him. It wasn't
often that she let herself acknowledge how handsome
he was, but he *really* was, more than Samuel or Sebastian or even that cold-hearted Duke Beatrix *thought* she
was in love with. With his muscular physique and serious, amber-brown eyes, there was something inherently
strong and dependable about him, too. He gave the impression of a man who wouldn't shift, once rooted, who
wouldn't falter or fail or betray, who would stand by his
word no matter what. Completely unlike her stepfather.

'Can I fetch you something?' He took a step towards

her, his broad shoulders seeming to fill her whole line of vision.

'No, I didn't come to shop.' She tossed the curl back again and then changed her mind, removing her bonnet and reaching up to unfasten her hair, letting it tumble in riotous waves over her shoulders. Or at least she hoped they were waves. There was a very real chance they might resemble snakes instead. 'I came to see you.'

'Me?' The pupils of his eyes swelled as they followed the scarlet tresses downwards.

'Yes.' She took a deep breath, fighting her natural instinct to pick an argument with him. 'You made me an offer a little while ago.'

'I remember.'

'Well, I've had some time to think and I've decided... if the offer still stands...that I'd like to accept.'

'You would?' His voice sounded very dry all of a sudden.

'Yes.' She turned and drew the bolts across the front door. 'Shall we go upstairs and discuss it?'

* * * * *